PRAISE FOR KRI[...]

"A Kristen Proby book is a g[...] [...]antastic romance. Proby always delivers when it comes to heat, heart, humor and ALL THE FEELS." —Lauren Blakely, *New York Times* and *USA Today* bestselling author

"No one packs as much passion and romance on each and every single page the way Kristen Proby does." —Jay Crownover, *New York Times* and *USA Today* bestselling author

"Kristen Proby's stories are all sexy, swoonworthy must-reads!" —Laura Kaye, *New York Times* and *USA Today* bestselling author

"Kristen Proby writes contemporary romance like no one else!" —Monica Murphy, *New York Times* and *USA Today* bestselling author

"No one does swoony alphas, strong women, and sexy love stories like Kristen Proby. She truly knows how to write romance with heart." —Laurelin Paige, *New York Times* and *USA Today* bestselling author

"Kristen Proby is a master at creating hot heroes and tender romance. I love her books!"

—Jennifer Probst, *New York Times* and *USA Today* bestselling author

CLOSE *to* YOU

CLOSE TO YOU

A Fusion Novel

Kristen Proby

wm

WILLIAM MORROW
An Imprint of HarperCollins*Publishers*

CLOSE TO YOU. Copyright © 2016 by Kristen Proby. All rights reserved. Printed in the United States of America. No part of this book may be used or reproduced in any manner whatsoever without written permission except in the case of brief quotations embodied in critical articles and reviews. For information address HarperCollins Publishers, 195 Broadway, New York, NY 10007.

HarperCollins books may be purchased for educational, business, or sales promotional use. For information please e-mail the Special Markets Department at SPsales@harpercollins.com.

FIRST EDITION

Designed by Diahann Sturge

Library of Congress Cataloging-in-Publication Data has been applied for.

ISBN 978-0-06-243476-0

16 17 18 19 20   RRD   10 9 8 7 6 5 4 3 2 1

This book is for Kara. Because you're my person.

CLOSE
to YOU

Prologue

~Landon~

"Are you packed?" my sister, Mia, asks through the phone. Her voice is husky with sleep, which makes sense since it's the middle of the night back home in Portland, Oregon.

"I leave tomorrow, Mia. Of course I'm not packed." She snickers. I just finished up my last debriefing meeting, my last day as an officer in the Navy. I grip the zipper of my flight uniform and sigh. "It's not right."

"I know," she says quietly. "But you're safe and whole, and you could be dead, Landon, so I'll take it."

I frown, staring at myself in the mirror as I unzip my uniform for the last time. I'll never wear it again, never pilot a plane again.

What the fuck am I supposed to do now? The Navy gave me options, but if I can't fly, there's no sense in it. Flying isn't just what I do, it's who I am.

"You're overthinking," Mia says.

"I'm a pilot, Mia. This is what I love. It wasn't supposed to end like this."

"You're alive," she says.

"Am I?" I murmur, then shake my head and wince at the neck pain that still nags me from time to time. Ejecting from an F-16 will cause a crick in the neck. And a loss of an inch in height that may never return, along with an entire Naval career.

Son of a bitch.

"This has been the longest four months of our lives, Landon. We're all anxious to see you."

"I'll be home in a few days," I reply as I pull a T-shirt over my head and throw the last of my belongings in a box that the Navy will have sent to me from Italy.

I loved being in Italy for the past few years, and God knows I didn't plan to leave it like this.

But I am. Maybe Mia's right; at least I'm alive and I can walk and live a normal life.

I just can't fly.

And that's what hurts more than any injury from the crash.

"What time should I come get you from the airport?"

"No need," I reply, regretting calling my sister and waking her up. I just didn't know what else to do when I came in here and was faced with boxes and the end of a career I love. "I'll get there."

"Landon—"

"It's okay, really. I'll see you in a few days."

"Be safe," she says. "And, Landon?"

"Yeah."

"It's going to be okay."

I force a grin and a nod, though she can't see either. "Of course it is."

We say our good-byes and I sit on the edge of the bed, scrub my hands over my face, and take a deep breath. I hope she's right.

Chapter 1

~Cami~

e's back.

I take a deep, cleansing breath and push my hands through my blond hair, scrutinizing my makeup. I don't wear much, and I'm certainly not as talented with it as my best friend, Addie, but it'll do. My green eyes are accentuated nicely, lips are pink, and heart is beating faster than ever.

"You've known him your whole life. It's not like he's new," I remind myself in the mirror. "You're just going over to say hi. It's no big deal."

I don't look convinced, so I narrow my eyes and lean in. "He's just an old friend. Suck it up, buttercup."

Landon is my other best friend, Mia's older brother. Addie, Mia, and I grew up together, and I've been in love with Landon for as long as I can remember. God, one look at him usually sends the giant birds in my stomach into over-drive. He's handsome—understatement of the year—and sweet and . . . *damn.*

I'm ridiculous.

I shake my head at my reflection and turn away to grab my purse and set out to Landon's parents' place, where he's been staying since arriving home a few days ago. Landon was in the Navy since he graduated from college. He was a pilot, until an accident a few months ago that resulted in him ejecting from the plane.

I've never felt fear like I did the day we received the call that he'd been hurt. And the past few months of him being on the other side of the world have been torture. I couldn't see him to make sure he was okay. He had to recover, then go through the process of being discharged from the Navy before he could come home.

Thank God he's back now. I gave him a couple of days to acclimate, but I just can't stay away anymore. I need to see him.

And I'm nervous as hell.

I park at the curb by his parents' house, gather my cour-age about me, and walk up the sidewalk to the front door, knocking with more conviction than I feel.

There isn't any movement in the house, making me frown. It's early enough in the day that he should be home.

I knock again, and just when I'm about to give up and leave, the door is yanked open and there he is.

Half-naked.

Hair rumpled.

Eyes blurry.

Did I mention that he's half freaking naked?

"What are you doing here?" he asks, his voice rough with sleep, snapping me out of my openmouthed stare.

"Were you still asleep?" I ask, squaring my shoulders and schooling my face to seem as though I see half-naked men every day.

Which I *don't*. Certainly not tall, dark-haired men with ice-blue eyes and olive skin and washboard abs.

Jesus.

"It's early," he mumbles, and scrubs his hand over his face. He's not asking me in. He doesn't look happy to see me.

He hasn't even hugged me, which probably isn't a bad thing considering that he's half-naked and I'd probably do something stupid like tackle him to the ground and molest him.

Down, girl.

"It's not that early," I point out, and he turns narrowed eyes on me and firms his jaw, and I realize that not only is he not thrilled that I'm here, he's . . . *irritated.*

"I'm still shaking the jet lag," he says. "What do you need, Cami?"

I take a small step back and shake my head. "I don't need anything, Landon. I just wanted to stop by and say welcome home."

"Thanks." His voice is a little flat. I was not expecting this at all. Landon has always been welcoming, happy to see me. I don't know what to do with this.

I do know one thing: I need to get out of here. I'm sorry I came.

"I'm sorry that I woke you up," I murmur, my eyes on my feet as I turn away. "I'll see you."

"Cami," he says, but I don't stop to see what he's about to say. My fight-or-flight reflex has kicked in, and all I can think is *Get out of here.*

"How embarrassing," I mutter, fighting tears. "Why would he want to see you, Cami? You're just his little sister's friend."

But it wasn't always that way. Back in the day, we were friends. He and I always got along well, and I refuse to believe that it was just because of Mia. We had things in common, and we had conversations. And when he left for the Navy, he left a hole in my life that I tried to fill with a mistake of a marriage.

I miss him. I've missed him for years. And now he's home and *he doesn't want me*?

I'll just have to learn to live with that. Besides, it's not like I can claim that I know him well. Ten years away is a long time. He only came home once a year, and after I got married, he stopped contacting me because he said it wasn't appropriate to continue to communicate with a married woman.

Divorced or not, why would I think that he'd suddenly be thrilled to see me and swoop me up in a tight hug, then want to share breakfast and conversation?

I sigh as I park in my driveway, kill the engine, and finally face the fact that despite our past, I don't really know Landon anymore. I know the young man who left here long ago, and that's not who he is anymore.

I'm not that girl anymore either.

I've been carrying a torch all these years for someone who doesn't exist.

"Stupid," I whisper, and slam my car door shut and climb the steps to my porch, unlock my door, and to my utter shock, see a gray-and-white streak run between my legs and into my house, then stop at the entrance to my kitchen, turn, and sit on its butt, as if he belongs here.

"Oh, no, you've got to go," I say sternly. "Come on." I gesture to the door, but the cat just blinks, then licks his tail twice before returning his gaze to me.

I've never seen this cat before in my life.

"Where did you come from?" I ask, propping my fists on my hips and giving the cat my best glare.

It doesn't seem to bother him.

"You need to go," I say, and march toward him. "Scoot. Outside."

He simply runs out of my reach into the living room, watching me. *"Meow."*

"No, you can't stay," I reply, as if I'm carrying on a conversation with the feline. "Seriously, I don't like cats."

"Meow."

"Because they're moody and snobby. I'm really a dog person," I say, trying to reason with him. He flicks his tail and turns away from me. "Seriously, I'm not even allowed to have pets here. My landlord doesn't allow it."

Great. Now I'm lying to the cat. I *own* this house.

"It's not you, it's me," I try, but the cat lies down on his back, exposing his belly, and stretches out on my expensive area rug, making himself at home.

"*Meow.*"

"You. Have. To. Go." I clap my hands and move fast, trying to scare him out and through the open front door, but he runs in the opposite direction. "Seriously? You're really starting to piss me off."

"*Meow.*"

He jumps up on the back of my couch and crouches, watching to see what my next move will be so he can dodge it, I'm sure.

"I said outside," I say, my voice heavy with authority.

Finally, he jumps down and runs through my legs, toward the front door, and when I turn around, there's Landon, with a shirt on now, leaning against the doorjamb with a smirk on his face and the cat weaving through his legs, purring.

"What are you trying to do to your cat?" he asks as he leans down and scoops the terrorist into his arms.

"He's not my cat," I reply, and blow out a gusty sigh. "He ran in here and now I can't get him to leave."

"Smart cat," he says, and scratches the feline's head. Landon's blue eyes are on mine as he closes the door and sits himself, and the cat, on my couch.

"By all means, both of you make yourselves at home." I roll my eyes and push my fingers through my hair. "What do you want, Landon?"

I frown. My voice has never been this hard when I spoke to Landon before. It doesn't sit well with me.

"I'm sorry, Cam," he says softly, watching the cat as it curls up in his lap and purrs happily.

"No need," I say, and sit on the love seat to the left of him. "I shouldn't have come over without calling first."

I trace the pattern in the fabric of the love seat, not wanting to meet Landon's gaze. I'm still embarrassed, and disconcerted about the cat.

"I didn't mean to snap at you," Landon says.

"I'm fine," I reply. "I was just going to say hi. No big deal. I have some stuff to do, so if you could just take the cat outside with you when you go, I'd appreciate it."

I stand and move to leave the room, but Landon catches my wrist in his hand to stop me. Since I was young, Landon's always caught my wrist when he wanted to take a bite of whatever I was eating, or just to catch my attention. He's a touchy-feely guy. I frown down into his face and my heart catches. His blue eyes are . . . *sad.*

And my arm is on fire from his touch.

"I really am sorry," he says. "I'm just not myself these days."

I gently tug my arm out of his grasp and sit back down, watching him. "Okay."

"I didn't want to come home," he says as he pets the cat, currently purring happily as if he lives here. "I guess things are just weird right now. But that doesn't mean I can snap at you. You're the sweetest person I know."

"You don't know me anymore," I murmur, remembering what I thought about in the car. Landon's brow furrows, but then he nods.

"Maybe not. But I do know that you're sweet, and I care about you, and I just wanted to say I'm sorry for being an ass."

"Thank you."

He looks over at me now and really *looks* at me, his eyes tracking me from head to toe, then finding mine again. "You look great."

"Thank you," I repeat, not knowing what else to say. I can see that he's hurting, and maybe confused, and everything in me wants to scoop him up and pet him, like he's the cat, to soothe him and comfort him.

But I can't. It's not my place. So I sit where I am, waiting for him to make the next move.

After a long minute, he stands, sets the cat on the floor, and walks to the door. "Thanks for stopping by, Cami," he says, nods, and walks out.

I sigh and stare at the cat. "You're not going to leave, are you?"

He simply jumps back up on the couch where Landon was just sitting, curls into a ball, and immediately goes to sleep.

"You're late," I inform Riley, who just walked through my door with a bottle of wine and a grocery-store sack full of ice cream.

"Sorry," she says as she hurries into the kitchen to stow away the ice cream and pop open the wine. "I got held up on a call with the Web designer. But I brought sugar and wine, so I should be forgiven. Besides, the show hasn't started yet."

I slap slices of pizza on plates for both of us, and we each take a plate and a glass to the living room and settle in for our date night.

Every week, Riley, another best friend of mine, and business partner, comes over and we watch our favorite shows back-to-back while eating bad food and drinking too much wine.

It's tradition.

"Meow," the cat says as he slinks into the room, his nose sniffing out the food.

"What the hell!" Riley says in surprise. "When did you get a cat?"

"I didn't," I reply as the opening credits for *The Vampire Diaries* begins. "He got me."

"Huh?"

I explain how he ran in the house and refuses to leave. "So I bought him some food and a bed and some toys."

"You got a cat," Riley says, grinning.

"He got me," I say again.

"What's his name?"

"Scoot. Because he *won't* scoot."

"I think it's awesome," Riley says with a smile, and scratches Scoot's ears, making him purr. "He's so pretty."

"And stubborn. He doesn't listen. I tell him he can't sleep on my bed, and he does it anyway. The only thing he does right is use the litter box."

"He's a cat," she says with a shrug. "That's what cats do."

We settle in to eat and watch TV as Scoot jumps up on the back of the couch and curls into a ball to sleep and watch over us.

"I'm telling you," Riley says as she sips her wine. "That Ian Somerhalder is going to eventually be my husband."

"He's already married," I remind her, and watch as young vampires feed on innocent bystanders while also saving the town from evil.

It's an amazing sort of irony.

"For him I could be a home wrecker," she says thoughtfully. "I mean, *look at him.*"

"Sexy for sure," I reply with a nod. "Except when he has blood dripping down his chin."

"I wouldn't kick him out of bed for having blood dripping down his chin," she says with a smirk. "Unless he wanted to do me in the bathroom."

"Ew," I reply.

"You don't like to do it in the bathroom?"

"No, the blood part. Ew."

We giggle, then settle in to enjoy the rest of the show. When it's over, I pause the DVR so we can clean up the pizza, refill our wine, and scoop ice cream. Because right after *The Vampire Diaries* is *The Originals,* an offshoot of *The Vampire Diaries.*

Just as I'm about to resume the TV, Riley says, "So, have you seen Landon?"

She's not looking directly at me, and she says it as if she's asking me if I've checked the weather forecast for tomorrow.

"I saw him the other day," I reply. "Just for a minute."

I really don't want to get into it. The girls all know that I've crushed on Landon for years.

"Kat said he came into the restaurant the other day," Riley says. Kat is the fifth friend of our group. The five of us co-own Seduction, a trendy restaurant in Portland. We've been open for almost a year, and business couldn't be better.

"Did he?" I ask.

"She said he looks pretty good."

No, he doesn't. He's sad and maybe scared, and it's not my job to help him.

"Good for him."

I press play and pretend to be engrossed in the show. When I'm finished with my ice cream, Scoot jumps down into my lap and curls up, but when I pet him, he hisses, so I leave him be.

"I know that Mia is glad that Landon's home," Riley says, and now I want to hiss at her.

"Why are we still talking about this?"

"Because you're not saying anything," she says.

"There's nothing to say. He's home."

"And you love him," she reminds me.

I shake my head. "I've been thinking about that. I don't know him, Ri. I've carried a torch for a boy I used to know. A lot has happened."

She's frowning. "But it's *Landon*."

"I'm fine," I say, exasperated. "It'll be nice to see him once in a while, but I'm not a teenager, Riley."

"Is it weird because of Brian?" she asks, making me frown.

"Why would it be weird because of Brian?" I'm deliberately being a pain in the ass. I don't like to talk about this. It just makes me feel guilty and *bad*.

"Look, people get divorced all the time." Riley's voice is calm and matter-of-fact. "I'll admit that being friends with your ex is odd, but people do it. I've heard."

"Brian doesn't have anything to do with Landon."

"Well, given that they didn't know each other before, and Brian's not even *from* here, you wouldn't think so. But I know differently." Riley's eyes are soft as she watches me. She's the only one who knows *all* of the reasons that my marriage to Brian didn't work.

And one of the reasons is Landon.

"I was young, and when I met Brian—"

"You were still hung up on Landon. I know."

"But I didn't marry Brian to spite Landon, Riley. That's dumb. I did fall in love with Brian, and our relationship evolved naturally to marriage. It was the logical next step."

"Logical," she says with a nod.

I blow out a gusty breath. I don't have to tell Riley that my marriage with Brian didn't work because I'd never allowed myself to fall in love with him the way he deserved. That I'd been holding a piece of my heart aside for Landon.

Even though I knew that Landon wasn't going to ever come back.

Except now he's back, and I'm no kid, and I'm still so attracted to him that it's silly.

"Can we not talk about this anymore and watch our show now?"

"Okay." She doesn't sound convinced, but I really don't want to talk about Landon. When the show is over, we clean up and Riley leaves, and I climb the stairs to my bedroom.

I don't argue with Scoot when he jumps onto the bed and curls up behind my knees.

I'm not a teenager anymore. I failed in a marriage with a good man because I was hung up on Landon. It's childish. It's ridiculous.

It needs to stop now. It's past time to move on with my life.

I LOVE OUR restaurant. We've worked our asses off for it. I walk through the dining room and stop to fuss over a centerpiece, enjoying the cozy color scheme and richness of the fabrics. It's inviting. Sexy.

Everything about our place is sexy. We made sure of it. From the warm atmosphere to the aphrodisiacs on the menu, Seduction screams classy sex.

And I like to think that it mirrors the five women who own and run it.

I walk through to the wine bar that Kat runs and grin when I see her and Mia, our master chef, with their heads bent over wine goblets, sniffing deeply.

"It smells like wine," Mia says.

"It smells like cherries and oak. It's full-bodied."

"Like me." Mia smirks and pats her round hip. Mia may carry a few extra pounds, but she's sexy as can be with it. Her long dark hair, usually worn up and under a hat, hangs in loose curls to her waist.

"I wish I had your curves," I say as I join them. "What are you doing?"

"Kat's trying to teach me how to smell wine."

"How's that going?"

"It smells like wine," Mia says with a shrug.

"I give up," Kat says with a frown, her red lips twisting in disgust.

"Kat, you're the one that needs to know this stuff," I remind her. "And you're excellent at it."

"Exactly," Mia agrees, nodding. "You're the wine expert. I'll keep doing what I do in the kitchen."

"Good plan," Addie says, her heels clicking on the hardwood as she and Riley join us. Addie's tall and rocks curves of her own. She's the most fashionable person I know, and since she's a former model, I'd expect nothing less.

"Kat, I just got off the phone with Leah, your new bartender. She'll be here by three to start training."

"Cool," Kat says with a nod. "Not sure why she called the front of the house and not my cell."

"She said she lost your number. She sounds a little—" Addie struggles to find the word.

"Not the brightest bulb in the shed?" Kat asks. "She's a little dense, but she's an excellent bartender, she's adorable, and she doesn't take shit from the customers who have had too much to drink. She comes highly recommended."

"I totally trust your judgment," Addie replies with a smile. "I'm just passing along the message."

"Do *not* try to set her up with Brian," Kat says, pointing her finger at me. "I mean it."

"I would not do that," I reply, as innocently as possible. "Like I would set people up with my ex-husband." I can't stop my lips from twitching.

"Right. Because you haven't tried to set him up with every single woman you know, including *us*," Mia replies, and rolls her eyes. "Finding dates for your ex is just weird."

"For your information, he's been finding his own dates lately," I reply, and sniff haughtily. My ex-husband, Brian, is a good man, and I want him to find an awesome girl. He deserves that. I just wasn't the girl for him, but we're still good friends.

"Now that we're all here," I begin, changing the subject and opening the folder I brought in with me, "let's talk about the expansion."

"I can't believe that we're expanding already," Riley says, eyeing Mia's wine. "We've been open less than a year."

"And we're bursting at the seams," I reply. "With Jake packing in crowds every weekend, and word spreading of what a fun, sexy place this is, our wait times are too long. I've made graphs and spreadsheets. Needing to expand isn't a bad thing."

"I agree," Addie says with a nod. "And I think we'd be packing in people with or without Jake. Just don't tell him I said that."

Jake Knox is Addie's husband, and a former rock star who's been playing at Seduction on the weekends. His voice is pure sex, and is perfect for the atmosphere of our place.

"Oh God, she brought graphs," Mia says, hanging her head in her hand. "This is all a foreign language to me."

"I was able to talk the former owners next door down far enough that we can pay cash for the space," I say, ignoring Mia, and pass around the report I typed up last night after

Riley left and I couldn't sleep. I've attached the graphs and spreadsheets to the back.

"We don't have to take out a loan?" Kat asks, surprised. "That's awesome."

"You are such a great financial officer, Cami," Mia says with a smile. "I used to hate your budgets, but it's exactly what we needed."

I grin. Mia's disgust over my budgets was never a secret. The passionate chef has thrown many a spatula at my head when I told her she couldn't have more money for extra truffles.

"Honestly, my only concern is time," Addie says. "I don't have time to oversee construction. I know that Mia practically lives in the kitchen, and with Kat running the bar and Riley dealing with marketing, who's going to take the lead on this?"

"I agree, and honestly, now that Seduction is my only client, I have the time to take on the project." I fold my hands over the folder and take a deep breath. As of two months ago, I closed my other CPA business and am now exclusively devoted to Seduction. Not that I wasn't before, but a girl can handle working sixteen-hour days for only so long before she starts to go a little nutty.

"Are you sure?" Riley asks. "It's going to be a busy few months."

"I'm sure."

"Awesome," Mia says. "You and Landon will do a great job."

"Excuse me?"

"Landon." Mia grins and nods toward the entrance, where Landon is walking our way. "He's taking the lead on the construction side."

"Hi, ladies," Landon says as he joins us. "I hear you have a project for me."

"We have a construction crew we work with," I sputter, but Mia just grins knowingly.

"Dad's thinking of retiring, and Landon's taking up some of the slack," she says. "We'll have the same crew, but Landon will be in charge of it."

"Cami's going to be in charge," Addie informs him. "So anything you need, you just call her."

"Great," he replies, and I finally glance up at him only to find him watching me with those shining blue eyes. "I promise to go easy on you."

I swallow and can't help but laugh at the irony. Just when I've decided to keep my distance from Landon, he takes on the job that I'll be working intimately on.

Murphy's Law.

Fucking Murphy.

Chapter 2

~Landon~

"So, what we need," Cami begins as she leads me into the empty space next to the restaurant, "is to expand into this space for more seating. We want to open it up and add a significant number of tables and booths so we have room to expand Mia's kitchen. She needs more staff, and that's impossible now, as the current kitchen is at capacity."

I nod and follow her, trying to keep my eyes off of her ass.

I've been working on keeping my eyes off of her ass for more years than I can count. It's habit.

But she still has a great ass.

"Are you listening?" she asks, crossing her arms over her chest.

"Yes, ma'am."

"Are you going to write this down?"

"I'm making notes," I reply, and tap my head, indicating that I'll remember what she says.

"Well, that's comforting," she mumbles, and turns away, making me smile. Cami has always been funny. She's giving and kind, and we once had a special friendship. I don't remember a time when I didn't want her. Had she been a couple of years older, there was a time when I would have pursued her romantically, but then I went into the Navy, and she got married, and life carried on. It's not right for a man to continue to call and send letters to a married woman, no matter how much it kills him that she belongs to another man. So we drifted apart.

Suddenly she stops pacing, links her fingers nervously together, and sighs. "Landon, I wanted to thank you for coming home when Mom and Daddy died."

I stare at her for a moment, then shake my head, shove my hands in my pockets, and shuffle my feet. "You don't have to thank me for that."

"Yeah, I do." She nods. "It was a weird time, and having you here was . . . well, comforting."

"I'm glad. How are you?"

"Better," she says, and smiles. "A lot has happened in the few years since then."

It's been a few years? I had no idea. Time sure goes fast.

"The restaurant keeps all of us busy." She takes a deep breath and looks around the empty space. "Speaking of, I think a row of booths, like the existing ones we have, would be beautiful over here," she says, gesturing to the far wall.

She continues to share her vision, her eyes shining with excitement.

She's professional and animated, and I can't look away from her. I never could. The dimple in her cheek winks when she grins, talking about the need for a larger storage space in the back. Her hair is up in a simple ponytail, and she's in jeans, sneakers, and a sweatshirt.

She still looks sixteen.

But when she turns, and her sweatshirt molds against her body, she's anything but a kid. She's all woman.

Beautiful, stunning, amazing woman.

"Seriously, you're not paying attention to me," she grumbles.

"Oh, I'm paying attention," I reply. Maybe not the way she wants, but I'm paying attention. "How are you and the cat getting along?"

She frowns. "He's taken over my house."

"He likes you. You're a likable girl." I shrug and watch as her frown deepens, then she shakes her head.

"We're talking about work."

"I think, for the first meeting, we did good," I reply, and glance about the room. "What used to be in here?"

"A toy store," she replies. "I guess most people buy stuff online these days."

"I think I can raise the ceiling in here," I say, studying the drop ceiling. "I can make it match your existing ceiling, open it up a bit."

"Good. I don't know why they made it lower."

"Probably to save on heating costs."

"Raising it will be much better." She's nodding, hands on hips, slowly sauntering around. "Can we match the floors too?"

"That shouldn't be a problem."

"Awesome." She pauses, smiles, and claps her hands. "I'm so excited!"

"Even if I'm your contractor?" I ask, and reach out to tug on her hair, but she ducks out of my way.

"I guess I can deal with you."

"You like me." The crush she's had on me since we were kids has never been a secret. I managed to keep mine hidden, but Cami never did.

"You're okay." She shrugs and chuckles, and for the first time that I can remember, she's not looking at me with that sparkle in her eyes, and I'm not sure what to do about that. Or if I even should do anything about that.

But I fucking miss it.

"I think I have everything I need."

"Great." She walks past me, but stumbles forward, and I catch her, wrapping an arm around her waist and pulling her against me.

"Hey, easy," I murmur, my face just inches from hers, and for just a brief moment, that sparkle is back in her eyes, making my gut clench. She's not nearly as immune to me as she'd like to believe. "I've got you."

"This is what I get for wearing sneakers," she grumbles as her little hands clench my jacket and she manages to get her feet under her.

"You don't usually wear shoes?"

"Not sneakers," she mumbles, and tries to pull away, but I tighten my arm and take a moment to enjoy the sweet way she fits against me. She smells good.

She feels fucking perfect.

For the first time in months, I actually feel alive.

"I have this, Landon," she says, but I don't let go. Not quite yet.

"You always have it," I reply softly, but when she just stares at me like I've lost my mind, the spark leaving her gaze, I set her away from me and move back, immediately missing her warmth. "Watch where you step."

"Yes, sir," she says primly, salutes—with the wrong hand—and walks ahead of me out the door and back to the restaurant. Her ass sways as she struts away, making me grin.

"Did you figure it all out?" Riley asks as we walk inside.

"I think we got a good start," I reply with a wink. "We'll make it beautiful, and you'll never be able to tell that it wasn't part of the original design all along."

"That's what we want to hear," Riley says.

"Have a good day, Landon," Cami says with a wave, and walks into her office, then firmly closes the door.

"Did I do something to irritate her?" I ask.

"Not that she mentioned," Riley says. "Maybe she's hormonal."

"And that's my cue to leave," I reply with a fake cringe. "Tell Mia I'll talk to her later."

"Have a good day!" Riley says with a smile and a wave.

I walk out to my car, and rather than measurements and supplies running through my mind, I have Cami and her slender curves and fresh scent front and center.

I need an hour in the gym to clear my head.

"WOULD YOU LIKE to see the pool?" Kelsie, the young woman showing me the first apartment I've stopped to look at today, asks with a flirty smile. I simply turn away, shove my hands in my pockets, and frown at the dark, outdated kitchen in the small space.

"I don't think so."

"I can show you the workout room," she says hopefully, but I shake my head.

"I think I've seen all I need to."

I walk out the door and down the steps to my car.

"I'll give you my card, so you can call if you want to look at anything else." She's hustling behind me. "Or, you know, if you'd like to get a drink sometime."

Kelsie is a pretty girl, not quite as curvy as I usually prefer, but she'd probably be a lot of fun in bed.

And I have *zero* interest.

"I appreciate the offer," I say with a smile. "But I just don't think I'm interested." *In either the apartment or you.*

I don't have to say the last part. She shrugs, as if to say, *Your loss,* and thanks me for stopping by.

This is the third place I've seen this week, and I haven't liked any of them. My things from Italy will arrive next week. I need to find a place.

I just hate doing it by myself.

Without giving it too much thought, I head downtown and park on the street near Seduction. It's midafternoon on Saturday, just one week after I had my meeting with the girls about the expansion. My guys and I spent the past week working on demo and cleanup so we can get to work on the actual building.

The girls will be pleased.

But it's the weekend, so there's no work to keep me busy today. I might as well see what the girls are up to.

"It's not busy," I say in surprise as I walk through the front door and see Addie talking to the hostess.

"Lunch was a madhouse," the tall blonde replies with a grin. "This is our brief lull before dinner."

"Mia's in the kitchen?" I ask.

"Of course," Addie replies. "Last I heard, she was throwing rotten tomatoes, literally, at the poor produce man."

"He shouldn't have brought her bad food," I say with a shrug. "I don't blame her."

"You Italians have quite the temper," Addie says, her eyes lighting up as her husband, Jake, walks in behind me. "Well, hello there."

"Hey Jake," I say, shaking the other man's hand firmly.

"Good to see you, man," he replies. "Are you gonna stick around to hear my set later?"

Jake Keller, or Jake Knox as the rest of the world knows him, is an international rock star who stepped out of the limelight to focus on producing and writing, and as of about six months ago, started focusing on our Addie.

"I don't know, I have to go house-hunting today." I shake my head mournfully.

"I like looking at houses," Addie says.

"I don't," I reply simply. "It's boring."

"What's boring?" Cami asks as she walks out of her office and joins us. My eyes immediately zero in on her feet—not in sneakers this time—and the mile-high gray boots she's wearing. My eyes travel up her body, taking in her stylish black-and-gray outfit, and sexy-as-hell body, and when I reach her eyes, her head is tilted, and she's gazing at me with a mixture of humor and reservation.

This is what interests me.

"Landon hates looking at houses."

"I've mostly been looking at apartments," I reply, still holding Cami's gaze with my own. "But I have appointments to see three houses this afternoon."

"Good luck with that," Cami says, and turns to leave, but I catch her wrist before she can walk away.

"Come with me."

"Excuse me?" She glances down at my hand and I pull it away, immediately missing the contact.

"Come look with me."

"I'm at work."

"I told her to leave two hours ago," Addie says helpfully.

"I've been busy," she replies with a frown. "The damn tills from yesterday were off."

"By a lot?" Addie asks.

"No, it was probably a mistake." Cami sighs and shakes her head. "I guess I could use a break."

"Perfect," I reply with a grin. "Looking alone is torture,

Cam. If I have to look at another bathroom, I'm going to . . . Well, I don't know what I'll do, but it won't be pretty."

She blinks at me, then finally shakes her head, mumbles something under her breath that I can't quite hear, then chuckles. "Well, we can't have you not being pretty."

"Great. Let's go." I gesture for her to lead me out the door, but she rolls her eyes.

"I need my jacket and handbag. I'll meet you outside."

"You might want to change your shoes too. We'll be walking a lot."

Both Cami and Addie laugh. "These are my walking shoes," she replies as she walks back into the office, then returns less than thirty seconds later with her bag, jacket, and shiny lips.

Great. Now I can't stop staring at her lips. I'm pretty sure women do that on purpose.

"Call me if you need me," Cami says to Addie, who just waves as we walk out of the restaurant and to my car. I open the door for her, then walk around and lower myself into the seat and pull out my phone.

"I have the appointments, with the addresses, in my calendar," I say as I pull the information up and hand the phone to Cami. "You be the navigator. Where are we going?"

She rattles off the address, then sits back silently as I drive to the first house. Cami and I have never had an uncomfortable silence in the twenty years I've known her, and I refuse to start now.

"How's business?"

"Great."

"How are you?"

"Can't complain."

She smooths her hand down her skirt and shifts in the seat, but doesn't elaborate.

"I like your nail polish," I say, nodding at the pink on her fingers, and for the first time, that dimple in her cheek winks as she smiles, just a little bit.

"Thank you." She points just ahead. "That's it."

"Got it." I pull up to the curb, and before I can tell her to wait, Cami shoves out of the car and walks up the sidewalk to the front door, where a Realtor is already waiting.

"Hello, Mr. and Mrs. Palazzo."

"I'm Cami LaRue, a friend of Mr. Palazzo's," Cami says immediately. The women lead me into the home.

"Nice to meet you. I'm Lacey. This is a 1956 Craftsman-style home," she begins, and leads us through the small house that probably hasn't been updated since the eighties.

"It's too small," Cami says when we're back in the car and pulling away. "And the pink master bathroom is so *not* you."

"We agree on that," I reply with a nod. "I don't need a huge place. It's just me."

"I know, but you don't need a broom closet either," she replies as she searches for the next address. "Aren't you afraid I'll snoop through your phone, look for pictures and messages from the many girls you date?"

"Yes, I'm horrified," I reply, my voice dry. "Contrary to popular belief, I don't date much, and second, you're not the snooping type. But if you do want to snoop, go for it. I don't have any secrets from you, Cami."

"I was being a smartass, Landon," she says, then gives me the address. "I don't know where this one is."

"I think it's in a newer subdivision. Can you pull it up on the map app?"

"Newer is better. Hopefully there won't be a pink bathroom." She wrinkles her adorable nose and directs me where we're going. It's not as far away as I thought.

"So far, so good," Cami says as she steps out of the car.

"I wish you'd let me open the door for you," I say as I join her on the sidewalk.

"Why?" She frowns and glances from the house to me. "This isn't a date."

I simply shake my head and follow her up the steps to the front porch.

"Oh, you could put a great rocking chair out here," Cami says as I see a note on the door, telling us to come in and look around. The property manager had to rush off to an emergency at another property.

"Let's check it out," I say, and lead us inside. This one already feels so much better than any of the others I've seen. It definitely is newer, it doesn't smell weird, and the floor plan is open.

"This is it," Cami says confidently.

"You just stepped inside."

"I'm telling you, that last one was haunted. This one is perfect."

"You didn't say anything about that last one being

haunted." I stop and stare back at her, but she's wandering around the living room.

"I didn't want to scare you, in case you decided to live there. But I would never visit you there."

"But you *will* visit me here?"

"I don't know, Landon; the last time I rang your doorbell, you snapped at me like I was trying to sell you on religion or vacuums."

My stomach clenches. "Cami, I told you, I'm sorry for that."

"It's fine," she says quickly, and walks into the kitchen, the click of her heels echoing through the empty space. "These countertops are to die for!"

I follow her into the kitchen and nod. "It's a big kitchen for someone who doesn't cook."

"Maybe someone will cook for you," she mumbles, not looking at me.

Everything feels off with her today. It's felt off since that morning when she showed up unexpectedly at my parents' house, waking me up and looking all sexy and sweet, and I didn't have my wits about me.

I fucked up. I seem to be the king of fucking up lately, and it's starting to piss me off.

"There's a lot of cabinet space," she continues, then opens a door in the back of the room. "And there's a large pantry here."

"Let's check out the rest."

We see two average-sized bedrooms, a nice guest bath, and then wander into a massive master bedroom, with a large closet and bathroom as well.

"Wow. Swanky," she says, that dimple winking at me as she grins. "You could get a lot of shoes in this closet."

"That's exactly what I was worried about."

"Hey, I'm just saying." She saunters into the bathroom. "Holy shit, you could host a party in this shower!"

A two-person-party-with-Cami-boosted-up-against-the-wall-with-me-inside-her party sounds just about perfect.

I don't dare go in there.

"Don't you want to check it out?"

"I'll take your word for it."

"But it's pretty."

"I believe you."

"Landon . . ."

I pop my head in and take in the spacious bathroom, see that the shower is indeed larger than the one in my last apartment, and turn away. "Yep, great bathroom."

"This is the house," she says confidently as she follows me out and back to the car.

"We have one more to see."

"No." She shakes her head and hands me my phone. "You don't need to see more."

"What if it's better than this one?"

"It won't be. You're sick of looking, Landon, and this house isn't too big, isn't too small, and is newer. And it's not haunted."

"I don't think that other house was haunted," I reply, agreeing with her. I like this house. I pull away and head back to the restaurant.

"Why are you renting instead of buying?" she asks.

"Because I don't know where I'll end up," I reply immediately, and slam on my brakes as we're almost T-boned in an intersection. "It's a four-way stop, asshole!"

"Nothing wrong with your reflexes," she says, and pushes her hair off her face. "So you don't plan on settling down in Portland?"

"I probably will," I say, and shrug. "I mean, the family is here, and I don't have any job offers elsewhere, but I want to keep my options open for a while, you know?"

"No, not really," she replies, and I glance over at her. "I like it here. I'll always be here."

"Well, especially now that you have the restaurant, I can see that."

"With or without it, this is home."

I shake my head. "Haven't you ever wanted to live anywhere else? I mean, you've been here your whole life. Now that you don't have family here—"

"Steven is here."

Her voice is hard as she reminds me of her nephew and when I glance at her again, her face is taut and lips pursed. I've pissed her off.

Again.

"I'm sorry, Cami." Shit, I don't know what else to say. I should know that Cami's always done what feels safe to her.

"You can drop me off at home," Cami says, and blows out a breath.

"You don't need to get your car?"

"No, I rode in with Riley this morning." She sighs and crosses her legs. "I think I'll actually take tonight off."

"Good for you," I reply, and drive the short couple of miles to her house, pull in her driveway, and glance over to see that she's fallen asleep. Her face is relaxed, her breathing even, and her lips—those amazing, plump lips—are slightly parted. I want to kiss her so bad I ache with it.

Instead, I get out of the car, and before she can climb out herself, I open the door for her and take her hand, helping her to her feet.

"Sorry I dozed."

"You're tired."

She nods and leads me into her house. "It's been a busy week."

"How many hours a week do you work?" I ask as she plops her bag on the table inside the door and toes off her shoes, instantly shrinking at least four inches. She looks so small.

So sexy.

"About sixty," she replies, and shrugs as if it's no big deal. "It's better than the eighty I was working before I stopped working for my other clients. I'll make dinner."

"No." My voice is calm, but firm. The thought of her working herself to the bone sets a fire in my stomach that I can't explain. "You worked your ass off this week, and I just dragged you all over Portland to look at houses."

"It was two houses," she says, and rolls her eyes.

"I'll order in Chinese."

Her eyes sharpen at that suggestion.

"That got your attention." I grin and reach out to tug a lock of hair, and this time she doesn't move away.

"You know it's my favorite."

I grin. "Of course I do. Sit." I point to the arm of the couch where Scoot has just jumped. He's sitting, his tail flicking back and forth, his eyes narrowed, watching us.

"I'm not a dog."

"Not even close," I agree. "Have a seat. Please."

"Since you said please," she says primly, and sits next to Scoot, who curls up next to her. "He won't get in my lap, at least not like he does you, and if he does, he won't let me pet him. He'll sit next to me like this, and he purrs, but he still won't let me pet him. He's the weirdest cat."

"He likes you," I murmur as I sit at the opposite end of the couch and dial the number for Cami's favorite Chinese place. After I order, I glance over to see that Cami's eyes are heavy. Her head is tilted back, leaning on the couch. Her bare feet are on the ottoman, crossed at the ankles.

I need to get my hands on her. But when I move to scoot closer, she flinches and eyes me warily.

I hate this. Did I fuck up that badly? Did I hurt her feelings that morning so bad that she's placed me directly in the friend zone? And I'm talking the don't-touch-me friend zone.

I hate that place, especially with Cami. I know that we'll never be like we were when we were kids, and hell, I don't want to be. I want to be close to her. I want to get to know her again.

"How is Steven?" I ask, trying to fill the silence. She smiles sweetly.

"He's great. He's living with his girlfriend, but he checks

in with me often, and we try to get together for dinner once a week. He's a good kid."

"You're close." It isn't a question.

"Well, given the age difference between me and Steve's mom, he's more like a brother to me. He's nineteen going on thirty. Were we that eager to grow up?"

I chuckle and rub her pinky toe. "You always seemed very grown up." I look up into her green eyes. "You acted so much older than your age."

"That's what happens when your parents are middle-aged when they have you, and your siblings have one foot out the door to college."

But did you ever get to just have fun? I don't ask it aloud, but I've often wondered if Cami is content playing it safe because being responsible was expected of her at such a young age.

The doorbell rings, saving me from my thoughts.

"I'll get it."

When I turn, after paying for the food, Cami's no longer on the couch, but walking back from the kitchen with plates and silverware. We sit in our normal, comfortable silence now, dishing up food and eating until we're stuffed. When the white boxes are empty and our dishes set aside, I surprise us both by pulling Cami's feet into my lap and digging my thumb into her arch.

"Oh, sweet Jesus, don't ever stop doing that."

I grin and watch as I knead her feet. Upon closer inspection, I see that they're callused, and despite being nicely painted, they're a bit of a mess.

"I hate my feet," she murmurs softly. "They're rough and callused and horrible."

"I don't mind," I reply honestly. "But you should spoil yourself sometimes and go get one of those froofroo pedicures."

"I do. But I wear shoes that are bad for me, and I hate socks, so this is what I'm stuck with." Her eyes slit open to watch me as she shrugs. "I don't care. My shoes rock."

"I'll rub your feet for you anytime you want."

She grins softly and I want to pull her in my lap and hold on tight. I want to kiss her madly and lay her back on this couch and uncover her body, inch by inch, discovering what makes her moan and what makes her sigh.

I want to do all of the things I've fantasized about for longer than I can remember.

Instead, I sigh and pat her ankle, then stand. "I'd better go."

She stands with me and follows me to the door. "Thank you for dinner. You didn't have to do that."

"Yes." I turn to her and push her blond hair back over her ear. Scoot is winding his way through my legs, purring. "I did. Thank you for today."

Before she can push me away, I lean in and press my lips to her forehead, breathing her in, and wanting to stay.

"Are you going to get that last house?"

"If you promise to visit." I pull back and see her bite her lip, then firm her shoulders.

"I'll visit."

I nod and leave her before I do something stupid like

scoop her up and take her up to her bedroom to spend the rest of the weekend with her.

She's not ready for that. I'm not sure I'm ready for that, which shocks the fuck out of me because I've never had a problem with carrying a willing woman off to a bed to have my way with her.

But this is Cami, and a fun romp on a mattress isn't the only thing I want with her. Not that I really know *what* I want with her.

I do know that she deserves more than a weekend in bed, and the thought of someone else giving it to her makes me crazy.

Chapter 3

~Cami~

*W*hat in the ever-loving hell was *that*?

I stare at my now closed front door, where Landon just left, and frown. This whole day has left me in a big bucket of confusion. I'd done so well all week, not seeking Landon out, keeping busy, truly believing that my girlhood crush was over and under control.

"And then *he* sought *me* out," I say to Scoot as I turn the lights off downstairs and head up to my bedroom. "Today was *not* my fault. He practically made me go with him to see those houses, and then he just didn't leave."

I peel back the covers on my bed and scowl at Scoot, who jumps up and promptly begins giving himself a bath.

"You're not supposed to be on the bed. Or in my house, for that matter." No response from the feline, so I shrug, shed my clothes, and get under the covers. Scoot climbs up on my belly and begins to purr.

"What was that kiss about? Like, was he kissing me as a *brother*? Because it didn't feel brotherly, but we all know that my hormones are ridiculous around that man." I reach up to scratch Scoot behind the ears but he lets out a low growl. "Sorry. I won't touch you. And what was up with him rubbing my feet? My good sense just leaves when he's around, and suddenly I'm sixteen again. It has to stop, Scoot."

I glance down into deep green eyes, currently narrowed as he purrs and rhythmically digs his little claws into my chest.

"Why am I talking to you about this?"

"Meow."

"Exactly. You don't even speak English." I sigh and check my phone, remembering that my ex-husband, Brian, is supposed to be out on a date tonight. I wonder how it's going. So I shoot him a text. *How's your date going? Don't forget to compliment her shoes!*

I bite my lip and watch the screen, but there's no response, so I call Riley.

"What are you doing?" I ask when she answers.

"I just got home from the restaurant."

"Do they need me?" I ask, and sit up, knocking Scoot off of me, and making him growl at me again before turning his back on me and resuming his bath.

"No, that's why I'm home. It's handled. What are you doing?"

"I'm in bed."

"It's early for bed," she says, and I check my phone, realizing it's not even nine in the evening.

Landon knocked me off my axis so hard that I just went straight to bed.

Not that I'm going to tell Riley that.

"I was tired."

"I heard you went house shopping with Landon. How was that?"

"Fine," I reply, trying to keep my voice neutral. "He found a house."

"And how are *you*?"

I cringe. It's actually mortifying that the other girls know all about my crush on Landon. I mean, it's my fault. I'm the one who couldn't keep her damn mouth shut. But it's still humiliating.

"I'm fine, Ri. We're adults now."

"Just checking." I hear her sigh. "Need anything?"

"Nah. I was just calling to see how you are. I'll talk to you tomorrow."

"Sounds good. Night."

I hang up and sigh. *We're adults now.* Get a grip, Cami.

"How in the hell did you get all of this crap in that tiny apartment in Italy?" Mia asks her brother two weeks later, her arms folded over her full breasts, scowling.

"You do have a lot of crap for a bachelor," Addie says in agreement as she unloads a box of books onto a bookshelf.

After being held up with the mover, Landon's things were finally delivered a couple of days ago. He'd bought furniture, which was also delivered and set up, and now Addie, Mia, and I are here to help him unload boxes and get settled.

I'm practicing the whole get-a-grip thing. So far, so good.

"Where do you want this?" I ask, my nose wrinkling as I pull the ugliest owl clock I've ever seen out of a box. "In the garbage?"

"No, it was a gift," Landon says, and rescues the clock from my hands. "I'll hang it in the kitchen."

"I'm going to have to disagree with that," I reply, shaking my head. "That thing will kill anyone's appetite."

"She runs a restaurant," Addie says with a smirk. "Trust her on that."

"Hide it in the spare bedroom you'll never use," Mia suggests, earning a high five from me.

"There's no need to insult my shit," Landon says.

"There is when it's ugly," I reply with a shrug, and open another box. This one is full of clothes. "Do these go in your bedroom?"

He peeks over. "Yep."

"Okay." I lift the box and stomp back to Landon's bedroom, kind of relieved to be out of the sea of boxes. Most of the clothes are still on hangers, so they're easy to put away. What I didn't factor in was that they all smell just like Landon.

Lord help me.

"You okay?" the man himself asks as he walks into his bedroom.

"Fine. Why?"

"I thought I heard you whimper."

And here I thought I was just doing that in my own head.

"I was clearing my throat." I've only seen him a couple

of times in the past few weeks, and every time has been at the restaurant. We've been professional and nice, but kept a safe distance.

Until today.

"You've always been a bad liar, Camille," he says, and sets another boxful of clothes next to the mostly empty one at my feet. "I appreciate you coming to help."

"No biggie."

"It's a biggie to me."

I move to hang a shirt and stumble on the empty box, but before I can reach out to catch myself, I'm suddenly surrounded by two very muscular, very warm arms.

"Easy," he says softly in my ear, sending goose bumps up and down my body.

"I'm fine."

But he doesn't let go, just like he didn't let me go a few weeks ago when I almost fell and he caught me at the restaurant. Instead, he takes a deep breath and kisses my temple.

"Whoa. Sorry to interrupt," Mia says, making me jump and try to pull out of his grasp, but he holds on tight. "The pizza guy is here."

"On my way," Landon says, dismissing Mia, then turns to me. "You okay?"

"I'm fine." His blue eyes hold mine as he brushes a piece of my hair behind my ear, then finally nods and follows Mia out of the room.

I take a long, deep breath before hanging the rest of the clothes, holding my breath so I don't inhale Landon's sexy, manly scent, damn him, and then return to the main living area, which now smells like pizza, which is much better than cardboard.

Also, there's safety in numbers in here.

"I'm hungry," I announce, and help myself to a slice of Hawaiian. "Hot!" I hide my mouth behind my hand as I breathe around the scalding-hot pizza in my mouth, and then Landon takes my wrist in his hand and pulls my pizza to his mouth, taking almost half the slice in one bite. *He's touching me again.* And I can smell him, and see his square jaw flex as he chews.

Where's that grip when I need it?

"Just right." He winks and walks into the kitchen, humming as he puts glasses in a cupboard.

It's a good thing my mouth is full right now because otherwise I'd be stammering. But the weird thing about all of this is, although he still makes my pulse speed up, my reaction to his nearness is . . . *different.*

I enjoy him, that's for sure, and he's as much a hottie at thirty-something as he was at twenty. But I realize that he no longer makes me nervous.

I guess we're all adults after all.

And the best part is, he's relaxed too. The sadness hasn't left his blue eyes altogether, but he seems much happier than when he first arrived in town.

"Your hair is pretty like that," Landon says quietly from across the kitchen island. I glance up to see him watching me.

"It's just in a braid," I reply. "But thank you."

"You usually wear your hair down."

"Unless I'm cleaning or working out," I say, and take another bite of pizza. "So far, this qualifies as both."

"Do you go to the gym?"

"Not if I can help it," I reply with a grin. "Addie makes me go sometimes, and I'm pretty sure it's because she hates me."

"I don't hate you!" Addie calls from the living room before returning to her conversation with Mia about a new walk-in freezer for the restaurant.

"So you don't go to the gym but you work out?" Landon asks with a smile.

"I go for walks. I shovel my sidewalk in the winter. I carry Christmas decorations down from my attic."

"That's all considered working out?" Landon asks.

"I have a lot of decorations," I mutter with a frown. "I jump over the cat."

"Wait. You have a cat?" Mia asks. "Since when?"

"About a month ago," I reply. "And I didn't get a cat, the cat got me."

"I'm so confused," Addie whispers.

"He came in my house and he won't leave."

"I've dated a few of those," Mia says with a laugh, then sticks her tongue out at her brother when he scowls.

"I'll make them fucking leave," Landon growls.

"Can you make Scoot leave?"

"Who's Scoot?" Addie asks.

"The cat," Landon replies as he crosses his arms over his chest and keeps his gaze level with mine. "And no. He loves you."

"He won't let me touch him," I counter. "That doesn't scream *love* to me."

"Just come to grips with the fact that you have a cat. He's cute." Landon brushes his knuckles down my cheek, but I barely notice. I'm still deep in thought about the damn cat. "Like you."

"He lets *you* touch him," I remind him, and roll my eyes and pull myself out of my own head. "What needs to be put away next?"

"These boxes are empty," Mia says.

"That's it, then," Landon says. "I'll finish up the kitchen."

"You are *not* to hang that horrible owl in the kitchen," Mia says, wagging her finger under his nose. "It's ugly as hell."

"It's my house," he reminds her. "I'll hang whatever I want in the kitchen. Maybe my underwear."

"Ew," Addie and I say in unison. "Do you hang your underwear in the kitchen?" Addie asks me with a laugh.

"I don't wear underwear," I remind her. "But if I did, they wouldn't hang in the kitchen."

"I can't even believe we're related," Mia says with disgust. "Mom raised you better than that."

But Landon isn't listening to her. He's watching me. His eyes are narrowed, just a bit, and his hands are clenched on the countertop. His jaw ticks.

"Landon." Mia waves her hand over his face, getting his attention.

"What."

"We're done. We're going to leave now."

Addie and I gather up the pizza box and our napkins and toss them in Landon's brand-new garbage can, and all the while I can feel his hot gaze on me. Landon's looked at me in a lot of ways over the years. He's laughed with me, been proud of me, irritated by me, and even mad at me.

But he's never looked at me like he'd like to strip me naked to see if I'm lying about the no-underwear thing.

With a look like that, if I *did* wear them, they'd be soaked by now.

"Landon!" Mia exclaims in exasperation.

"Thanks for coming," Landon says, shaking himself out of his daze. "It was sweet of all of you."

"You never know when one of us is going to move and need the favor returned," Mia says with a shrug.

"I'll hire movers," Addie assures him, and pats his arm.

"I'm not moving," I add, and push my feet into my heels. "I'm gonna be in that house until it's time to go to the home."

"It's a good house," Mia says. "I like it."

"Me too," Landon says, and brushes his hand down the back of my hair. "Thank you, Camille."

"You're welcome."

"Mia and I were here too," Addie reminds him with a sweet smile. "Just in case you forgot."

"Thank you too, smartass," Landon says, ruffling Addie's hair the way he knows she hates it.

He follows us out of the house and stands on the porch as we all climb into Mia's car and pull away.

"So, what's up?" Addie asks from the passenger seat. She turns around to smile at me.

"Well, we just helped Landon unpack, and now I'm going home."

"No, jerk, with you and Landon," she clarifies.

"We've been friends for a long time. Do you have amnesia?"

Addie rolls her eyes and looks over at Mia. "Help me out here."

Mia looks at me in the rearview mirror. "You're being obtuse."

"There's nothing to say."

"Didn't look like nothing to me," Mia says, and turns down my street. "Especially when I caught you two all cozied up in the closet."

"They were cozy in the closet?" Addie asks, her voice shrill.

"We're friends," I insist. "I almost tripped on the box and he caught me. That's all."

"He kept watching you all day," Addie says. "And not in the *friends* way, if you know what I mean."

"Then ask him what's up," I reply. "Also, I need to talk to you about Steven."

"Trying to change the subject," Mia mutters as she pulls into my driveway.

"That's just a side benefit," I reply. "I want to hire Steven to bus tables. He could use part-time work."

My siblings are both significantly older than me, and have children that are closer in age to me than they are. I was an afterthought for my parents. Despite my not having a close relationship with my brother and sister, Steven and

I are super close. He's more like a brother to me than any-thing, and I feel an obligation to look after him, especially since his parents moved to Seattle last year.

"No problem," Addie says. "Can he start this week?"

"He can start whenever you tell him to. I'll text you his number. It'll seem more official if you're the one to call him. Use your scary-boss voice," I reply as I climb out of the car and wave on my way through the front door.

"*Meow.*"

"You know, you could give me three minutes to take my shoes and jacket off before you start demanding food," I inform Scoot, who simply watches me shrewdly. "Not gonna wind between my legs, huh? You only do that to humans who don't feed you?"

Scoot blinks, not finding me humorous at all, and follows me into the kitchen just as my phone rings.

"How was it?" I ask immediately.

"Well," Brian replies with a sigh, and I know immedi-ately that it didn't go well. "I left before dessert."

"Why?" I frown and shake cat food into Scoot's bowl, then grab a bottle of water from the fridge and lean against the counter, listening.

"Because when you texted me during the date, she wasn't impressed that I'm still friends with my ex-wife."

"This is why you need *me* to find you someone new!" I insist, and slap the counter. "Anyone I set you up with won't care that we're still friends."

"Cami, you really need to stop trying to set me up," he says with a laugh. "I don't need the help."

"Whatever. The bimbo you dated two weeks ago tried to date-rape you and the chick from last night was a jealous bitch."

"Both of those points are exaggerations," he says, his voice dry.

"I just want you to be happy, B. Like, seriously happy."

"You let me worry about my happy, and you just worry about your own, Cam. You deserve it too."

Maybe.

"I'm happy."

"You know what I mean."

I shrug, not caring that he can't see me. "I can help you find the perfect girl."

"I don't want your help, Cami. Seriously, I'm fine. I date more than anybody I know."

"I'll just keep my eyes and ears open, just in case the perfect girl for you comes along and I need to tell you about her."

"Can we change the subject now?" he asks, resigned.

"Sure."

"What's up with you?"

"I just got home, was gonna do some work before Riley comes over to watch our show."

"That's not what I mean," he says calmly. "I can hear it in your voice, Cami. What's going on?"

Absolutely nothing that I feel comfortable telling you about.

"I'm great."

"You're a bad liar."

"Why does everyone keep reminding me that I'm a bad

liar?" I ask, pacing the kitchen. "I'm not lying. I *am* great. Business is good. Friends are healthy. Steven's gonna work at the restaurant part-time. I have no complaints."

"When was the last time you got laid?" he asks, making my jaw drop.

"I think there's a law written somewhere that says that you should never, ever discuss your sex life with your ex-husband."

"I'm over being jealous. Spill it."

"No."

"Tell me. I'll tell you."

"Absolutely not! I don't want to know that."

"Are *you* jealous?"

I was never jealous. That was the problem.

"I'm ending this conversation, Brian. Have a good night."

He's still laughing when I end the call and toss my phone on the countertop.

"Well, that was uncomfortable," I inform the cat, who's still washing himself after his dinner. "Not that you care."

My phone rings. I answer it without checking the caller ID.

"I am *not* going to tell you the last time I got laid!" I exclaim. "And I definitely don't want to hear about your sexcapades."

"Bummer."

I freeze. Fucking hell, it's Landon.

"I thought you were someone else." I laugh, not sure what else to say.

"Clearly," he replies, chuckling in my ear, and I'm immediately transported back to his bedroom and his face pressed to my ear as he saved me from falling. Everyone's right. I *am* a bad liar. We *were* all cozied up in his closet, and damn it, I liked it too much.

"What's up?" Damn it, my voice is squeaky.

"You forgot your iPad here," he says. I'd taken it with me so I could show him some general design ideas I'd found on Pinterest for the renovation.

"Damn. Sorry. You can just give it to Mia and she'll give it to me."

"Cami, can I ask you something?"

"Of course."

"Have I done something to piss you off or hurt your feelings?"

I frown. "No, not that I recall."

"Then why are you so determined to avoid me?"

Now Scoot chooses to wind himself between my legs, purring, making me almost trip. "Crap!"

"Cami?"

"Sorry, I just tripped over the cat." I swallow hard. "I'm not avoiding you, Landon. I'm just living my life."

"And living your life includes not seeing me?"

Yes, because it's easier that way!

And better on my libido.

"I see you."

"I don't think you do, Cami. I'll just run this over to you."

"Oh, you don't have to—"

But before I can finish, he's gone.

Chapter 4

~Landon~

$\mathcal{N}$ow I can't stop thinking about the last time Cami got laid. It's not a thought that I'm comfortable with. Since I've been home, the thought of anyone else putting their hands on her makes me a little crazy.

Okay, to be honest, I haven't been comfortable with other men putting their hands on her in . . . ever.

But damn it, the *next* time she gets laid is going to be with me if I have anything at all to say about it.

And I think I do.

Damn right I do.

I climb her stairs and ring the doorbell, frowning at the burned-out porch light. That's an accident waiting to happen.

I'll replace it for her.

"Hey, Landon," she says with a smile as she opens the door. "Thanks for bri—"

CRASH.

She closes her eyes, hangs her head, and sighs. "Damn cat. Sorry."

And with that, she turns and runs for the kitchen, her ass swaying nicely in her jeans, her blond hair bouncing around her shoulders. I step in and shut the door, slip out of my shoes, wet from the rain, and follow her.

"You're such a menace," she hisses at the cat, who simply lies down and watches her sweep up broken glass.

"I'm so glad to see that y'all are still getting along so well."

"Why do I suddenly feel like I didn't get a cat, but rather *he* got a human?" She chuckles and shakes her head. "Wait. I've always felt like that. I'm his slave, for God sake. Thanks for bringing that by. You can just leave it on the countertop. I don't want you to step on glass."

She's not looking at me. Come to think of it, she's avoided looking me directly in the eyes since I got home. I lay the iPad on the counter, shove my hands in my pockets, and lean against the doorjamb, watching her sweep, scoop, and dump the glass.

When she's finished, she turns and her eyes widen as she comes to an abrupt stop.

"You're still here."

I nod. "You know, Cami, it used to be that we had a great friendship. We could talk for hours, just about anything. We laughed. We weren't uncomfortable around each other."

"I'm not uncomfortable now," she lies, and bites her lip.

"We never lied to each other," I continue calmly. "You once knew more about me than anyone else in the world."

"Yep, I was your ol' pal Cami," she says sarcastically. "And I'm still your friend, Landon, but you've barely spoken to me over the years."

"I've spoken to you," I reply.

"Not the way we used to. And I get it." She holds a hand up. "You made it clear that you didn't think it was right to have a close friendship with a married woman."

It was a cop-out. I just couldn't stand hearing about the new husband.

"I should have kept in contact," I murmur, suddenly regretting my cowardice.

She frowns and leans her hips against the countertop. "That was a long time ago." Her voice is soft as she stares at Scoot. "But I missed you."

"I did too," I reply. "I've missed you for a lot of years."

"I've always been right here." She holds her hands out at her sides.

"And I'm the one who went away," I finish for her. "But I'm home now, and I don't want to keep having this uncomfortable distance between us, Cami. We're better than that."

"So, you want to be friends again?" She tilts her head to the side, her dimple winking at me as she bites her lip. "Not that we were ever *not* friends, but you know what I mean."

"No." Enough of this talking-in-circles bullshit. I begin to walk toward her, slowly. "That's not what I mean." Her shoulders straighten as I approach. Green eyes widen and are fixed on me now. "I want. To take you. On a date."

Finally, I'm inches from her, but I'm not touching her. My

hands are braced on the countertop next to her hips and I'm leaning in. She licks her lips. Her pupils dilate.

She's not immune to me, and damn if I don't want to boost her up on this countertop and take her, right now.

"A d-d-date?" she stutters.

I nod slowly. "A date. Dinner. Conversation." My eyes skim over her, from her hair to her lips. "The kind of date that might end with a kiss."

"What kind of kiss?" she whispers, staring at my lips.

"The good kind," I reply, also whispering.

"I don't know if that's a good idea."

I frown. "Why?"

"Because you're Mia's brother." Her eyes find mine. There's heat there, but there's more. Fear? Uncertainty?

"I've been more than that for a long time, Cami."

Redness fills her cheeks, and I suddenly feel like a grade-A asshole.

"Hey." I tip her chin up so I can see her eyes. "It's just dinner."

"And maybe a kiss."

"Probably a kiss," I say with a grin. "I could just kiss you now to get it over with."

"No, that's okay," she says quickly, placing her hand on my chest to push me away, but instead she grips my shirt in her fist. "I haven't brushed my teeth."

God, she's so fucking adorable.

"Tomorrow, then," I whisper before I lean in and kiss her forehead. Her skin is so damn soft. Everything about her is welcoming and sweet, and I want to stay and soak her in.

So I'd better go.

"Have a good night."

She nods, staring at my shoulder.

"Cami?"

"Yeah?"

"You have to let go of my shirt so I can go."

"Oh!" She lets go and tries to smooth out the wrinkles, which only makes me hard as a damn rock. Her small hands rubbing all over my chest—covered in a shirt or not—should be goddamn illegal if I don't get to strip her naked as a result.

"I'm okay." I take her hands in mine and kiss her knuckles. "Make sure you got all that glass."

"Glass?" She frowns, and I can't help but chuckle. "Oh! The glass. Damn cat."

"*Meow.*"

I glance down to find Scoot sitting by my feet.

"Stop being mean to your mommy." I point at him, but he just blinks at me. "And both of you be nice to each other." I wink at Cami as I turn to walk away.

"Landon," she says. I turn and raise a brow. "Are you sure?"

I'm going to do my best to wipe away any of that uncertainty. I smile at her and nod. "I'll pick you up at seven."

"I'll be ready."

"I know."

Cami's never late. And now I have to fill the next twenty-four hours until I can see her again.

"HEY BOSS, WE'RE gonna knock off for lunch," Jay, one of my crew members, says the next day. "We're just gonna go get some burgers. Welcome to join us."

I shake my head and measure out a board. "Thanks, but I'm good. I'll see you in a bit."

The guys stow their tools and head out, laughing and giving each other shit, which is the norm. My crew is tight-knit and reliable, and I get along well with them, despite only being back for a short time. But most of them have worked for my dad for many years. Hell, a few of them taught me in the summers when I'd work for my dad, and not just about drill presses and table saws.

There might have been a few inappropriate magazines that made the rounds a time or two. I smile at the memory and measure a board.

"How's it going over here?" Mia asks as she walks in carrying a covered plate.

"It's going," I reply.

"I saw the others leave for lunch, so I decided to bring you something to eat."

"I'm quite sure you couldn't have seen that from your kitchen lair," I reply with a chuckle. "But thanks for the food."

"Maybe I wanted to talk to you too," she says in her direct way. Mia's always been the kind of person who speaks her mind. You never have to guess where you stand with her. It's one of the things I love the most about her.

"Is something wrong?" I take a bite of her lasagna with white sauce and sigh in happiness. "This is damn good."

"I know." She grins. "I don't know if something's wrong. That's why I want to talk to you."

"Okay."

"What are you doing with Cami?"

"I'm not doing anything with her right now."

"Don't be a dick," she says calmly. Mia can be wildly passionate, or the calmest person in the room. She would have made an excellent pilot.

As it is, she's a scary woman.

"Why don't you tell me what your concerns are?"

"My concern is Cami. I saw you yesterday, Landon. You weren't just doing your harmless-flirting thing that you usually do with her."

"No, I wasn't."

Her big brown eyes narrow. "You know, Cami is maybe the sweetest person I know. She's giving and loyal and she's the best person to have in your corner."

"Yes, she is."

"And she's had a crush on you since the beginning of time. And you knew that. So don't do the flirty thing with her and then turn around and date someone else under her nose the way you used to do when we were teenagers, Landon. It's mean and she doesn't deserve that."

"I wouldn't do that to her."

"You *have* done that to her," she says, getting heated now. "I know that you're not thrilled to be home, and that you didn't want to leave the Navy, especially the way it all went down. But don't start something with Cami because you're home and bored and want to fill your time with someone that you know will hang on your every word."

"I'm not sure who you just insulted more; Cami or me," I reply, and toss the disposable plate of food in the trash, not able to eat any more. "But I do know that if you were a dude, I'd be decking you right now."

"I'm not trying to insult anyone," Mia replies. "I'm being honest. I don't want you to hurt her."

"I don't want to hurt her either, Mia. We haven't even been out on a date."

"But you're taking her to dinner tonight. She told me."

I want to ask her what Cami said, but that sounds way too much like high school. "The crush wasn't always one-sided," I admit quietly, then shove my hand through my hair and pace away from her, my boots echoing through the space. "But we were young, and then I left."

"And then she got married," Mia says, completing my thought. "I'm sorry. I didn't know."

"No one knew. Well, except for Dad."

"Dad?" she asks, surprised. I nod.

"Dad saw the lust written all over my face when she was around." I sigh. "And he warned me that she was too young. And he was right."

"So you left."

I nod again.

"And now you've decided to scratch an old itch?"

"Watch yourself, Mia." My voice is hard.

"Hey, I'm just asking. We've always considered her

family, but now that her folks are gone, and her brother and sister moved away, I feel even more protective of her."

"I'm going to see her. Get to know her. I like her, Mia. Not because I'm bored or I think she'll hang on my every word. Hell, she's barely looked at me since I've been home."

"She notices you," Mia says.

"I want her to do more than notice me," I reply.

"It feels like it's moving fast. You just got home, and I know it's been rough on you."

"It's getting easier," I reply, surprised to discover that it's the truth. "And it's not fast, Mia, I've known her forever. But, something I've learned through all of this is that life's damn short. I could have died up there." I swallow hard as tears fill my sister's eyes. "And in those seconds when all hell broke loose and I knew I'd have to eject, Cami was my only regret."

"Oh, Landon." Mia wraps her arms around me and hugs me tight. "I hope that whatever you both want to come from this is what happens. I love you both. I don't want to see anyone with their feelings hurt."

"You'll hurt my feelings if you don't bring me lunch again tomorrow."

"You only ate half." Her eyes flare as she pulls away. "You threw my food away."

"You pissed me off," I reply with a shrug.

"I have to work." She turns to walk away, then stops and looks back at me. "She loves sunflowers. She says they always look happy."

"Where am I supposed to find sunflowers in February?"

"That's not my problem," she says with a laugh.

"You always were a pain in my ass!" I call after her, but she just waves and keeps walking.

"Love you too!"

I frown, suddenly wishing I hadn't thrown the last of that food away, and pull out my phone to start calling florists.

If Cami likes sunflowers, then she'll have sunflowers.

IT'S BEEN A long day. Maybe that's because we had a tool malfunction, requiring me to drive out to another job site to get another one. Maybe it's because I know I'll get Cami all to myself in just a few hours and that's making the seconds drag by.

Either way, I'm itching to get the hell out of here.

"I'm gonna run next door for some water," I tell my guys, and saunter over to the restaurant.

Who am I kidding? I want to get a glimpse of her. I'm pathetic.

But I don't want to change it.

I walk through the door and smile at Addie. "How's your day, Blondie?"

"I can't complain," she says with a smile. "Lucas is here. He's back at the bar. I told him you were next door, but he said he wanted to say hi to the girls first."

"Awesome, thanks." Lucas has been my best friend since we were in the second grade and he gave me a black eye over a G.I. Joe. We went into the Navy at the same time, went to boot camp together, then flight school. He's my closest friend in the whole world, and there's no one else I'd rather have as my wingman.

But when I walk into the bar, I want to lay him flat.

He's hugging Cami close, his lips pressed to her cheek. And one hand is planted squarely on her skirt-covered ass.

"It's so good to see you," Cami says with a smile, and pulls back to cup Lucas's face in her hand. "Landon will be happy to see you."

Landon will be happy to see him unhand Cami.

"You look beautiful, as always," Lucas says, and that's all I can take.

"Hey man," I say, and move in to shake my friend's hand, effectively pulling him away from Cami. "When did you get to town?"

"This morning," he replies as he eyes me with concern. "Decided it was time to come check on you, since I couldn't make it over to Italy."

"I'm fine." *Now.* I wasn't for a while.

"Well, you can tell me all about it tonight while we drink too much beer and embellish flight stories."

Cami has discreetly backed away, talking quietly with Kat.

"No, I can't. I have a date tonight."

"Of course you do," Lucas says, barking out a laugh. "Didn't take you long to snag some hometown bimbo. Do I know her?"

"She's me," Cami says, surprising me. "I'm the hometown bimbo."

Lucas looks from me to Cami in surprise. "No, really."

"Really," I reply with a smile. "So you'll have to come over to the job site next door and fill me in on your fictional flightscapades."

"Hey Cami, I don't really think you're a bimbo—"

"It's okay," Cami says, waving him off. "I'm sure the others he's dated have been bimbos."

"I've always liked you," Lucas says.

"I'll see you tonight," I say to her, and grin when she nods and elbows Kat, who makes gagging noises.

"Is Kat single?" Lucas asks as he follows me out of the bar.

"Pretty sure she is," I reply. "But not positive."

Lucas continues to chuckle as we walk into the construction zone. "Cami?"

"What's wrong with Cami?"

"She's a kid."

"She's almost thirty," I reply, and motion for him to follow. "Hardly a kid."

"Well, she's hot, I'll give her that."

"She's a lot of things," I reply. "And we should change the subject now. What are you really doing home?"

"I'm checking on you," he says, his face sobering now. "I want to know how you really are."

I sigh and pick up a hammer. "I'm better than I was."

"Have you wrapped your head around being home for good yet?"

That's the thing. I don't know. It was never my plan to be home for good. I was going to be in the Navy until I retired, and then probably still work for the Navy.

Civilian life is as foreign to me as living in Italy was when I first got there.

"I'm fine," I repeat.

"You scared the piss out of me. Literally," Lucas says, and rubs his hand over his mouth. "What happened up there?"

"I don't know," I reply, and shake my head slowly. "I don't remember much of it, thankfully."

"Brain injury?"

"No, the doctors call it a traumatic injury." I smirk. "I don't recommend ejecting out of your plane, man."

"So noted." He sighs. "So this is what you're going to do now? Construction? Have you been medically cleared for this?"

"I'm cleared," I reply. "And as for now, yes, I'm going to help my dad out with the construction. Long term? Who knows?"

"I'm only here until tomorrow morning. Are you sure you can't take a few hours to hang?"

"I'm sure. You should have called, man. I'm not ditching Cami for your ugly ass."

"Fine."

I toss him a measuring tape. "But while you're here, you can make yourself useful."

"You're an ass."

I laugh. "That's not the first time I've been called that today."

I HAVEN'T BEEN nervous to pick up a date since I was sixteen fucking years old. But here I am, palms sweaty, sitting in my car outside of Cami's house.

Cami would laugh at me and tell me I'm being silly.

Which I am.

I lift the sunflowers out of the passenger seat and walk up to her door. But before I ring the bell, I quickly replace the burned-out lightbulb and shove the old one in my jacket pocket.

With a deep breath, I ring the bell.

And wait.

No answer.

I glance over at the window and see lights on. She's definitely home. So I ring the bell again, clear my throat, and wait.

Is she okay?

I pull my phone out of my pocket and text her.

Are you ready? I'm at the door.

"I'm sorry!" Cami yells, just as I hit send. She's upstairs, yelling out of an open window. "The door is unlocked. I'll be down in a second!"

"What are you doing?" I yell back.

"It's girl stuff! You don't want to know! Just be thankful that you're a boy."

I haven't been a *boy* in a very, very long time. I'll set to reminding her of that tonight.

I walk inside and back to the kitchen, foraging under the sink and in the cabinets until I find a vase, then arrange the flowers and carry them to the living room and set them on the sofa table.

When I turn around, my tongue glues itself to the roof of my mouth, making it impossible to speak. But Cami's eyes are warm with female recognition, and she knows.

She knows that she's a fucking knockout in that dress.

She knows that her hair looks touchable the way it's pinned up in that messy knot. And she definitely knows that her legs look long and lean and would be perfect wrapped around my waist.

Oh, she knows. And I fucking love it.

Chapter 5

~Cami~

He's downstairs. In my house. And of course, he's on time because he's always on time.

And I'm not ready.

I slip my feet into my new Jimmy Choo heels and take a last look in the mirror. Short skirt, carefully sculpted messy hair, sparkly heels.

I'm ready.

I take a deep breath and try to remember what Riley said last night when we watched our show. Or, rather, when we tried to watch our show, but I was too keyed up.

He's just a man. Just a regular ol' man. Nothing special there at all.

From the bottom of the stairs, I stand and watch Landon arrange a bouquet of sunflowers in my vase, fussing over them just like I would, then he turns around and sees me, and all the blood drains from his face. I'm not going to lie, it's a great ego boost to watch as his eyes rake up and down my body. He has to swallow hard, and when he tries to speak, he has to swallow again.

Ego boost, indeed.

Every emotion shows on Landon's face. It always has. He can be playful and arrogant and, well, a typical confident man, but his face doesn't lie. That's what drew me to him from the beginning. I was a young girl being raised by elderly parents, my siblings already out of the house, and this boy would smile at me, and I felt like I was at home.

I never saw him as a brother, but I did see him as a protector, a friend, and in my girlish fantasies, my prince charming.

He's no prince, but he can be charming.

"Wow," he finally says with a soft smile. "You're just beautiful."

"You're not so bad yourself," I reply, meaning every word. He's in black pants and a blue button-down, sleeves rolled to his elbows. His hair is still a bit wet from his shower, curling around his collar.

I could eat him with a spoon.

"Are you hungry?" he asks.

I'm too nervous to be hungry. "Starving," I lie.

"Well, then let's feed you." He reaches for my hand, but stops himself. "Oh! These are for you."

"They're lovely." I touch the petals of the yellow blooms and then turn to him. "How did you know they're my favorite?"

"I have my ways," he replies with a wink, and holds his hand out for mine. The fact that this is the first time that Landon has ever held my hand is not lost on me. And the sixteen-year-old in me might be squealing right now.

But all I can think is how good his big hand feels wrapped around mine. He leads me to his car and opens the door for me, and we're off. But rather than driving to a restaurant, Landon pulls into his own driveway.

"Did you forget something?" I ask.

"Nope. This is where we're going." He smiles. "Stay. I'm opening your door, since this is an official date and all."

We're going to *his* place. What does this mean? I'm not stupid, and I'm no virgin. That ship sailed many moons ago. So this has seduction scene written all over it. Am I ready for that with Landon?

On the one hand, absolutely. On the other . . . I'm not sure.

"Stop thinking so hard," Landon says as he helps me out of the car and leads me to the door. "I am not going to try to poison you with my cooking."

"Thank goodness," I reply with a laugh. "Mia definitely got all of the cooking skills in your family."

"I've cooked for you before," he says defensively as he closes the door behind us.

"I remember." I shudder, teasing him, then glance into the dining room and feel my jaw drop. "Wow."

Candles are lit and more sunflowers are on the table. Soft music is playing through a speaker on the kitchen counter.

"Dinner is in the oven," he says. "Have a seat. Would you like some wine? A beer?"

"What's for dinner?" I ask.

"Burgers."

"I'll take the beer." I sit at the table and watch all six feet of sexy man clumsily pull dinner out of the oven and plate it, then walk toward me. "Is that from Burgerville?"

"Of course. It's your favorite."

I blink at the plate before me, then look up at Landon as he sits next to me, rather than across from me. "You remember that?"

"No onions, right? With extra pickles."

Now I'm hungry. "I haven't had this in a very long time." I take a bite and sigh. "So good."

"I got you a strawberry milkshake too."

"I'll have it for dessert." I grin and sip my beer, immediately relaxing. "Remember that time that you, Mia, and I went to Burgerville and Mia tried to tell the cooks in the back that they were doing it wrong?"

Landon laughs and nods. "She's always been bossy when it comes to food."

"She's just always been bossy." I munch my fries. "But her heart is in the right place. I love that girl."

"She loves you too," Landon says as he reaches over, grips my wrist in his hand, and takes a bite of the fries in my fingers.

"You have fries."

"Yours taste better."

"Okay, tell me the truth."

"Always my goal," he replies, and sips his beer.

"Are you okay with being home?"

He smiles. "Lucas asked me the same thing today. It was something I had to wrap my head around. It's not that I hate Portland. My family is here, and this is a fun city. But—"

"But you enjoyed saving the world," I say.

"I didn't save the world, but I enjoyed what I did."

"So how do you feel?" I raise a brow. "You didn't answer the question."

"I feel better every day." He sits back and watches my face. "I feel really good."

"I'm glad. You were so sad when you got home." His eyes narrow and he cocks his head to the side. "I saw it. But there's less sad now. I'm glad."

"And how are you, Camille?" he asks, still watching me. "We haven't talked much since you and Brian split."

"I didn't think people were supposed to talk about their exes on dates."

"We're more than *people*. Besides, I really want to know." He gathers our empty plates and sets them in the sink, then lifts his beer. "Shall we sit in the living room?"

"Sure." I follow him to the couch, toe off my shoes, and sit, my feet pulled up under me. "I'm doing great. Brian and I are still friends. He's a really great man, and he'll always be my friend. I just shouldn't be married to him."

"Well, that's a CliffsNotes version if I ever heard one." He shakes his head and watches me, willing me to spill more, but I don't know if I'm ready for that yet.

"I'm glad that you're okay." Landon's voice is soft. "You look fantastic."

"Thank you."

"What else is new with you?" he asks.

"Honestly, not much. With the business, I pretty much just work. Which sounds pathetic."

"No, it sounds like you're dedicated. So, you work and sleep?"

"That about sums it up."

"Hmm," he says, eyeing me with humor-filled eyes. "When was the last time you went to the movies?"

"It's been a long time. But there's a new one I wouldn't mind seeing."

We spend another hour talking about movies we've seen or want to see, laughing and just enjoying each other. I haven't enjoyed myself so much with a man in . . . *ever*.

Even with my ex-husband, and that's a sad state of affairs all on its own.

"I should take you home," Landon says, looking at the time on his phone. "We both have to get up early for work."

I keep my face neutral, but I'm a bit thrown. I was expecting him to try to seduce me, here on this couch.

But he stands and throws our empty beers away as I slide my feet back in my shoes, then escorts me to his car and drives me home.

I reach for the handle, but he stops me. "Date's not over," he says with a wink.

He walks just behind me to the door. I can feel his body heat in the cool winter evening, and I want to lean back against him.

Instead, I unlock the door and turn around to face him.

"I had a good time."

"Me too." He brushes his fingertips down my hairline, tucking a stray strand behind my ear, as he leans in and brushes his lips tenderly over mine. He grips my neck in his palm and proceeds to give me the sweetest, most gentle kiss of my life. "Good night."

He backs away and I turn to open the door, but the next thing I know, I hear Landon whisper "Fuck it," and I'm spun around and pushed against the still-closed door, and Landon's hands are fisted in my hair and his lips are on mine. More urgently this time, licking and tasting me as if he's been starving for me.

I grip his shoulders and hold on for dear life, praying this never ends. His lips are ridiculous. His touch is firm but reverent. And when he growls deep in his throat, I'm completely lost to him.

As the kiss slows, he whispers against my lips, "That's the good kind."

Finally, he eases back, brushes his nose over mine, and with a deep breath, turns and jogs down to his car.

I walk into my house in a fog. Did that just happen? I stare at the sunflowers on the sofa table and touch my lips with my fingertips. They're still wet. I can still taste him.

It totally just happened.

I WAKE TO the smell of coffee. Which is impossible because I don't even own a coffeemaker. I frown and throw an old T-shirt and yoga pants on and pad downstairs. Someone is moving about my kitchen.

I stop in the doorway, completely surprised. Landon is at

the stove, flipping bacon in a pan and jumping back when it spatters at him. Scoot is nibbling at kibble in his bowl.

"How did you get in here?" I ask.

Landon's head whips around. He smiles, allowing his eyes to rake up and down me. "Good morning, beautiful."

"Good morning. How did you get in here?"

"Well, babe, I don't want to lie to you." He sighs and turns to place the cooked bacon on a paper towel, but doesn't finish his thought.

"And?"

"That's it. I don't want to lie. Or, I could just say, it's none of your business."

"Uh-huh. Okay, then *why* are you here?"

He shakes his head. "It's really flattering how excited you are to see me. I thought you could use a nice balanced breakfast before work. You say you don't have time to eat in the morning, and I'm making time."

"I *am* happy to see you," I admit softly. "I'm just surprised." And that might be the understatement of the year.

He leans over the island and kisses me chastely, then hands me a piece of bacon. "This will tide you over until I scramble the eggs."

"When did I get a coffeemaker?"

"This morning. Mia told me you didn't have one."

"You didn't have to buy me a coffeemaker." *But oh dear God, how good does it smell!*

"I don't have to do much of anything," he replies, and pours me a cup, then passes it to me. "I wanted to bring you breakfast."

"I didn't think you could cook."

"I'm not half-bad at morning food."

"No, you're not," I murmur as I chew the bacon, still not completely awake. I take a sip of the coffee and hum as the hot liquid works its way down my throat. "Thank you."

"You're welcome."

"I should go get ready for work."

"Eat first. Then you can go get ready and I'll answer some e-mails and wait for you."

"Why would you wait?"

He glances back at me like I'm just not keeping up with him. "Because I'll drive you to work. I'm going to the same place."

I frown, but he walks around the island to me, and before I can speak, he plants those lips on mine. "Don't argue," he whispers.

"You're bossy."

"It's good that you recognize that now, sweetheart."

"I don't know how I feel about you being so bossy."

"That's just because you're still half-asleep."

"LANDON'S HERE FOR you," Riley says later that afternoon. "He says he's taking you home?"

"We rode together this morning," I reply, and hit send on an e-mail to our payroll lady, then shut down the computer.

"You spent the night with him?" she squeals. "And you wait until right now to say something?"

"No, I didn't spend the night with him. He came over this morning and made me breakfast, and drove me to work."

"Huh."

"What?"

"Nothing." Riley shakes her head and sits at her desk. "It's just interesting, that's all."

"What's interesting?"

"The whole situation." Riley laughs and points at the door. "He's waiting. Have a good night. Use protection."

"You're weird," I reply with a frown, grab my bag and jacket, and walk out of the office. Landon is waiting by the front door, looking at his phone with a frown on his handsome face. "Something wrong?"

His head whips up and he smiles when he sees me. "Not a thing. Are you ready?"

"Ready." He opens the passenger door for me and I sink back in the seat of his car and take a deep breath. "I'm so ready to go home."

"Well, the thing is, we're not going home."

"We're not?" I glance over at him in surprise. "Where are we going?"

"To the movies."

"It's not even five in the afternoon."

"Matinee," he replies, and takes my hand in his, kisses my knuckles, and drives us into the heart of downtown Portland. He finds parking and escorts me into a mall, then up about five thousand escalators to the top, where the theater is. "Popcorn for dinner?"

"That's healthy."

"You had a balanced breakfast. You're good."

When we're seated in the theater, I can't help but wonder again if this is really happening. I'm at the movies with Landon, who has his arm around me rather than eating any popcorn. I, on the other hand, am inhaling it.

The movie is a chick flick that I mentioned wanting to see last night while we had dinner at his house. He pays attention, I'll give him that. And the fact that he thought to do this is flattering, not to mention it makes my heart melt more than a little.

I lean my head on his shoulder and sigh when I feel his lips on my temple. The movie is a good one, but a bit sad at the end. When we leave, I yawn, but I'm so damn happy.

"Tired?" Landon asks as he drives us home.

"A bit. Thank you for that."

"You're welcome. Are you hungry? I can buy you dinner."

"I had a whole tub of popcorn myself," I reply with a laugh. "I have a little work to do tonight from home."

Landon nods and takes me home, and when he walks me to the door, he kisses me just as passionately as he did last night. His hands are firm and warm on my arms as he pulls me closer, and his mouth devours mine, in the absolute best possible way.

"I'll see you tomorrow." It's said with promise in his voice.

When I get inside and shut the door, I can't help but do a quick, undignified happy dance, startling Scoot. "He's into me. You don't kiss a girl like that unless you're into her. I haven't dated like this in ten years."

Scoot's eyes narrow, and he flicks his tail and turns his back on me.

"Don't judge me, you little judger."

SOMETHING CRASHES, WAKING me up out of a dead sleep and scaring the fuck out of me. I sit up, looking around my bedroom, but it's pitch-black. The power's out.

Suddenly lightning flashes, brightening up the room, and is followed immediately by the loudest thunder I've ever heard. Scoot is crying and pacing the bed.

"It's okay, baby." I reach out to pet him, and he hisses, but then runs into my lap and huddles against me. "I've got you. It's just a storm. It'll go away."

But more lightning and deafening thunder hit again, making us both jump. Rain is pelting against my window so hard it sounds like it could break the glass.

This is one hell of a storm.

As the rushing in my ears slows, I swear I can hear a scratching noise, which only scares me all over again. I grab my phone and call Riley.

"This better be good," she mumbles sleepily into the phone.

"I think someone's trying to break into my house," I whisper to her. "My power is out and I hear noises."

"Why are you calling me and not the cops?" Riley asks. "Jesus, it's two in the morning."

"I wouldn't know that. My power's out. And there's a murder-death-kill person here."

She giggles and I scowl at the phone. "This isn't funny!"

"You're right. Did you lock your door?"

"Yes."

"You need to get an alarm."

"Not the time to berate me," I say, and take Scoot to the bathroom, locking him in. "I'll protect you, baby."

"Who are you talking to?"

"My cat."

"Jesus, you're the crazy cat lady."

"Not helping," I hiss, and drop to my hands and knees to find the baseball bat under the bed. "Seriously, I heard a noise."

"It's a storm, Cami. It was probably a tree on your house or something."

I take a deep breath and sit on the edge of the bed, bat in hand.

"You're probably right. I don't hear anything now."

"Go back to sleep. The storm will blow over."

I nod. "Okay. Good night."

"Night."

I hang up and shine my phone around the room. It all looks normal. Riley is probably right, I'm just scared because of the storm.

Just when I stand to let Scoot out of the bathroom, I hear another noise. I tiptoe to the door and peek my head around, petrified to see my front door creaking wide open.

Holy fucking hell.

I clutch the bat in my best grand-slam stance and take a deep breath.

"Whoever you are, you need to get the fuck out of my

house!" I yell, sounding much more confidant than I feel. "I have a gun and the cops are on their way!"

"Jesus, don't shoot me."

Landon.

I drop the bat just as Landon reaches the top of the stairs and I launch myself into his arms. And I do mean *launch.* My arms are wrapped tightly around his neck, most likely cutting off his air supply, and my legs are wrapped around his waist.

"You scared me!"

"I'm sorry." He's holding my ass, but when he realizes that I'm glued to him and he doesn't need to hold me up, he runs his hands up and down my back, soothing me. "I didn't mean to scare you. I wanted to come see if you're okay."

"Why didn't you just knock like a normal human being?" I ask with my face buried in his neck.

"I didn't want to wake you up if you were sleeping." He sits on the bed with me in his lap.

"So you thought that me waking up to a tall man at the side of my bed would be less scary?" He chuckles and kisses my cheek. "You seriously need to stop breaking into my house."

I pull back.

"Wait. Is that how you got in yesterday morning? You picked the lock?"

I can't make out his face in the dark, but I feel his shrug. "Old habits die hard."

We used to break into each other's bedroom window when we were kids. We'd sneak in and talk, especially during storms. I hate thunderstorms. I always have. I'm surprised Landon remembers.

"Here I thought you had some kind of magical powers," I say. "But in all reality, you're just a felon. I couldn't pick a lock these days if my life depended on it."

"I'm not a felon," he says with a laugh. "And if I am, then we all were when we were young. And if memory serves, it was *you* who taught me how to pick a lock."

I laugh softly. "No one lived in that old scary house by the river when we broke into it. It was empty."

"It wasn't ours to break into. I'm pretty sure I could turn you in for breaking and entering."

"*I'm* pretty sure the statute of limitations has expired on those adventures," I reply, and poke him in the ribs. "Besides, it was *you* who used to taunt me and Mia about how it was haunted, and horrible ritual killings used to happen there."

"I was hoping to scare you away from there, not entice you even more." He kisses my forehead. "I never would have guessed that the cute, responsible girl we all knew would have been up for trespassing."

"I was up for a lot of things back then," I reply softly. "The consequences don't seem so dire when you're young. It seems *you* never outgrew your trespassing tendencies."

"You would have opened the door to me."

"Just freaking knock next time."

"Or you could just give me a key and save us all the trouble," he replies, and kisses my forehead. As the adrenaline slows down, I realize that he smells delicious. His muscles feel amazing under my hands.

He just feels so damn good.

"They tore it down, you know," I say, still staring into the dark. "That old house."

"I know. I drove by the other day and it was replaced with a row of town houses." His hands are roaming soothingly up and down my back. "Are you okay?"

"I'm fine."

"Where's the gun?"

Silence. I smile against his neck.

"You don't have a gun, do you?"

"No, but I wasn't going to tell a potential rapist that."

"You're so funny," he says, his hands moving over my back again. "I don't have power either."

The sky lights up and I can see him for just a split second. His hair is still messy from bed. His eyes look tired.

"Thank you for coming to check on me." I rest against him. "You didn't have to."

"You hate storms," he murmurs.

"That hasn't changed," I agree, and then I panic all over again. "Shit! Scoot's trapped in the bathroom!"

I shimmy off his lap and run to the bathroom, almost tripping on my new Choos on the way.

"Why is he in the bathroom?"

"Because I put him there to protect him," I reply, and open the door. A pissed-off cat scurries out of the bathroom and jumps up on the bed. "He'll be pissed at me for a while. Although, he's always pissed at me."

"Now that I know you're okay, I'll head home."

"Stay."

He stills in the darkness. "Cami—"

"You don't have to have sex with me," I rush on. "But I'd rather not be alone."

"Come here."

I cross to the bed and reach out when I can see his silhouette against the windows, careful not to fall into him. He takes my hand and pulls me down into his lap.

"When we have sex, it won't be because either of us *has to*." His lips are just barely touching my cheek as he speaks. "It'll be because we're both ready and can't keep our damn hands off of each other. Making love to you will never be a chore."

"I should hope not."

"And as for tonight, I'll happily stay if it makes you feel better."

"It does."

"Do you want me on the couch?"

"No. I want you to lie in my bed with me and hold me." I'm breathing easier now. "Please."

He groans as he lifts me, and with me in his arms, he toes out of his shoes and lies down in my bed, gently lowering me beside him.

"You're strong."

"You're sweet," he says as he pulls me against him. I lay my head on his chest and wrap my arm around his waist and sigh deeply. "Go to sleep, sweetheart."

"Don't go away." I've relaxed against him, feeling safe and calm once again.

"I'm here."

Scoot climbs onto Landon's belly and lies against my arm, purring, and before long I feel myself drifting back into sleep.

Chapter 6

~Landon~

"Hello?"

"Where are the screws?" Cami asks in my ear as I lay my drill down and frown at the room in general.

"What screws?"

"The ones at the home supply store."

I grin and fold my arms. "You're at Home Depot?"

"Yes, and I can't find the damn screws." Her voice is thick with exasperation and I can't help but wish I was there to witness this. It's been more than a week since the power went out and I spent the night with her in my arms, and I've barely seen her since then because of both of our work schedules. I'm determined to spend the weekend with her.

"Do you see the signs at the ends of the aisles? Nails and screws should be listed somewhere."

She grumbles in my ear as I motion for my foreman. I put her on mute.

"I'm gonna run an errand, but I'll be in back in less than an hour."

"Sounds good, boss."

"Cami? I'm coming down there."

"You don't need to come here, Landon, I just don't know where anything is."

"You're not far away. I'll see you in a few."

I hang up and hurry out to my work truck. The truth is, I miss seeing her beautiful face. I've talked to her on the phone a few times, and there have been plenty of texts, but I need to see her.

I pull into the parking lot, finding a slot close to the door, and jog inside. I find her in the nail and screw aisle, her nephew Steven standing next to her, fuming.

"I'm telling you, Cami, those screws are too small. The shelf won't hold."

"Don't yell at me!"

Steven looks up and sees me. "She called both of us."

I reach out and shake his hand, then turn to Cami. "How's it going, Bob Vila?"

"I want these screws." She's frowning, her lips twisted in frustration. "But Mr. Know-It-All says they won't work."

"What are you building?"

"I'm redoing my pantry."

I nod. "Why did you call both of us?"

"Because it's always better to get more than one opinion," she says reasonably. "And he didn't tell me what I wanted to hear."

"Oh my God, Cami, I'm out." Steven pulls at his hair and looks up at me. "She's all yours."

"I love you," she tells him sweetly.

"Yeah, I love you too, and it's a good thing because otherwise I wouldn't put up with your shit." He grins and leaves as she blows him a kiss.

"Steven grew up," I say, surprised.

"He's in college now," she says with a nod, still staring at the screws. "He's working at the restaurant a few days a week."

"Awesome. Still living at home?"

"No, he's living with his girlfriend. Amanda and Brock moved to Seattle about a year ago for a job opportunity, and Steven wanted to stay here. I offered him my guest room, but I think he likes having a little freedom. He checks in with me."

"Okay, tell me more about your pantry."

"Okay. So, I want to redo the shelving and paint it. It currently has wire shelves, and whoever put them in there should be hung by them." She scoffs, making me grin. "I can't put granola bars on them. Or little packets of taco seasoning. They fall right through!"

"So you want wood shelves."

"Yes." She nods. "So what screws do I buy?"

I survey the packages of screws on the wall and pull a few down. "These."

"Okay. Now I need shelves."

"Let's go." I take her to the organization aisle and we

pick out the shelves she wants, along with brackets and bins.

"Now, since you're here . . ." She bats her big green eyes at me.

"Yes?"

"I need paint and a door."

"A door?"

"I really want to replace the plain one with one of those pretty ones with the glass in them that says 'pantry.'"

She bites her lip and looks up at me, and in this moment, I'd give her just about anything she asked for.

"Okay, a door it is. This way." She follows me all the way to the other side of the store, stopping on the way to pick out a paint color, brushes, and other painting supplies. After we've chosen her new door, we make our way to the check-out counter.

"I can't fit this all in my car."

"I have the work truck," I say, leading her to it. "I'll just take this stuff with me and meet you at your place after work. I'll help you put it together."

"Well, at least let me take the paint and I'll get that done before you get there."

"Good plan." She helps me unload the flat cart, takes the paint, and sends me a winning smile.

"Thank you, Landon."

"You're welcome." Before she can walk away, I grab her hand and tug her to me, lower my head, and kiss her softly. "I'll see you a little later."

"Looking forward to it," she breathes. She sends me a

sassy smile, then turns and walks to her car, a little extra sway in her step, her pretty blond hair bouncing around her shoulders.

I want her.

IT'S LATER THAN I anticipated when I pull up to Cami's house, thanks to a bunch of snafus at work this afternoon and then getting tied up at my dad's office discussing a new job.

Work is really interfering with my love life.

I use the key Cami gave me to let myself in, and find Scoot lying on the back of the couch, sleeping soundly. He opens his eyes when I walk past, but then falls right back to sleep, not caring in the least that I'm here.

Suddenly I hear . . . giggling. I walk into the kitchen to find a war zone. Food, bins, and appliances cover every surface. The pantry door is standing open. I can't see inside it, but I hear a loud thud, then Cami giggle, and another female voice says, "Ow! That was my knee!"

"Sorry." More giggling. I quietly walk around the island until I can see inside the pantry, then stop, fold my arms over my chest, and watch the show.

Because it's quite the show.

All of the old wire shelves have been taken out. Cami's on her hands and knees, painting along the baseboard. Kat is rolling up high, and they're chattering away.

"Dick size is important," Kat says, as if she's talking about the weather. "I mean, if it's too small, it's like, *Are you in yet?* And if you have to ask that question, it's not a good sign."

"Definitely not," Cami says, slurring her words. She sits

back on her haunches, giving me a prime view of her back and ass, and takes a sip of wine, right out of the damn bottle. "And if they're too big, it's like, *ouch!* I prefer a medium-sized dick."

"Yes!" Kat says, nodding. "Medium-sized is perfect. Not fun-sized. Why do they call it fun-sized, anyway? What's fun about small pieces of chocolate? Or small cocks?"

"Or small dicks," Cami adds, then laughs. "Oh, you just said that."

"It's worth saying twice," Kat says. "Also, the last douche I dated? What was his name?"

"Craig?"

"Yes!" Kat exclaims, pointing at Cami. "Craig. He wouldn't go down on me. What the fuck is up with men who won't go down on a girl?"

I smirk, completely agreeing with Kat, and more than a little shocked. Jesus, girl talk is a hell of a lot more explicit than locker room talk. Who knew? This is fascinating.

"Right? Like, we're supposed to suck them off like some kind of sucking Olympian, but they won't return the favor?" Cami asks before drinking more wine. "It's ludi-ridicu . . . It's dumb." I cover my mouth to keep from laughing at her stumbling over her tongue.

God, she's fucking hilarious.

"So dumb," Kat agrees. "Does Landon do it for you?"

Now my interest is very piqued. I wish we'd already made love so she could brag a bit. But then again, I'm not so sure how I feel about her sharing our intimate time together.

Which is a change for me. I don't think it would have ever bothered me in the past.

"We haven't done any of the sex stuff." Cami takes a sip of wine, then bends over to touch up some paint, showing me her perfectly round, begging-to-be-kissed ass.

"None?" Kat looks down at her and frowns. "Like, at all?"

"We kiss sometimes," Cami says. "Maybe he doesn't want to do the sex."

Oh, he wants to do the sex, sweetheart.

"He does," Kat says, her voice confident. I nod.

"How do you know?"

"Because he's a man. Trust me, he wants the sex."

"I think he likes me," Cami says.

Oh, I like you.

"I hope so. Otherwise I'll have to remove his manhood," Kat says, and they both giggle.

"Don't do that," Cami says right before snorting, which makes her laugh even harder. "I have plans for his manhood. I think he'd be really good at the sex stuff. Like, really, *really* good."

"You know, if he doesn't initiate sex, you should just drop to your knees and suck him." Kat nods once. "Just go to town on him."

Jesus. Just the thought has me rock hard. I need to interrupt this conversation, but just before I step forward, Cami says, "I thought about it. I might just attack him."

"Yessssss!" Kat says. "Do it. Seriously."

I clear my throat and walk toward the pantry like I just

got here. If they keep talking like this, I'll scoop Cami up and take her upstairs to rectify the no-sex-yet situation, and she's way too drunk for that to be our first time.

"Hello, ladies."

"You're just in time!" Cami says with a smile and staggers to her feet, then gives me a big hug.

"I am?"

"Yep, lover boy," Kat says, and lifts her bottle of wine. "We've painted the pantry."

"Say that five times fast," Cami says with a giggle. "Painted the pantry. Painted the pantry. Printed the pinto."

"Ha! Printed the pinto." Kat laughs.

"I like the color," I reply, admiring the deep coral that looks happy and cheerful in the nice-sized pantry.

"Me too," Cami says happily. "It's pretty."

"Your kitchen is a hot mess," Kat says with a frown as she walks out of the pantry and throws her empty bottle of wine in the trash. "This is going to require a small army."

"Or a box of matches," Cami says. "I could burn it all down and start over."

"But we just planted a pantry," Kat replies, then snorts. "Boy, we're drunk."

"Drunk painting is good for the soul," Cami says, smiling up at me. "You're pretty."

"Pretty?" I drag my fingertips down her cheek and she snuggles close to me. "I don't think guys are supposed to be pretty."

"But you are," she says with a sigh. "With your dark lashes and thick hair and all your . . . prettiness."

"She thinks you're hot," Kat says, and shrugs when Cami scowls at her. "What? You just told him he's pretty. I'm translating."

"Thank you," I say, chuckling. "I'll take you home, Kat."

"I have my car."

"And you're way too drunk to drive. You don't live far."

"I'll call an Uber," she says, waving me off and pulling the app up on her phone. "No need for you to leave and come all the way back."

"This was fun," Cami says. "But we forgot to eat."

"No wonder we got so drunk," Kat says. "I knew we were forgetting something. According to this, my driver will be here in three minutes. I'll go out and wait."

"Thank you," Cami says, and hugs Kat around the neck. "You're pretty too."

Kat snorts again. "You *are* drunk. You're welcome. See you when I see you."

"I'll go wait with you," I say as we walk to the front door. "It's dark."

Cami crashes on the couch as Kat and I walk outside and down to the sidewalk.

"I think you're good for her," Kat says out of the blue. "She's happy. And it's been a long time since I've seen her be really happy."

"I'm glad." This is an awkward conversation.

"Just don't hurt her." She points her finger into my chest. "Seriously, don't. Because then she'll be sad, and she's had her share of sad, with her parents dying and her divorce and stuff."

"I don't want her to be sad either," I reply. "And thank you for being such a good friend to her."

"Well, duh. She's awesome. Oh, there's my car." A black car pulls up to the curb and the driver rolls down the window, verifying that Kat is his passenger. She climbs in the backseat and waves at me, blows a kiss, and they drive away.

I take a deep breath, enjoying the crisp night air, then walk back inside and smile softly at my girl passed out cold on the couch. She's curled in a ball, her head resting against the back cushion, and Scoot is curled up in her lap, purring away.

I take the blanket off the back of a chair and drape it over her, leaving Scoot's head poking out, and bend down to kiss her forehead.

"Sleep well."

And now it's time to get started on the pantry.

SOMEONE'S KISSING ME. My face, my neck, my ear. I crack an eye open and find Cami smiling at me, lying on top of me. After I finished the pantry, at around two in the morning, I simply picked Cami up and joined her on the couch, and we slept here all night.

Scoot is lying on my feet.

"Good morning," Cami says softly. "I don't remember falling asleep here."

"You were in a wine coma," I inform her dryly. "What time is it?"

"I don't know. It's Saturday. Do you have to work?"

"Nope, I'm off today. I'd like to spend it with you, if that's okay."

She smiles happily. "It's okay."

I drag my knuckles down her cheek and kiss her forehead. She feels so good lying on top of me. The only way this would be better would be if I was inside her.

But we'll get there.

"I'll make you breakfast," I offer softly.

"I can make it." She's playing with my hair and watching her own fingers as they comb through the strands, then her eyes widen. "Oh no! I have to put my kitchen back together!"

I kiss her, then sit up, taking her with me, and when we're both on our feet, I guide her back to the kitchen, where she stops cold, eyes wide, surveying the clean room.

"Was I robbed?"

"No." I laugh and kiss her head, then walk over and open the new pantry door.

"Oh my God." She walks over and studies the door, then peeks inside. "Oh, it's so pretty."

"You did a great job on the paint," I say, loving how her cheeks have gone pink and her eyes shine as she walks into the pantry and checks it out. "I wasn't completely sure where you wanted everything, so you can obviously change it, but it's put away for now at least."

"You did this for me." It's not a question. She turns and looks at me with confusion and elation, all mixed together.

"Of course I did."

"Why?" She shakes her head, then looks around again. "I mean, I'm grateful, and it looks amazing. It's exactly what I wanted. But this must have taken you all night."

"I was done by two," I reply proudly. "And I did it because I knew you'd like it."

And because it seems I'd do just about anything for this woman, but I'm not ready to tell her that. Not yet.

"Thank you," she says, and walks into my arms, her head pressed to my chest, and hugs me tightly. "It's so great."

"You're welcome."

"Now I have the whole day free." She kisses my chest, then pulls away, shuts the door of the pantry, gives it a grin, and moves to the fridge. "How do you want your eggs?"

"So you *are* making breakfast?"

"Yes, sir. I haven't cooked for you. Eggs?"

"Scrambled."

She nods and begins pulling ingredients out of the fridge. "Scrambled it is. I'm also going to make ham, potatoes, and toast."

"That's quite a feast."

"It's all part of a balanced breakfast," she says with a wink. God, she's sassy. Has she always been this sassy? This much fun? "Plus, you've earned it."

"Have I earned a shower?"

"Definitely." She keeps gathering supplies. "Go help yourself. This should be just about ready by the time you're done."

"I can stay and help."

"I'm good. Go ahead." She waves me off, already concentrating on the task at hand. "Oh, I have to feed you, little man." She bends over to scratch Scoot behind his ears and he doesn't even bat at her this time.

They're making progress.

Before I leave to take my shower, I pull her into my arms and kiss her soundly. She melts against me, her hands planted on my arms. She kisses me back, as if I'm the best thing since sliced bread. Her tongue tangles with mine, and one of her hands glides up over my shoulder and into my hair at the back of my head.

I growl. She tastes amazing, and she feels even better. Her grip on my hair tightens. She clenches her fist, almost pulling my hair, and I can't stand it. I boost her up onto the countertop and grind my now hard cock against her crotch, squeezing her ass and pulling her tightly against me. She groans and rotates her hips, pushing. I slip my hand under the shirt she's still wearing from last night, skim up over her ribs, and cover her small breast with my palm, and squeeze gently. She covers my hand with hers and encourages me to squeeze harder.

Suddenly the smoke alarm goes off, startling us both, and we stare at each other for a moment as we breathe hard, both our mouths wet and swollen, her eyes are glassy.

I glance over at the stove. The pan she put on the burner to heat up is smoking.

"Oops," she says, and giggles, twists out of my hold, and moves the pan. "Go get in the shower. I'm hungry."

"I'm hungry too," I reply, and her gaze meets mine again. She gives me a naughty grin, licks her lips, and winks. I can't help but let out a laugh as I shake my head and leave the room.

I'll make it a cold shower.

Chapter 7

~Cami~

"I love the Esplanade," I say happily as Landon takes my hand and we begin walking down the paved path that loops around the waterfront of the Willamette River, giving us amazing views of the city.

"It's a good day for a walk," he says, smiling down at me. "Not raining."

"Nope." I look up at the blue sky, then fish in my purse for my sunglasses. "But it's a little chilly."

"We'll warm up the more we walk," he says.

"You know, we'll be walking just about a block away from Voodoo Donuts," I remind him with a grin.

"We just had a big breakfast."

"Oh, come on, there's always room for donuts," I reply with a scoff. "When was the last time you had a Voodoo?"

"Oh God, it's been a few years," he says, and guides me to the side so we avoid a cyclist.

"Well, I say we stop in." I pull him down the sidewalk toward the famous donut shop. "And look! No line."

"That doesn't happen often, especially on a Saturday morning."

"See? Good luck." I wink and lead him inside. "Smells good."

"How can I possibly be hungry for this right now?" He stares longingly at a maple with bacon. He looks at me like that too. Usually he has his hands on me when he has that look on his face, and holy shit, does it make me crazy.

It was all I could do to not rip his pants off in my kitchen this morning.

"I'll take one," he says to the guy behind the counter, pointing at the donut, then he turns to me. "What would you like?"

"I'll take one without the bacon," I say. "You don't have to put it in a bag. It won't last that long."

When we're outside, I pull my phone out and take a photo of Landon biting into his ridiculously big donut, laughing at how his nose squishes up as he bites.

"If you post that anywhere, it'll ruin my political career," he says, his face perfectly sober.

"I'm sure there are other photos in existence that would do that more than you eating a donut," I reply, and bite into my own treat. "Dear God, these are good."

I glance up to find him staring at me.

"What?"

He licks his lips, then leans in and whispers in my ear, "I want to make you make noises like that."

"Oh." I stop walking and stare up at him, his lips, his hot blue eyes.

Dear sweet Jesus, the man makes me hot. I've always been attracted to him, but this is different. It's *more*.

He just grins and keeps walking, and I have to hurry to catch up to him.

"Come here. Let's take a picture." We turn our backs to the river and hold up our donuts, but my arms aren't long enough to get a good shot. "You take it. Your arms are longer."

"I'm not good at the selfie."

"I'll show you." I instruct him on holding the phone, and we pose for a few photos. On the last one, he leans down and kisses my cheek as he takes the photo.

"Aw, that's cute," I say, looking through the pictures, eating my donut, and walking beside him. "You did just fine with the selfie."

"I learn something new from you all the time," he says with a laugh, and takes the last bite of his donut. "Ah, the Rose Garden." He points at the stadium and smiles. "I've seen many a concert in that place."

"They changed the name, you know. It's the Moda Center now."

"Hmm. It'll always be the Rose Garden to me." Since I've finished my donut, he takes my hand back in his and tucks them both in the pocket of his jacket. It's very chilly today. I can see our breath as we walk, but the sun is nice on my face, and our brisk pace helps. "What was your first concert?"

"Britney Spears." I grin and break out in a really bad

rendition of "Hit Me Baby One More Time," which Landon joins me in, making me laugh so hard my stomach hurts.

"Wasn't that for Addie's birthday?"

"Yep, we were fourteen," I reply with a nod. "We had a blast. Britney puts on a good show. She's quite the dancer. What about you?"

"Metallica," he says. "It was fucking awesome."

"So you're a metalhead? I didn't know that about you."

"Not really, but I love Metallica," he replies. "I saw Springsteen, the Cure, Garth Brooks, and Madonna in that stadium."

"I remember when you went to see Madonna! I was so mad. I wanted to go."

"You did?"

"Of course I did. But you took Natasha What's-her-name." I scowl. "Bimbo."

"Natasha *was* a bimbo," he agrees with a nod. "And my seventeen-year-old self was elated."

"Ew."

"Don't worry, babe. You're the only bimbo I'm interested in now."

"I'm so relieved," I reply, and push him playfully. Our walk goes by fast, and before long we're back in the car and headed to my house. When we pull up, I'm surprised to see Brian's car in my driveway and the man himself walking down my steps.

"Hey!" he says as we approach. He glances at Landon, down at our linked hands, then back at me, and smiles widely. "I was just going to leave."

"I'm glad we caught you," I reply, and squeeze Landon's hand. "What's up?"

"I was wondering if I can borrow your KitchenAid mixer?"

I frown. "Why?"

"Stephanie wants to bake cookies this afternoon, but I don't have a mixer."

I unlock the door and step inside, then turn and stare at my former husband. "Who's Stephanie?"

"A girl." He rocks back on his heels. "That I met." Shoves his hands in his pockets. "You know, on my own. Without your help."

"Oh my gosh! That's so great!" I hug him quickly, then walk back to the kitchen, the guys in tow. "I want to know all about her. Do I know her?"

"I doubt it."

"How did you meet her?"

"Does she give you the third degree like this?" Brian asks Landon, who just laughs and shakes his head. "I met her in the grocery store."

I stare at the tall blond man I know so well, and then a slow smile spreads over my face. "What aisle?"

"Why does that matter?"

"Humor me. What aisle?"

"I met her by the ice cream."

"Did she have wine in her basket?"

The guys look at each other in confusion, and then Brian says, "I don't remember."

"Think. Really hard."

I lean on the counter, waiting, and watch Landon's eyes travel down to my chest. I glance down, and sure enough. Cleavage, front and center.

I send him a sassy wink. *You're welcome, handsome.*

"Honestly, Cam, I wasn't looking in her basket," Brian says, and then chuckles. "That sounds dirty."

"Ew." I shudder. "I don't want to know about the dirty stuff. Of course you can borrow my mixer." I open the pantry and fetch the appliance.

"You remodeled," Brian says.

"I painted, Landon did everything else." I grin and hand Brian the mixer. "Have fun."

"That's the plan." He winks. "Thanks. I'll talk to you later. Good to see you, Landon."

Landon nods, and he and I just look at each other as Brian leaves.

"You seem very excited for someone who just found out her ex is seeing someone."

"Hell, yes, I am," I reply, and wash my hands in the sink. "I've been trying to set him up for over a year."

"Really." He takes his coat off and hangs it on the back of a chair. "That's . . . unusual."

"I know. But it's okay." I turn to him. "Brian is a really great guy, and I want him to be with someone equally great."

"So you've been trying to set him up."

I nod. "I felt guilty."

Landon takes my hand and leads me to the couch, sits, and snuggles me against him. "Why guilty?"

"Because I left him," I reply softly. "The divorce was

all me. He didn't put up much of a fight, but he probably wouldn't have asked for it. I left him alone, and that made me feel bad."

"You were alone too," he reminds me, and kisses my forehead.

"But that was *my* decision." I drag my nails up and down his thigh. "But, I guess I didn't have to set him up after all. The fact that he's doing any kind of cooking or baking with her says a lot. He claims to be allergic to the oven."

"I hope it works out for them," he says. "Wanna watch movies and veg for the rest of the day?"

"Hell yes."

THIS HAS BEEN, hands down, one of the best days I've had in a very long time. Exercise in the morning, and an afternoon on the couch, snuggled up, watching movies and eating junk food is exactly how I needed to spend my day off. I feel rejuvenated and happy.

We're in the middle of an action movie that Landon picked. We took turns choosing the movies today, which seemed fair to me. Right now action movie stars from the eighties and nineties are all banded together to fight . . . something. I'm not sure what. But Landon is laughing and pointing, and generally having a good time, so I'm having a good time too.

I traded my jeans for cropped yoga pants long ago. Landon ran home to get some lounge clothes as well, so we're as casual as can be, with a blanket over our laps, and Scoot is curled in a tiny ball beside Landon, snoring happily.

This just feels good. I'd forgotten how much I love to snuggle. To feel a solid, warm body next to me. I slip my hand under the blanket and drag my fingertips up and down Landon's thigh, like I did earlier, but this time it's on bare skin thanks to his running shorts. I like to touch him. His skin is smooth, but his muscles are just . . . yum.

I glance up at him, and realize that he's staring down at me, his eyes hot, and the next thing I know, I'm on my back and Landon and his harder-than-should-be-legal body are covering me, his mouth is on mine, and his hand has traveled up my shirt.

"Jesus, you're sweet," he whispers against my lips. "Arch up."

I comply and he unfastens my bra, giving him easier access to my breasts. He doesn't take my shirt off, but his hands are doing amazing things to my nipples and his mouth is teasing mine, nipping, licking, then devouring.

I feel like I'm sliding straight into a high that I've never had before. My head starts to buzz, along with every nerve ending in my entire body. He eases between my legs and presses his pelvis to mine, grinding against my core, and moans as I push my hands in his hair and hold on tight.

"I want you," he whispers as his hand glides down my belly to the waistband of my pants, but he stills and pulls his head back, staring down at me, panting.

"Why are you stopping?" *Please, God, don't you dare stop.*

"Cami, I—"

He just doesn't want me like this.

"It's okay," I say quickly, and wiggle out from under him, not able to look him in the face. "I get it."

"No. You don't." He grips my arm, but I don't want to look him in the eyes and see the apology there. "Cami, look at me."

"Landon, it's okay." Why do I keep saying *it's okay*? Because I'm so embarrassed I don't know what to say. Except, *he* started it.

"Cami, I want you." My gaze whips up to his. "I want you so bad I'm aching with it. But I don't want to rush things. We don't have to hurry."

"I don't feel like we're rushing," I reply. "We've been seeing each other for a few weeks now. We spend a lot of time together. Every time you walk in a room, I want to rip your clothes off. Trust me, I'm more than ready."

He takes a deep breath, stands, and just when I think he's going to leave, he scoops me up and carries me—*carries me*—up the stairs and into my bedroom.

"You are so beautiful," he says softly, his face close to mine as he sets me on my feet near the bed, then makes quick work of our clothes. "And I want to take my time exploring every gorgeous inch of you. We've waited this long, there's no need to go fast."

"That sounds nice," I reply as my eyes rake over his long, lean body. The feel of his muscles over his clothes is nothing at all compared to what they look like naked. "I didn't think people really looked like that."

"Like what?" he asks with a grin.

I just point at him. "Like they've been airbrushed."

"You're good for my ego, baby." His eyes narrow. "You really don't wear panties."

"Nope."

"Why?"

I lift one shoulder. "Panty lines. I hate them. And thongs are just damn uncomfortable."

He laughs. "That's my Cami, always logical."

I bite my lip and cup his perfectly sized, not-too-big, not-too-small dick in my palm. "I'd say that by the look and feel of this, the compliment is returned," I reply, and look up into his blue eyes. "You're rather hard, Landon."

"I'm hard as a fucking rock, and it's definitely your fault," he replies, walking me backward to the bed. "Lie down."

He doesn't have to ask me twice. I lie on my back and he covers me, just like he did on the couch. But this time, there's plenty of naked skin for both of us to explore. Hands glide and lips nibble as we discover each other.

He kisses his way down my chest, paying attention to my breasts, rolling the nipples between his fingertips. My back arches off the bed. I can't stay still as he bites my belly near my navel, then licks his way to the promise land.

Holy. Fucking. Hell.

With one swipe of his tongue, I'm lost. A sheen of sweat breaks out over my skin, and I cry out, not giving even one shit about making noise. When most men would think they've done their part with one or two swipes of the tongue and move along, Landon proves yet again that he's not most men. He settles in and continues to explore me with his mouth and fucking me with his tongue, then sweeping up to tease my clit and back down again.

I'm writhing, my legs shifting, hips circling. He's making

me absolutely fucking crazy. Someone shouts for more, and I'm pretty sure it's my voice. His hands are traveling over my body, and then scoop under my ass and lift me, and I'm spread open to him like a feast.

And boy, does he feast.

Finally, when I'm nothing but a shaking, trembling hot mess, he licks and kisses up my torso, my shoulder and neck, and kisses me deeply. I can taste myself on him, and that only turns me on more. I can't get enough of him.

I grab his bare ass and try to tug him to me, but he holds strong, making growls.

"In a minute," he says.

"Want you," I reply.

"Oh, baby, I want you too." And then he takes himself in his hand and rubs the tip of his dick up and down my wetness, through my lips, and up over my clit. His eyes are on mine, watching what he does to me.

"Holy shit, that's good."

I close my eyes, but he leans in and kisses me, then says against my lips. "I want you to open your eyes for me, sweetheart. I want you to look at me when I push inside you."

I look up at him, and slowly, so fucking slowly, he guides himself inside me. He pushes all the way in and stops, sweating, staring down at me with a mixture of awe and pleasure and everything I've ever wanted to see from him.

"Fuck me, you feel good," he says, and lowers himself to his elbows so he can bury his hands in my hair and kiss me. I hitch my legs up over his hips and he sighs.

"So deep," I whisper. "God, Landon."

"Too much?"

"No." I shake my head and grip his ass in my hand once again. "But I'd love for you to move."

I clench around him, making his eyes roll. "God, babe."

I kiss him. Sweetly at first, then more insistently, and his hips begin to move. The thrusts become harder, but they're still shallow, and I can feel every single glorious inch of him.

Even my lips are tingling as I feel the orgasm start low in my belly.

"Fuck."

"I love it when you talk dirty," he growls, and bites my neck, which only makes the tingling spread, and before I know it, I'm clenching down on him and crying out as my whole world explodes into a million bright pieces. I can't see. I can't hear. I can only feel him, in me, around me, and suddenly he groans and joins me, shaking and panting.

He collapses on top of me, his face buried in my neck, and we stay like this for long minutes while our hearts slow down and our bodies cool.

Landon just made love to me. And it was better than any fantasy I've ever had. I lie quietly and just let my hands roam over him, from his tight ass to the soft hair on the top of his head, loving him.

After he catches his breath, he kisses my neck and rolls to the side, taking me with him, so his weight is off of me. He brushes my hair behind my shoulder, drags his knuckles down my cheek and neck, down to my breast, and gently grazes over my nipple, keeping it erect.

"You're amazing," he says, holding my gaze.

I don't know what to say to that. I'm suddenly a bit shy. I reach for the covers, but Landon takes my hand in his and kisses it.

"Are you cold?"

"No."

He smiles softly. "Bashful?"

"A little," I admit.

"After what we just did, there's no reason to be shy," he says softly. "Your body is beautiful, and I plan to spend the rest of the night exploring you."

I feel my eyes widen and he chuckles.

"That's right. But first, let's nap." He pulls me against him, tugs the blanket over us both, and in the dark, under the covers, his hand roams over my bare back, my side, my thighs.

There's no way I'm going to sleep.

Chapter 8

~Landon~

I couldn't move now if I tried. Jesus, she surprises me at every turn, and learning her body, being buried deep inside her, is no different. Have I ever felt this connected to anyone in my life? I rack my brain, but all I see is Cami.

After having her just once, I know without a doubt that I'll never get tired of her.

She's lying quietly in my arms, breathing softly, but she's not sleeping. Her fingers brush lightly through the light spattering of hair on my chest and her foot rubs up and down my calf.

I didn't bother to turn the light on when I brought her up here, but the moon is full, casting plenty of light into the room. Scoot jumps onto the bed, looks at both of us, then curls up at our feet to give himself a bath.

I could get used to this.

Cami's hand travels down my chest to my stomach, and suddenly the thought of moving again doesn't seem so impossible. Surprisingly, my cock is ready to go again already.

And then it occurs to me: we didn't use a condom.

Fucking hell.

I've never forgotten to suit up before. Ever.

"Baby?" I ask softly, and bury my lips in her hair.

"Hmm?" It's more of a purr than a question.

"We didn't use a condom." My voice is calmer than I feel inside. But I don't want to upset her. We're adults, for Christ sake, there's nothing to freak out over.

Unless there is.

She tips her head back and looks up at me, her eyes shining in the moonlight.

"I'm on the pill," she says calmly. "Have been for years. And I haven't been with anyone since I was married."

What?

I stare down at her, shocked. Cami is breathtaking. She's funny and warm and wonderful, and she hasn't been with *anyone* since Brian?

"Why are you looking at me like that?" she asks.

"I'm just surprised."

"That I'm on the pill?"

"No." I laugh and pinch her, making her squirm, but it backfires when she rubs her thigh against my already hard dick. "That you haven't been with anyone in so long."

She shrugs and is quiet for a minute. "It just wasn't a priority."

"Well, I haven't been with anyone since before I was

home on leave last year," I reply, and drag my hand down her back, then draw hearts on her ass.

"That was quite a while ago," she says, and looks up at me with raised brows.

"I guess it wasn't a priority for me either." My hand slips farther down and my fingers slip down her crack and between her folds and back up again.

With my other hand, I grip her hair and tilt her head back, giving me access to her lips and neck. Her lips fit mine perfectly. Her mouth is delicious.

She moans, deep in her throat, as I push her onto her back and cover her with my body again, but rather than slip inside her, I flip her over, pull her hips back, and slap her ass gently.

She gasps and tosses a smile over her shoulder.

"You like that?"

"What's not to like?" she asks with a laugh, and lowers her head. Her slender shoulders are bathed in moonlight, and to my utter surprise, there's a tattoo on her right shoulder blade. A small anchor.

I lean down and kiss it, then drag my lips up her neck. "Do you have any idea how fucking sexy you are?"

"Am I sexy enough for you to fuck me again?" she asks, surprising me yet again.

"Such a dirty mouth," I mutter, and grin. Rather than answering her, I slip inside her quickly, pushing all the way in and making her gasp. "How's that?"

"So damn good," she says, and grabs on to a rung in the headboard, white-knuckling it. "You can go harder."

I bite the fleshy top of her shoulder, grip her hip in my fist, making marks with my fingertips, and begin to fuck her, hard. Her pussy grips me like a vise.

Jesus, how am I supposed to keep it together when she does shit like that?

Using the headboard as leverage, she pushes back on me, her ass slapping against my hips, and propels the speed.

"Faster?" I ask.

"God, yes," she says, and cries out when I speed up further. I release her hip and shove my hand under her, circling her clit with my fingers, and she loses her mind. "Oh God, Landon."

"That's it."

"Fuck me harder."

"Baby, I'm already fucking you into the mattress. If I go any harder I'll split you in two."

"I won't break." She shakes her head vigorously. "Please."

With both hands gripping her hips now, I thrust as hard and fast as I can, and suddenly she screams my name and comes violently, shaking and pushing back on me, milking my cock like crazy.

I can't hold back anymore. I push inside and come, my forehead on her back, panting, shocked at what we just did.

It might have been the most passionate sex I've ever had. And not even an hour ago we made the sweetest love.

Both blew my mind.

She's fucking perfect for me.

I guide us to our sides and spoon her from behind, holding her close.

"I get lost in you," I whisper, wishing I could see her face, but not wanting to move her.

"Mm," she says. "But it's the kind of lost that's like being found."

I blink, processing her words, and know, in this moment, that there will never be anyone else for me.

"I'M SO GLAD your birthday fell on a Sunday," Kat says to Riley the next afternoon. We're all at Jake and Addie's home for a barbecue to celebrate Riley's birthday. Mia, Jake, and Kat are in the kitchen. Riley, Addie, Cami, and I are in the adjoining family room, watching with interest as Jake and Mia fight about who's going to man the grill.

"I'm happy to oblige," Riley says with a grin, and then rolls her eyes when Mia throws a mushroom at Jake. "Jesus, Mia, it's *his* grill."

"I'm the chef," Mia replies, her nose in the air.

"That's the same look you gave me when you were little whenever Mom let you have your way." I smirk when she glares at me.

"She never stopped throwing that look around," Cami says with a laugh, and links her fingers with mine.

"I didn't realize that Riley's birthday was also known as give-Mia-shit day," Mia says with an indignant sniff, then turns back to Jake. "I know what I'm doing with a grill."

"Do you say that to all the guys?" Jake says, then ducks out of her way when she throws a punch at him. "Go enjoy your friends, Mia. I got this."

"They've kicked me out of my own kitchen on Sundays," she says mournfully. "And now you're kicking me out too?"

"We are villains for making her take one day off a week," Addie says, and shakes her head when Kat offers her a glass of wine. "You're going to kill yourself if you keep going at this insane pace, Mia."

"Hello, pot, I'm kettle," Mia says. "I'll whip the potatoes."

"Fine," Jake says, shaking his head. "Landon, want to help me with the grill?"

"Why does *he* get to help?" Mia cries.

"He's a guy," Jake says, and laughs when Mia just glares daggers at him.

"Addie, you married a sexist pig."

"Hi, everyone!" We all turn our heads as a pretty blonde walks into the room. "Sorry I'm late. My children are demons."

"Cici!" Cami jumps up and gives the woman a hug. "I'm so happy you came."

"I'm just happy that I had a reason to leave my house and enjoy some girl time." Cici smiles and looks around. "Or, sort-of girl time."

"This is Landon," Cami says as I shake Cici's hand. "I don't think you've met."

"No, but I've heard all about you," Cici says with a smile. "Welcome home. I'm glad you're here safely."

"Thank you." I turn to Jake. "Let's give them some girl time, whatever that means, and go tackle the grill."

"Sexist pigs," Mia mutters again, making us laugh as we step outside.

"Has she always been this bossy?" Jake asks me as he opens the already lit grill.

"She's mellowed out with age," I reply, and chuckle. "Mia has always been headstrong. It might be the Italian in her. Or maybe it's just her."

"She's awesome," Jake says with honest affection in his voice. "But man, can she be intimidating."

"I like to think of her as badass," I reply. "But don't tell her I said that. We'll never be able to live with her."

"Your secret is safe with me, man." He sets the steaks on the grill. "I'll add the salmon when the steaks are half-done. It cooks faster."

"Was that also a Mia instruction?"

"I think she said it about six hundred times."

I shake my head and lean against a cement pillar, looking out over the pool that's covered for the winter.

"How are things with Addie?" I ask.

He closes the grill and pulls two beers out of a small fridge next to the grill, hands me one. "I don't remember my life without her now."

"In case you need a refresher, you were an international rock star and you've won Grammys for your songs, Jake. FYI."

"I know it sounds dumb," he says with a shrug. "I don't care if I'm sappy or whatever. In less than a year, she became the center of my universe. Of course I work, and she works, and we have lives to run, but at the heart of it, it all comes back to her. And I didn't think that I'd ever say that about anyone."

I nod, thinking about Cami and how much she's come to mean to me in less than a month's time.

"What's going on with you and Cami?"

I raise a brow.

"Come on, you knew that question was coming."

"What's going on? We're seeing each other." I take a sip of my beer. "I've known Cami for a long time."

"As a friend," Jake says reasonably. "That's not the same thing."

"That's what I'm learning," I reply. "I thought I knew her so well, but she's proving that to be wrong every day."

"Cami's sweet." Jake turns the steaks, then laughs when he sees Mia with her nose practically pressed to the window watching him. "Go away!"

"You should put the salmon on now!" she yells, but Jake shoos her away and turns his back on her.

"I'm going to wait an extra two minutes to put the salmon on now."

"I knew I liked you," I reply with a smile. "And yes, Cami's sweet. Are you going to warn me too?"

" 'Too'?"

"Mia and Kat have already pretty much said they'll cut my balls off if I hurt her."

"Nah. I'm not going to do that. You're both adults, and you know what's what. Besides, they all warned me off of Addie. I'll never divorce her just to preserve my manhood."

"If you hurt Blondie," I reply, perfectly serious, "you won't have to worry about your manhood. I'll simply kill you and make it look like an accident."

"Point taken." Jake laughs and pulls the meat off the grill. "Come on, let's listen to Mia tell me all about how I did this wrong."

"I just don't want any wine," Addie says, and looks to Jake for help when we step inside. "Seriously, babe, they won't leave me alone."

"You know, peer pressure is bad," I say slowly. "Just in case you forgot from when you were teenagers."

"Addie loves wine," Kat insists, but Cami's watching with a thoughtful gaze. She's rubbing her lips with her fingertip. She glances over at me and gives a slight nod, and I know what she's thinking.

I know what's happening here. Just wait and see.

"So tell them," Jake says with a shrug. "I told you to tell them a month ago."

"Holy Mary, Mother of God!" Mia shrieks. "You knocked her up!"

Cami grins. Everyone gasps and stares at Addie wide-eyed as tears gather in her pretty blue eyes.

"He totally knocked me up," she says, getting choked up. "Isn't it just the sweetest thing ever?"

The girls squeal and rush over to Addie to give hugs and kisses and belly rubs.

"How long?" Riley asks.

"Do you throw up all the time?" Cici asks.

"I want to throw the baby shower!" Cami says.

"I feel great," Addie says, and smiles brightly at Jake as he walks over and kisses her cheek, then hugs her from behind. "I'm about three months along. I wanted to make sure everything was okay before we announced it. I know, that seems silly because it's you guys, but—"

"We get it," Riley says, patting Addie's hand.

When the girls are all finished fussing over Addie, I saunter over and pull her in for a big hug. "I'm so happy for you, Blondie."

"Thank you, handsome."

"You should stop wearing those shoes. You don't want to fall and hurt yourself." The room goes absolutely quiet at my statement, and then all of the girls bust up laughing.

"You're so sweet," Addie says, patting my cheek like I'm a little boy who just said something funny. "But you'll get my sexy shoes off my cold, dead feet."

"Addie and Cami are very serious about their shoes," Kat says.

"And you're not?" Cami asks Kat, looking pointedly down at her cherry-red high heels.

"Not like you guys. You make shoe shopping into an Olympic sport. Have you seen Cami's shoe-closet dream board on Pinterest?" Kat asks me.

"No," I reply, smiling at Cami as she blushes.

"Oh God, you have to see it," Riley says as Jake motions for all of us to file through the kitchen and dish up buffet-style. "The girl knows how to daydream about a pretty closet."

"My shoes deserve a pretty closet," Cami says softly, then latches on to my arm and buries her face in my shoulder. God, she's funny. "I spend a fortune on them," she mumbles into my shirt.

"I want to go play in Addie's closet. Since we're here anyway," Mia says, and sniffs at the salmon. "These spent about a minute too long on the grill."

"Sorry, chef," Jake says, and rolls his eyes. "Eat steak instead."

"I'm trying to steer clear of red meat," Mia mumbles, and takes a piece of salmon, along with salad. No dressing. My heart hurts a bit for my sister. She's beautiful, extra pounds and all, but she's beat herself up for not being thin enough her whole life. "Addie, let's go stare at your shoes after dinner."

"We can totally do that," Addie says happily, shoving mashed potatoes in her mouth. "God, I'm hungry."

"I was constantly hungry when I was pregnant," Cici says with a laugh. "I gained ninety pounds with my first."

"Holy fuck," Addie whispers, staring at her potatoes, but then she shrugs and keeps eating. "Jake's stuck with me. Even if I do gain another whole preteen person."

"Eat, baby," Jake says, kissing her cheek.

I glance down at Cami and frown when I see tears in her eyes. "What is it?" I ask softly, so only she can hear. She shakes her head and looks up at me.

"I'm just happy. Everyone's happy."

I lean in and kiss her gently. "If you're happy, I'm happy."

"What did you think of today?" Cami asks as we finally walk into her house later that night.

"I had a good day. I always enjoy hanging out with you girls."

She smiles and hangs our coats, then absentmindedly leans down to scratch Scoot's ears. "I'm glad you had a good time. I did too."

"Your mood has been hard to read today," I say honestly, and watch as she thinks it over and then shrugs.

"I don't know why I've had this weird mood on today. I'm so happy for Jake and Addie. I love celebrating my friends' birthdays, and Riley seemed to enjoy herself. Everything was great today, but I've felt kind of . . . *melancholy*."

"Come on." I hold my hand out to her, then lead her up the stairs. "Show me where you'd put this shoe closet of yours."

"Oh, it's just a silly daydream," she replies, but I shake my head.

"So daydream with me for a minute. Where would you put it?"

She bites her lip and watches me warily for a moment, then walks into the bedroom adjacent to her master bedroom and flips on the light. There are three bedrooms up here, not including her master. One is her office, one is a guest room, and this one is currently being used for storage.

"Okay, talk to me."

"Really, Landon, it's silly."

"No, it's not. Talk."

She sighs and rolls her eyes, then walks about the space. "I would close up the doorway and make a new one that goes into my bedroom," she begins. "Then I'd make this whole wall nothing but shelves for shoes. The walls on either end would have racks for clothes and this last wall would have hooks for scarves, my dresser, and more shelves for bags.

"In the middle, I'd put a vanity table and chair. Maybe. I don't know, I don't have it all figured out, but I'd essentially turn this bedroom into a kick-ass closet."

I'm looking about the space as she describes it. "That wouldn't be difficult, Cami."

Her eyes light up.

"Seriously, it would maybe take a weekend and a few hundred dollars. Where do you have your shoes now?"

She motions for me to follow her, turns out the light of the closet-bedroom, and leads me into her master, opening a small walk-in closet that would be too small for most women I know. She has all of her clothes hung, and about three dozen shoe boxes stacked under them.

"I just leave them all in the boxes so they aren't just in a huge heap," she says. "It works fine."

I know exactly what I'm getting her for her birthday in a few weeks.

I simply nod and pull her in for a hug. "Let's take a bath."

"A bath?"

I nod and pull her shirt over her head, toss it aside, and reach for her bra. In a matter of seconds, I have her undressed and sitting at the side of the bed as I strip off my own clothes.

"Stay."

"Still not a dog," she says with a sigh, and watches, her eyes on my stomach, as I turn away and walk into her bathroom. She has a separate shower and tub. The tub is a big jetted tub, the perfect size for two.

I run the water, adjust the temperature, and walk out to find that she's flopped onto her back, her feet still on the floor. Her eyes are closed. I wish I knew why she seems so down today.

"Did you fall asleep?" I ask before laying my lips against hers and kissing her sweetly.

"Mm-mm," she says, and grins against my lips. *There's her pretty smile.*

"Have I mentioned how much I love this dimple in your cheek?"

"You used to tease me about it when we were teenagers," she says as I pull her to her feet.

"Did you ever stop to think that teasing you was my way of flirting with you?" I ask as I guide her into the bathtub. I sit behind her and tug her back against me, then wrap my arms around her stomach and simply hold on.

"Well, if you were trying to flirt, you were bad at it," she says, and bats at the bubbles with her hand.

"I was a teenager. Of course I was bad at it." I chuckle and kiss her neck, just under her ear. "Are you sure you're okay?"

"I'm just quiet, Landon," she says, and leans her head back on my shoulder, takes a deep breath, and relaxes against me. "There's nothing wrong."

"Will you tell me if that changes?"

"If you like," she says.

"I want you to talk to me. I want you to tell me anything and everything."

"You'll get sick of hearing my voice," she says, and looks up at me with a smile.

"Impossible." I kiss her nose. "Your voice is the best part of my day."

"My voice? Not my body, or my mouth?"

"Those are both impressive," I reply, and tuck her arms under mine, hugging her around her shoulders now. "But it's your voice that makes my day."

"That could be the sweetest thing that anyone's ever said to me," she says.

"Oh, there's more to come, sweetheart."

Chapter 9

~Cami~

"What's up with you?" Addie asks me as I walk into the office and close the door behind me. I stop and look over my shoulder, as if she might be talking to someone else. "Yes, you."

"Well, I was going to balance our corporate checkbook," I reply, and walk over to my desk. "And I need to write a check out to the newspaper for the ad we bought. I also need to balance the tills from last night."

"Not that," Addie says, and rolls her eyes. She sits in the chair by my desk and crosses her legs. "The other stuff."

"What other stuff?"

"I noticed it at Riley's party on Sunday," she says, watching me closely. "When you get quiet, it's because your brain is in overdrive."

"It is?" I frown and sit back, thinking over the past four days. "I thought I just got quiet."

"Yeah, because you're thinking." She smiles. "Spill it."

"Well, this is new information," I reply.

"Are you happy?"

"Yes." I think about all of the time I get to spend with Landon. I love my house. I love my job. I even have a cat that's beginning to tolerate me. "I have no complaints."

"Okay, good. But something is bothering you."

I frown and sigh. "So, things with Landon are good."

"It looked like it, if the way he looks at you and can't keep his hands off of you is any indication," she replies with a wink. "But I can hear a big, fat *but* at the end of that sentence."

"It's a little *but*."

"Okay, hit me with it."

"But when's the other shoe going to drop?" I ask, and sigh in relief. I didn't even realize that I'd been agonizing over it, I just knew that there was *something* that was bothering me.

"The designer heel, or the steel-toed work boot?" she asks.

"I don't have any shoes to drop," I reply, spreading my hands wide. "He knows all about my past. It's no secret."

"And you think he has secrets?"

"I don't know." I stand and pace the large office that we all share. "Maybe. Probably not *secrets* per se, but there's things that bother me."

"Like?"

"Like the Navy," I reply, spinning to look at her. "He loved the Navy. He loved to fly, to live all over the world, and now he has to settle for being here, and what if he gets tired of being here?"

"How do you know he *will* get tired of being here?" she asks.

"Landon's always had a wandering soul. He's talked about living in far-off places for as long as we've known him. I like it here, Addie. I don't want to move away. I don't think I could. I have a home and a business to run."

"Whoa, Cami. He hasn't even said anything about moving away."

I blow out a breath. "I know, I'm overthinking it."

"What are you really worried about?"

I bite my lip and feel the tears that I've been trying so hard to keep at bay fill my eyes. "What if he doesn't feel the way I do?"

"How do you feel?"

"I love him. But I'm afraid to tell him because what if it sends him running?"

"Sometimes you just have to take the risk," Addie says.

"I'm not a risk taker, Addie. I always play it safe. I'm the numbers girl. But being with Landon has been the biggest risk I've taken because I've fallen completely in love with him, and not in a childish crush way, and he could just be in it because I'm a distraction that he needs. This whole thing makes me very, very nervous."

"I think you're way overthinking all of this," Addie says. "Which shouldn't surprise me because you've always been an overthinker. Cami, he's always cared about you. *Always.* You're the one that he'd pull aside to ask your advice, or hang out with. And the way he looked at you at my house on Sunday? A guy doesn't look at a girl like that if she's just a convenience."

"Maybe."

"I'm not blowing smoke up your ass."

"Well, that's a relief, because that just sounds uncomfortable."

Addie smirks. "Right? I don't understand that expression."

We laugh and glance at the door as Riley comes inside and looks back and forth between us. "Did I interrupt something?"

"Just me trying to talk some sense into her," Addie says.

"Did you lose your sense?" Riley asks. "Because I can help."

"She thinks that Landon's just biding time with her."

"That's not exactly what I said," I reply, glaring at Addie. "I said it all makes me nervous."

"Girl, he looks at you like you're an ice cream cone and he wants to lick you all day long."

I purse my lips. "He *is* good with his tongue."

"Atta girl," Addie says, giving me a high five. "Is he good with the other stuff too?"

"Why does this feel icky?" Riley says, her face pinched like she smelled something gross.

"Because it's Landon and he's like a brother to us," Addie says. "But, he's her man, so we have to still ask the questions."

"He's good at all of it," I reply. "Better than anything I might have daydreamed about over the years."

"That must be good because you've had a lot of time to daydream," Riley says, smiling. "I'm happy for you. And I know you. Don't overthink it. Just enjoy him. Take it one day at a time. Don't worry about what *might* happen, because you're not a psychic. You don't know what's going to happen."

"That's a lot of advice," I reply. "And how is it that you all knew I overthink everything and I didn't know it?"

"Because we've known you forever," Addie says. "And we love you."

"We pay attention," Riley agrees.

"I have one more thing," Addie adds. "If you love him, tell him. Life's short, and sometimes even the girl who doesn't take risks needs to make the leap. Just be honest."

"I'll think about it," I reply. "Thank you."

"Can we have chocolate now?" Addie asks hopefully.

"We can always have chocolate."

I go to the safe and pull out the deposit bag for yesterday. Each evening, the last waitress and bartender on shift close out the tills, put the cash and credit-card receipts in this bag, and stow it in the safe. I reconcile it the next day.

Riley and Addie are chatting about going shopping for baby clothes and Addie wants us to come over later to help her design the nursery. I'm listening with half an ear as I count the money for the fourth time.

It's still short by eighty dollars.

I frown and count it again, still coming up eighty dollars short.

"What's wrong?" Riley asks.

"The bar till is short eighty dollars." I glance up at the girls, then back down at the cash and receipts on my desk. This is weird. The numbers *always* add up. We may be a dollar short here and there, but never this much. "It's so odd. This is the fourth time this week. I'm losing it, guys. I can't even balance the damn daily till. I'm supposed to be the numbers girl, and all I am is a big, giant mess!"

"Take a deep breath there, tiger," Addie says, and stands to come look over my shoulder. "Want me to count?"

"Sure, a second pair of eyes is never a bad thing." I stand so she can take my chair and add all of the money, coming up with the same conclusion. "Seriously, what's wrong with me? My personal life may be in chaos, but the numbers *always* add up. I'm losing it."

"You're not losing it," Addie says as she counts the money. "You've been working your ass off, and we're only doing as well as we are because of you."

"She's right," Riley adds. "Take a deep breath and give yourself a break."

"Is it always the same amount?" Addie asks.

"No, but it's never big. It varies from forty to a hundred."

"You don't think the new girl, Leah, is stealing from us, do you?" Addie asks with a frown.

"Maybe she doesn't know how to count back change?" Riley asks diplomatically.

"I don't know, but we should talk to Kat about it," Addie says.

"Leah's here now, so I'll text Kat to come in here," I reply, thumbing out a message to Kat. A few seconds later, she walks through the door and we tell her what we've found.

Kat's eyes narrow. "I'm going to get to the bottom of this right now. I won't tolerate this in our place."

She stomps away, out the door, and we all look at each other, then hurry to follow her into the bar.

There are no customers right now. We haven't opened for lunch yet.

"Leah," Kat says as she walks behind the bar toward the petite blonde. "Are you stealing from me?"

Leave it to Kat to just lay it all out there.

Leah's eyes widen in shock. "What? No!" She glances over at us, then back to Kat. "I would never do that."

"Cami, can you please tell Leah what you found?" Kat asks, her eyes pinned to the girl's. Leah's reaction seems sincere.

"The tills have been short after you've been on shift," I say, and show her the reports from each day, how much there should be, and how short it is. "Do you know where the money could have gone?"

She shrugs, looking thoroughly perplexed.

"Could you be giving back too much change?" I ask, grasping at straws.

"No, the register tells me how much to give, and I always count it out." She bites her lip and looks at Kat imploringly. "Honestly, I'm not taking money that doesn't belong to me. At the end of my shift, I take my cash tips, and I add up the credit-card tips and take those too."

"Wait." I hold my hand up, stopping her. "You take your credit-card tips at the end of the shift?"

"Yes."

"That's it," Kat says, her whole body sagging in relief. "I must not have told you, Leah, but the credit-card tips are added up during the pay period and added to your paychecks."

"Oh!" Leah clasps her hands over her mouth. "I'm so sorry! I didn't know."

"It's okay," Addie says with a nod. "Now you do. Crisis averted."

The next morning, Landon and I are having coffee and getting ready for our day ahead when his phone rings. I make myself busy feeding Scoot, trying not to eavesdrop.

Who am I kidding? I'm totally eavesdropping.

"Are you kidding me?" he asks, a frown on his handsome face. "They couldn't have caught this before I left Italy?" He sits back in his chair and scowls at his coffee. "So I have to take a day off of work and drive two hundred miles out of my way because someone else fucked up."

Uh-oh.

He's quiet for a moment, and then says, "I'll be there this afternoon."

He hangs up and sighs. "What do you have going on today?"

"Just the usual, why? What's wrong?"

"I have to go up to the Naval base north of Seattle to sign some paperwork that the morons in Italy forgot."

"You have to go all the way to the base? They can't fax it to you?"

"No, I have to sign it in person." He crosses his arms over his chest. "Come with me."

"Sure, I'll just blow off work and go up to Seattle with you."

"Great."

"You're serious."

"Absolutely," he replies, and smiles. "Let's make a night of it."

He wants me to spend the night in Seattle with him. In the middle of the week. I bite my lip while I think about work. I don't have anything that won't keep a couple of days.

"What do you say?" he asks.

"Let's do it. I'll make some calls."

"Great." He tugs me into his lap and kisses me firmly. "I get you all to myself for a while."

"I'll be a captive audience in the car," I reply with a laugh.

"Good."

In less than an hour, I've called Addie and Kat to fill them in, and Kat agreed to stop by to feed Scoot tonight. I packed an overnight bag and we are on our way north. Thankfully, there is no winter weather to speak of, so it should be a smooth ride.

Landon lets me choose the music, and we sit in silence for about an hour, listening to music, holding hands, just being with each other. Sometimes, these are my favorite moments with him. When we just are.

He squeezes my hand and I look up to find him smiling at me. "Doing okay?" he asks.

"I'm great." I lean in and kiss his shoulder. "You?"

"I'm great too. A bit irritated that we have to take a trip up for this."

"So, this is paperwork that they should have had you sign before you came home?"

"Yes. Pain in the ass." He shakes his head and then offers me a smile. "You're welcome to sleep if you want."

"I know, but I'm fine." I shrug and look out the window, watching western Washington pass us by. "It's been a mild winter."

"I prefer it that way," he replies. "Makes it easier to work."

"How much longer until the restaurant is done?"

"Just a couple of weeks. The floors are going in today. It'll be mostly finishing work for a bit, and rehabbing Mia's kitchen. Odds and ends."

"I'm so excited," I reply. "You guys have done great. What's next?"

We spend the next hour talking about work, until he pulls up to the gate of the Naval base. "You don't have to bring me with you. You can drop me off at the hotel."

"No need, this will only take a minute," he replies, and asks for my driver's license to show the armed guard at the gate. We're cleared through and he drives to a simple building and parks. "Come on."

Once we're inside, he's recognized by several guys, and Landon waves or says hello as he leads me to an office where a man in uniform is sitting at his desk. He waves us in.

"It's good to see you, Palazzo."

"Sir," Landon replies, his *Navy voice* sounding very hot. "Do you have the paperwork?"

"I do," the man replies, and opens a file, then sets one paper before Landon. "I'm sorry you had to come all this way."

"It should have been handled," Landon says, sounding not pleased at all. "Are you sure this is the last of it?"

"It is." Landon signs and passes the paper back. "Thanks for coming in."

"You're welcome, sir."

And with that, we turn right around and leave. We're back in the car less than ten minutes after we parked it.

"We seriously came all the way up here so you could sign one piece of paper?" I ask.

"Gotta love the Navy," Landon replies grimly. "Shall we go find lunch?"

"Maybe we can check into the hotel early?" I suggest, my wheels turning. "The men in that office recognized you."

"I was stationed up here for a couple of years," he replies. "Some of them worked here then."

"Do you miss it?" I ask, turning in my seat so I can see him.

"Living up here? No. The weather is worse than in Portland."

"That's not what I mean. Do you miss the Navy?"

Landon sighs and rubs his fingers over his lips. "There are days that I miss it a lot," he replies honestly. "I miss some of the guys. There are things about Italy that I loved. And it's only been a couple of months, so I guess it's safe to say that I'm still adjusting."

He pulls into the hotel parking lot before I can ask any more questions. We check in and find our room, which is nicer than any room I've stayed in before.

"You booked us a suite," I say in surprise.

"Might as well make it worth the drive," he replies with a wink, then pulls me to him and hugs me close. "Okay, spill it. What's going on in that gorgeous brain of yours?"

"What if I'm just a stand-in for the Navy? I don't want to be a replacement to keep you busy because you're sad about what you lost." I can't believe the words came out of my mouth. I look up to find Landon frowning thoughtfully, watching me closely. "I'm not saying that that's how you're making me feel. You've been so great. But the thought is there. I just don't want you to wake up one morning and realize that this thing between you and me has been fun, but it's served its purpose."

"Come here." He takes my hand and leads me to the sofa on the far side of the room, and doesn't just sit next to me, he tugs me into his lap and wraps his arms around me tightly. "Cami, it's recently occurred to me that joining the Navy and moving away was a replacement for *you*." My gaze whips up to his in surprise. "You were too young for me, and going into the Navy was the right thing to do, but you were what I wanted. I had such a crush on you."

"No way."

He raises a brow. "I'm not lying to you. I won't lie to you. You didn't know because it was easy to keep my feelings to myself from thousands of miles away."

"I don't know what to say."

"You don't have to say anything, sweetheart. I'm simply trying to reassure you that you are *not* a replacement for the Navy, or for flying. Do I miss it? Sometimes, yes. But I have you. I have my family, and a job that I surprisingly enjoy for now. I'm not discontent, and I don't want you to think that I am, even for a minute. You are way more than a diversion, Camille."

I grin. "I hate that name."

"I don't."

I drag my fingertips down his face, feeling as if the world has been lifted off of my shoulders. "I've always envied the way you take risks."

"I probably take too many risks," he murmurs. "And you rarely take them at all."

"That seems to be changing lately," I reply, and grin as a genius idea occurs to me. I kiss his cheek, then his neck. "Maybe you're a bad influence on me."

"Oh, I can pretty much guarantee that's true," he replies, then sighs when I nibble on his collarbone. I slip off his lap and onto my knees, between his legs, and lift his shirt up, exposing his stellar abs.

"These are delicious." I lick him, from sternum to navel, and smile when he groans. My fingers slip inside the waist of his jeans, then unfasten them and spread them open. He's already hard. "No underwear?"

"You've been a bad influence on me too," he replies, his blue eyes hot with lust. He licks his lips as I drag my lips from his scrotum, up the thick vein in his cock to the head, and then I lick him lightly. "Holy shit."

"I have oral skills I haven't showed you yet," I inform him as he shimmies his jeans down his hips and I take him in my hand firmly. "Don't make me stop."

"Oh, honey, I'm not going to make you stop."

"I mean, when you're close, don't make me stop. I want to taste you."

"Fuck me," he groans as I sink down on him, just taking the head in my mouth and running my tongue over the tip, then around the rim. I watch him bite his lip and throw his head back as I sink farther and swallow around him, massaging him with my mouth.

Oral sex is empowering. I love watching his face as awe, surprise, and pure unadulterated lust wash through him. His hips begin to move, slow at first, then picking up their rhythm as he fucks my mouth. I slip one hand under his balls, massaging gently, and rubbing my finger over the sensitive skin beneath, while my other hand continues to jack him and I suck him.

His hands dive into my hair, but he doesn't force me down, he simply holds on, as if he doesn't know what else to do with his hands. He's completely lost to me, and it's the most powerful thing I've ever done in my life.

"I want to fuck you now, Cami," he says, but I don't stop. I keep sucking and licking, hard and then soft, driving him mad. I can taste the little drops of dew that escape, and I know that he's close.

"I know you don't want to stop, but damn it, Cami, I want to come inside you, not in your mouth." He gasps when I drag my teeth up his shaft. "Please."

I pull back and grin, release him, and free myself from my jeans, then climb on top of him and lower myself onto him.

"God, you're so wet."

"Going down on you is sexy," I reply, and wrap my arms around his neck. "You taste amazing."

"Jesus, Cam," he groans. He plants his hands on my hips and guides me up and down, his eyes pinned to mine. When I circle my hips, he grins and glides his hands to the globes of my ass.

"You like my ass," I say as I lean in and kiss his lips.

"I like all of you," he replies. "Every glorious fucking inch."

I push down and clench hard, rocking back and forth, and his eyes close. He pushes up hard, and I slip one hand down so I can play with my clit, and that's it. We're a mess of sweaty limbs as we both come, crying out, watching each other.

When we're both spent, but still breathing hard, he stands, still inside me, and wraps my legs around his waist.

"Where are we going?" I ask with a laugh.

"Shower," he replies. "Let's clean up."

"And then get dirty again?"

"Have I mentioned how fond of you I am?" he asks with a laugh, and moans when I laugh with him, squeezing his still-semihard dick.

"Once or twice," I reply. "But you're welcome to keep reminding me."

"Don't mind if I do."

Chapter 10

~Landon~

"Have you been eating enough?" my mother asks two weeks later as she comes out back, where Dad and I are measuring a two-by-four to cut for the covered patio we're adding to their backyard. Or, I should say, extending the patio. Mama decided that the existing one was too small, and it needed to be enlarged now, not this spring.

I'm just thankful that we've had a bout of warm weather this week, so we're not building this thing in a blizzard.

"I eat plenty," I reply with a smile. She's a very typical Italian woman, always trying to feed everyone. The board falls on my thumb, and I pull it against my chest, sucking in a breath. "Motherf—"

"If you finish that sentence, I'll twist your ear right off your head," Mama threatens, wagging her finger at me, then smiles. "Here, let me see."

"I'm fine," I reply, my throbbing thumb anything but fine, but I've had worse. "Hazard of the job."

"Put ice on it," she says, and pats my shoulder. "It'll help the throb."

"It's not throbbing," I lie with a mutter, and kiss her forehead before she turns around and heads back for the door.

"I'll make sandwiches," she says. "You're thin."

"I'm not thin," I say to Dad when she's out of earshot.

"It makes her happy to feed you," he says, and motions for me to lift the other end of the board. "I've discovered that whatever makes her happy is what we do. That simple."

"Happy wife, happy life?" I ask with a wink, and Dad nods. For a man nearing sixty, he's in excellent shape himself, thanks to many years in the construction business.

"Nothing more true," he says and nods. "Speaking of women, how are things with you and that pretty Cami?"

I look up, surprised, but Dad rolls his eyes. "I have eyes in my head, don't I? And my memory is a good one. If I remember correctly, I warned you to keep your hands to yourself when she was just sixteen and you were an adult."

"And I did what you said," I reply. "I went off to college, and then the Navy, and I left her be to grow up."

"Because you're smart as well as handsome. You get the brains from your mother." He laughs and lifts the nail gun. "How long are you home for?"

I frown and shake my head. "What do you mean? I live here."

"For now." He doesn't look me in the eye as he places a board and nails it. "But I know my son. You don't stay anywhere long. I figure it won't be long before your wanderlust kicks in and you decide it's time to move on."

"I'm not leaving, Dad. The Navy moved me around—"

"Are you going to tell me that you didn't enjoy it?" he asks.

"No. I did. But I'm not in the Navy anymore. I'm home, and I love it here. I have Cami and you guys, and I love being back in Portland."

I stop and sigh. "I admit, it hasn't been an easy adjustment. I loved flying, Dad."

"I know you did."

"I was good at it. And I felt like I was doing something good."

"You were," he says proudly. "But this is good too. Makes your mother happy."

I nod. "I like it too."

"For now."

I shrug. "Maybe for good."

"It's not a bad idea to keep your options open," Dad replies simply. "Nothing wrong with that at all. Does Cami know you're keeping your options open?"

"I'm not keeping them open where it comes to her," I say quickly, my voice hard. No damn way. Now that I have her, I'm not letting her go, just to watch some other asshole move in and claim her. She's *mine*. "Work and women aren't the same thing."

"No, but women are a lot of work," he says. "The ones worth keeping are, anyway."

"She's worth keeping."

"I've always liked that girl. All of Mia's friends are good girls."

"They are." I glance over as Mom comes outside with a plate of sandwiches. "Thanks, Mama."

"You're welcome," she says, and smiles over her shoulder. I'm surprised to see Cami walk out behind her.

"Speak of the devil," Dad says with a smile as he walks over to kiss Cami's cheek. "We were just talking about you."

"All good things, I hope," she says, her gaze finding mine.

"Always good things," Dad says. "I think I'll wash my hands and eat my lunch inside with my beautiful bride."

And with that, he leads Mom inside and I'm left outside with Cami.

"I'm sorry to just drop by."

"You're welcome to just drop by anywhere, anytime," I reply, and pull her in for a long hug, swaying back and forth. "I'm not going to apologize for the way I smell."

"You don't smell bad," she says, and buries her nose in my chest. "And you're warm."

"You should have worn a warmer coat."

She shrugs. "It looked toasty out here with the sunshine."

"It's deceptive," I murmur, and kiss her head. "Did you need anything in particular, or did you just want to see my manliness as I build a patio?"

She smirks and pulls back. "Your manliness is a perk."

"Why do you sound sarcastic? Are you saying I'm not manly?" I lift an arm and flex my bicep. "Feel that."

"You're such a man," she says, and feels my arm. "Very impressive."

"Damn right."

"I came by on my way home to see if you want to go to the movies tonight with me and Riley?"

"We can't," I reply, and smile when she scowls.

"*We* can't?"

"No, ma'am. I have a surprise for you tonight." I push her hair over her shoulder and kiss her cheek.

"Are you going to tell me what it is?"

"Are you not aware of what a surprise is?" I ask, and dodge to the left when she swats at my arm. "You just need to be ready by seven when I pick you up."

"Do I need to look fancy?" she asks, worrying her bottom lip.

"You always look beautiful. Be comfortable."

"Are we going out in public?"

"Yes," I reply with a laugh.

"So, public comfortable. Got it." She nods and grins. "Fun."

"You like surprises?"

"Not usually." She shrugs and checks the time. "But this is fun. If I'm going to be ready in time, I'd better get home."

I pull her back into my arms and kiss her, the kind of kiss that would make my mother blush, but I don't care. When I pull back, I drag my finger down her nose. "You know, something skimpy and lacy under your comfy clothes wouldn't hurt my feelings."

"I'll see what I can do."

"So, I KNOW it's not Madonna, but I thought you might enjoy this." I pull into the parking garage for what I will always refer to as the Rose Garden and find parking.

"Are you freaking kidding me?" Cami exclaims, practically dancing in her seat. "This is awesome. I love Bruno Mars."

I find parking and lead her inside, holding her hand tightly. She's dressed in a simple black sweater and jeans with black boots.

I can't help but wonder what's under those clothes.

"I thought this show was sold out," she says as we find our section.

"I know people," I reply, and locate our seats, to the right of the stage, and only a few rows back. We'll have a great view.

"You're good at this date-night thing," Cami says with a grin. "You're hired."

"I'm relieved," I reply, and lean in to kiss her cheek, just as the opening act takes the stage. I can't take my eyes off her. She's watching the show with wide green eyes, taking it all in. She laughs at the band's bad jokes and claps for them. And when it's time for Bruno Mars to take the stage, she loses her ever-loving mind, screaming like a teenager.

She's adorable.

We dance and simply soak it all in.

And when the song "When I Was Your Man" begins to play, I pull her into my arms and we sway in the aisle, moving back and forth, and for this moment, we're the only people in the room. She sighs and melts against me, her whole body pressed to me. I bury my face in her hair, kiss her softly, and then the song, and the moment, are over.

"This is incredible!" Cami exclaims, smiling up at me. "Thank you!"

"It's my pleasure," I reply.

Everything with Cami is my pleasure.

"So HOW ARE your siblings?" I ask on Thursday night. Cami and I are in her kitchen, cleaning up from dinner. "I know you said Amanda and her family moved north. What about your brother? I haven't seen him in years."

"They don't live here anymore either," she replies with a shrug. "Bobby and his wife moved to Arizona to be closer to her family."

"I always liked your brother," I reply, watching her closely. "I'm just surprised they left you all alone here."

"They didn't." She frowns. "I have the girls and Steven. Plus, I talk to Amanda all the time, probably more since they moved."

"Good," I reply, not sure why I suddenly feel the need to hug her.

"Riley will be here any minute," Cami says, and bites her lip just as we hear the front door open and Riley calls out hello. "Or right now."

"Your cat tried to kill me," Riley says as she walks into the kitchen, peeling her coat off. "I'm pretty sure he hates me."

"He's a lover," I say in the cat's defense, and grin down at the feline as he winds his way through my legs, purring happily.

"He only likes men," Cami says. "He doesn't like me either."

"What other men has he been around?" I ask, raising a brow.

"Oh, you know," Cami says, waving me off. "Just Jean Claude and Ricardo. But I always make sure they're gone by the time you get here."

Not giving one shit about having an audience, I pull Cami into my arms and kiss the hell out of her, plunging my hands in her hair and fisting, holding her still as I plunder and explore her mouth, nibble her lips, then kiss my way down her jawline to her ear and whisper, "Do you want to change that answer?"

"Just you," she says, then clears her throat. "I told Jean Claude and Ricardo to take a hike."

"That's better," I reply, and drag my knuckles down her cheek. "I'd hate to go to jail for murder."

"A little possessive, aren't we?" Riley asks, and helps herself, pouring a glass of wine. "You want some?" she asks Cami.

"Yes, please."

"Speaking of possessive," I reply, not directly answering her question, "what's going on tonight?"

"It's Thursday," Riley says, as if that explains everything. "It's our TV night."

"Hot vampires," Cami says, nodding. "Want to join us?"

"In watching vampires? No thanks," I reply, and shake my head. "I guess you get her tonight," I say to Riley.

"Sorry not sorry," Riley says with a smug smile. "And just so you know, when summer starts, there will be a *Real Housewives* night too."

"*Real Housewives*?" I ask. "Do I even want to know?"

"Probably not," Cami replies, and sips her wine. "Riley

and I love trash TV. It's sort of an addiction. You should probably know that from the get-go."

"I believe the get-go was a while ago," I say, and then laugh. "Okay, have a good night. I'll see you at work tomorrow."

"You don't have to leave," Cami says, and worries her bottom lip. I can see that she's torn between hanging out with Riley and me leaving for the night, and that's never a worry I want to give her. She doesn't have to choose. She can have all of us.

"I'm fine," I reply, and kiss her forehead. "Have fun with Riley tonight. I'll see you all weekend."

Her face lights up. "Do we have plans?"

"Do we need them?" I ask.

"No." She shakes her head. "I don't care what we do, as long as I get to do it with you."

"I'm going to gag," Riley says, and starts for the living room. "I'll take my chances with your homicidal cat while you all play kissy face."

"He's not homicidal," Cami calls after her, then stares up at me with a happy smile. "Thanks for understanding."

"I'm a guy, babe. I'll never understand hot vampires." I kiss her nose, then her lips. "But I understand needing time with your friend. Seriously, enjoy yourselves. Do you need anything?"

"Ice cream!" Riley calls from the other room.

"So much for privacy," I mutter.

"The walls are thin!" Riley yells, making us both laugh.

"I'll go get your ice cream."

"You don't have to," Cami says.

"I know." I walk through the living room and wave at Riley on my way out.

"Cherry Garcia, please," Riley says with a sweet smile.

I nod, but rather than walk out, I turn back to look at Cami. She's just sat down next to Riley, and she's laughing at something Riley said. Cami's head is tossed back, her hair fallen back so I can see the soft curve of her neck.

I want to bury my face there and breathe her in.

I rub my chest as I walk out of the house and down to my car. It aches.

I'm in love with her.

I can't imagine my life without her in it. She's it for me. And this isn't just a childish crush. It's the real thing.

Holy fuck, I'm in love with her.

Now I have to figure out a way to tell her without scaring the shit out of her.

Chapter 11

~Cami~

"Seriously," Riley says, her eyes glued to the TV, "Stephan makes my insides tingle."

"Your insides?" I giggle and sit back, giving Scoot room to jump onto my lap, give me the stink eye to make sure I don't dare try to pet him, then settle in to sleep. "Are we fourteen? Your girlie parts are tingling?"

"Stop judging me," she replies. "You know what I mean."

"We really should go to a Comic Con sometime. They are always there."

"Why haven't we done that?" she asks as Landon walks back into the house, carrying a bag.

"I have several kinds of ice cream here," he says with a grin, passing over the bag. "I also grabbed spoons so you don't have to get up."

"I like you so much," Riley says, reaching eagerly for the

bag. "Oh my God, seriously! Look at him!" She's pointing at the screen where a very mostly naked Stephan is standing. "Hubba hubba."

"He looks twelve," Landon says, frowning. "You like the young ones, Ri?"

"He doesn't look twelve," we reply in unison.

"He's over a hundred years old in the story," Riley says, her face perfectly serious. "But he was in his late teens when he was turned, so he'll always look young."

"I'm so relieved," Landon says, laughing.

"Well, I think we have everything we need," I say.

"Does that mean, please leave?" Landon asks.

"It means, thank you very much, I'll see you tomorrow." I wink at him, enjoying the way he looks at me with those hot, blue eyes. He kisses my cheek and waves, then leaves. When we hear his car start, Riley pauses the show.

"Hey!"

"Spill it."

"Spill what?" I open a tub of Chunky Monkey and sigh happily after the first bite. "You should have some of this."

"Spill your guts," Riley replies, also digging into the ice cream. "This is going to be much better than the show."

"I really don't have anything to say." I keep my eyes on my spoon as I eat.

"Lies." Riley sighs. "All lies. The electricity zinging between you almost electrocuted me. I want the details."

"Okay, fine. I've already admitted it to Addie and Kat. And I'm sure Mia knows."

"Why am I always the last to know?" Riley demands.

"I'm in love with him," I mutter, and stare at the ice cream. "Like, head-over-heels, can't-feel-anything-else in love."

"That's awesome. I'm assuming you guys are flinging around the L-word?"

"Nope." I take a gulp of wine. "No L-words have been spoken."

She stares at me, her brow furrowed in confusion. "Why not?"

"I'm not saying it first."

"Now who sounds like a kid?"

"I don't care if it sounds dumb," I say, and shrug. "I really don't. I'm not saying it first."

"Whyever not?" she asks, completely confused. "I mean, who cares who says it first, as long as it's said?"

"Because what if he just says 'thank you'? Or 'you're so cute.' Jesus, Riley, I would die. Dead. Deader than a door-nail."

"But what if he says, 'I love you too, Cami'?"

"Well, that would be nice," I admit softly. "But what if he just thinks that it's all just a part of the crush I've had on him forever? Because it's *not*. What I feel for him now is so much bigger, so much better. He's not perfect, not by any means, and sometimes he makes me a little crazy, but he's good to me. He listens to me. I care, more than I ever have about *anyone*, and I was married, Riley."

"I know," she murmurs softly, watching me with happy hazel eyes. "And I watched you be unhappy in a marriage that was just mediocre for far too long."

"Yeah." I nod and sigh and absently pet Scoot. "I don't

think anything with Landon could ever be mediocre. He's not a guy that seems like he'd settle for mediocrity in anything."

"Do you feel safe with him?" she asks, surprising me.

"Of course."

"Honestly, Cami, I think you should tell him."

"Maybe it's too soon?"

"Oh, please." Riley rolls her eyes and takes a scoop out of my tub of ice cream. "You and I both know that falling in love happens when it happens. You may have only been dating him for about a month, but you've known him most of your life. You *know* him, Cami."

"I do." I nod and stare at the paused screen. "Maybe you're right. Maybe I should just let it slip out when we're making love—"

"Bad idea," she says, shaking her head. "That shouldn't be the first time."

"Why not? It's as intimate as it gets."

"Exactly. Don't force it." She's staring at Scoot now. "How long have you had this cat?"

"I don't know, a little more than a month, I guess."

"You should probably take him to the vet."

I frown down at him and realize that he's been letting me pet him. Without trying to kill me. He's coming around. "You're right. I'll make an appointment tomorrow."

Scoot glares, as if he knows what I'm saying. "He's smart," Riley says.

"I know." I chuckle when he slips out of my lap and curls up next to me on the couch to give himself a bath. "Want to help me take him to the vet?"

"Not a chance in hell of that happening," she says, shaking her head. "I have a meeting with the Food Network tomorrow."

"What?" I squeal, staring at her as if she's just grown a third arm. "Why didn't you tell us?"

"Because I don't want to get all our hopes up for nothing," she says. "But I admit, I'm nervous."

"Is this a phone meeting?"

"Video chat," she says. "They might be interested in featuring us on a reality food show, and they have questions. I'll be chatting with a producer and a publicist, a few others too. I'll let you know if anything comes of it."

"Well, duh. This is so exciting!"

"If the show wants to intrude on Mia's kitchen, it won't be. She'll put up a fight."

"She *is* territorial," I agree. "But she'll do what's best for the restaurant."

Riley and I stare at each other for a moment, then giggle.

"Okay, she'll put up a fight. But wow, this could be really cool."

"I'm ready for more wine and more Stephan."

"Me too." I nod and reach for the bottle. "Hit play, sister."

THERE IS SOMETHING furry on my face.

"Mmmph," I mumble, muffled. With my eyes still closed, I take stock of my body. My head is lying on something bony, and my feet are up.

What the hell?

I open my eyes, but all I see is gray fur. Scoot is sleeping on my chest. I glance up, and there's Riley, sleeping with her head back on the couch, and my head is in her lap.

"Good morning," Landon says, startling me.

"Holy crap." I stare at his smiling face. "Is this a dream?"

"Yes, I'm your dream lover," he says, and then laughs. "You weren't answering your phone."

"I don't know where it is."

"What the hell is happening?" Riley asks, stirring.

"Landon just woke us up."

"Why?"

"You guys didn't show up to work and neither of you was answering your phone," Landon explains again, and circles around the couch, crouches in front of me, and nudges Scoot off my chest. "How are you, sweetheart?"

"Sleepy." *Hungover.* "We stayed up late watching our shows."

"There's more than one?" he asks.

"We were behind by a few weeks," Riley informs him. "Damn, my neck is stiff."

"You were worried when we were late for work?" I ask.

"A little."

"You know, I don't know if you know this, but we own the joint," Riley says, always grouchy when she doesn't have her coffee. "We don't have a set schedule." She scowls. "Wait. What time is it?"

"Nine fifteen," he replies.

"Fucking hell!" Riley exclaims, and wiggles out from under me. "I have a meeting at ten! Cami, I'm stealing some clothes."

I slap her ass. "How are you going to fit this luscious ass in my clothes?"

I envy Riley's ass. She's curvy where I'm just not.

"I'll find something."

She dashes upstairs, and Landon and I just stare at each other until she's out of earshot. "I missed you last night," he says, and leans in to kiss my lips softly.

"Aw, I missed you too," I say, smiling against his lips. "And I'm pretty sure I smell bad."

"Not too bad." He kisses me twice more. "Want to ride in with me?"

"I can't." I sit up and glance over at Scoot. "I have to take him to the *V-E-T*."

"You have to spell it out?"

"Yes, because I'm pretty sure he knows what that word means. I've had him awhile. It's time to have him checked out."

"Want me to stay and help?"

God, yes. But I square my shoulders and do my best to look brave. "No. I'm fine."

"Do you have a carrier?"

"Yes. I bought one when I bought his other things."

Landon nods. "Do you think he'll let you put him in there?"

"God, I hope I don't die."

He laughs and pats me on the leg. "I'll put him in there for you. Do you think you'll be okay at the vet's?"

"Yes, thank you." He brushes my hair back behind my ear and kisses my forehead as he stands.

"Where is it?"

"In the laundry room, on the dryer."

He disappears through the kitchen to the laundry-slash-mudroom and returns quickly as Riley makes a mad dash down the stairs, wearing a cute winter dress I forgot I had. "That looks better on you than it does on me."

"Thanks, I'll keep it." She winks at me and hurries into her jacket. "Are you going to stick around tonight for Jake's set? He's bringing Max."

Max is Jake's business partner and a former member of their band. Jake brings him once in a while to join him on-stage, and when the two sing together, the harmonies are magical.

"Yep, that's my plan. Wanna hang at the restaurant to-night and listen to music?" I ask Landon.

"I can do that."

"Awesome, I'll see you later." Riley waves and runs out. And then, as calmly and easy as you please, Landon reaches over and picks Scoot up in his arms. Instead of the bloodshed I'm expecting, Scoot nestles against Landon's chin, purring.

"You have got to be kidding me," I mutter, glaring at both of them. "He barely lets me touch him."

"I don't know what to say. I'm irresistible."

"You're something." I shake my head and watch as he easily slips Scoot into his carrier.

"There. All done." I stand and sigh happily as Landon pulls me into his arms for a big hug. "Good luck. Will you be coming into work when you're done?"

"Yes, I'll just run him back here and go in."

"Okay, babe. Let me know if you need anything."

"Well, it might help if you're on standby with an ambulance and some Neosporin."

He just laughs and kisses my head, then leaves. Scoot glares at me from behind his cage door.

"You're not in jail," I inform him. "You just have to go to the doctor."

He growls.

Shit.

"So, HOW DID it go?" Landon asks that evening as he joins me at the bar. I've been locked in my office all day and into the evening, trying to catch up on work. Being with Landon is awesome, but it's been bad for my productivity.

Not that I'm complaining.

"Well, it was fine—"

"Good."

"Until we got to the office."

"Oh no." He chuckles and smiles at Kat as she joins us. "She took the cat to the vet today."

"Oh, I've heard the story," Kat says, and pours Landon his usual gin and tonic. "I just want to hear it again."

"What happened?"

"The cat is evil," I reply calmly, and take another sip of my wine. "Like, certifiably evil. I could call in a priest, and the priest would agree."

"He's so mild-mannered."

I stare at Landon, and then bust up laughing. "Right." I

hold out my arm so he can examine the scratch marks from my elbow to wrist. "I made this up. Of course, this didn't happen until *after* the vaccinations. When we first got there, all was fine. I opened the carrier, and he came out, meowing, looking all innocent and cute. He let the *male* doctor hold him and examine him. He's perfectly healthy, by the way."

"Good to know," Landon says with a smile.

"He thinks that Scoot is about two years old. He was malnourished at some point." I frown, not enjoying the thought of the evil cat being hungry. "I guess he can tell by his teeth? I don't know. Anyway, he got a couple of shots since we don't know if he's ever had any before. He's been neutered, so probably, but we can't be sure. So, he got some shots. He sat perfectly still, looking around like, whatever.

"And then." I swallow hard. "The vet left me alone with him."

"Take a sip of wine," Kat suggests, and I comply.

"So I opened the cage and reached for him, and he became this . . . *wild creature.*"

Landon is holding his hand over his mouth, trying to stifle his laughter, but it's not working.

"His ears went back, and his eyes got super wide and all wildlike and he *hissed at me.*"

"He doesn't like the cage," Kat says, nodding sagely.

"You weren't there, Kat. You didn't see it." I take another sip of wine. "He actually scratched me. And I was so surprised, I practically threw him into the cage!"

"Aw, poor Scoot," Landon says, earning the glare of death from me.

"Poor Scoot?" My voice is calm, but I feel my cheeks flush. *"Poor Scoot?"*

"You know what I mean," he says, reaching for my hand, but I jerk away.

"I *bled*. And then he screamed at me all the way home, and when I opened his cage, he ran out super fast and tried to trip me . . . and the worst part?"

"There's a part that's worse?" Landon says, laughing.

"He freaking *peed in his cage!*" Both Landon and Kat are laughing now. "Have you ever had to clean cat pee? It's the most disgusting thing *ever*."

"But tell him the rest," Kat says, waving at me and holding on to her stomach. "Seriously, it's the best part."

"Oh God," Landon replies. "I have to hear it."

I square my shoulders, trying to wrap a little dignity around myself and failing miserably, I'm sure. "Well, I took the cage into the laundry room, and I had it in the big sink back there to wash it out."

Kat doubles over, lays her forehead on the bar, and hits it with her fist. "Oh my God, I can't handle it."

"So, I'm running hot water into it, and swishing the water around."

"Oh my God, I'm gonna pee!" Kat exclaims.

"And suddenly, out of nowhere, Scoot jumps into the sink! Which isn't such a bad thing because after he peed in the cage, he needed a bath anyway. He starts flailing about and howling, and sending water all over me and over the side of the sink onto the floor, and to try to climb out, he latches on to my other arm." I pull my sleeve up so Landon can see.

"And proceeds to almost amputate me as he launches himself across the room!"

Now they're laughing so hard that I wouldn't be surprised if one or both of them has a stroke.

"I'm so happy that my bloodshed is funny to you."

"Oh, baby," Landon gasps, trying to gather himself. "I'm sorry. It's just that it's so horrible."

"Horribly funny," Kat agrees, wiping tears from her cheeks. "Damn, my makeup is a mess."

"Yes, and my arms are a mess," I say, which only makes them laugh more.

"Seriously, it hurts." I pout, but I have to bite my lips because I want to bust out into laughter with them, but now it's the principle of it all.

Jake and Max are onstage, singing one of their old hits, the restaurant is packed, and I'm back here with these two being ridiculed.

"I'm sorry, sweetheart." Landon pulls me against him to give me a hug. "I should have gone with you."

"Why does he like you so much and not me? I feed him! I give him a place to live. I'm nice to the little bastard."

"He's just temperamental," Landon says reassuringly. "Are you set on staying through the show, or can I steal you away?"

"I guess we can go," I reply with a shrug. "I'm not really in the mood for this anyway."

"Come on." He takes my hand and leads me out back where his car is. He must have swapped out the work truck earlier and come back.

"Where are we going?"

"Nowhere fancy," he says, and takes my hand as he pulls away from the restaurant. He looks down at my arm. "Boy, he really got you good."

"No kidding. I wonder if I need a rabies shot?"

"It's not that deep, and I am quite sure that Scoot doesn't have rabies."

"No, he just has a bad case of the assholes," I reply, sulking, which only makes Landon start chuckling again. "Keep laughing and you'll be sleeping by yourself again tonight, funny man."

"Oh, come on, I saw your lips twitch earlier. A year from now, this will be the funniest story ever."

"I'll wait until the wounds heal to laugh about it."

The car comes to a stop in the parking lot of our old high school. I frown and glance over at Landon. "Did you forget your homework?"

"No." He smiles and unfastens his seat belt, then mine, and turns to face me. "Do you remember that day when I was home from college for the summer and you had just graduated but needed to come back to the school for something or other—"

"I had to pick up my diploma," I add, already knowing where he's going with this. Of course I remember that day.

"Right, and you asked me to drive you over here. When you came back to the car, we just sat here for like an hour and talked about so many things."

He leans toward me, his eyes on my lips. "I knew it then, but I was so young, and didn't know what in the hell to do about it. And you were so fucking young too."

"You knew what?" I ask with a whisper, but he keeps going.

"I had to take a step back and give you room. Time. Time to grow up and experience some life. But I'm not going to keep giving you room."

"I don't want room," I say. He smiles softly, in that way he does when I've done or said something that he finds particularly cute. He brushes my hair behind my ear and rubs my earlobe between his finger and thumb. "You were the one that got away, Cami."

"I didn't go anywhere."

"I'm not doing this right." He licks his lips, and then leans in and stops talking altogether when his lips meet mine. I sigh into him, the way I always do when he kisses me because it feels so damn good. I fist his shirt and pull him closer, then moan when his tongue meets mine.

God, I can't get enough of him.

But suddenly he takes my hands in his and pulls back, and when I open my eyes, he's staring at me with wide, sincere eyes.

"What's wrong?" I ask.

"Absolutely nothing." He takes a deep breath. "I just wanted it to be here, in this place, where I wanted to say it then and couldn't, for all of those reasons.

"I love you, Cami."

Chapter 12

~Landon~

She's not saying a fucking thing.

She's staring at me with those incredible green eyes, unblinking. This can't be coming from left field for her. Jesus, after all we've shared, she's had to have felt it from me.

"Sweetheart, I need you to say something."

She frowns, and that's it. I'm positive that she's going to say that she doesn't feel the same way, but suddenly tears fill her eyes and she squeezes my hand as a smile spreads across her lips.

"I love you too," she whispers, and my heart begins beating again. I lean in and rest my lips against hers.

"I couldn't hear you."

"Yes, you could."

I simply wait, and after a moment, she says, "I love you too, Landon."

"Thank God. For a second there, I thought I'd just made a huge ass of myself."

"No, that was me today at the vet's office," she says, her lips still tickling mine. "Telling me how you feel isn't being an ass."

"I've loved you for a long time."

She smiles and drags her fingertips down my face. "Ditto."

I need her. Right now. I kiss her, taking it from sweet and soft to pure need. She reaches for my jeans, but I take her hand away and kiss her palm. "I'm not going to do this here, in the high school parking lot."

"Why not?" She looks around, making me smile. "We're the only ones here."

"Because we're not teenagers." I sit back in the seat, put my belt on, and start the car. "But make no mistake, I'm taking you home right now. If I'm not inside you very soon, I'll go crazy."

She doesn't put her seat belt on, but she sits back and crosses her arms. "But it's so far away to your house! Why did you have to choose the house so far away?"

"Well, I didn't anticipate telling you I love you at the high school and then need to make love to you."

"You're a bad planner," she says, and makes me laugh. I glance over when I stop at a red light.

"You're in a skirt."

"I'm aware."

"You don't have to wait." She raises a brow and hitches her skirt up around her hips.

And of course she's not wearing any panties. Is it any wonder that I love her? She grips her legs in her hands and pulls up, from her knees to her hips, making me absolutely crazy.

My dick is so hard I'm surprised I don't bust out of my jeans. When she tries to reach for my pants again, I shake my head.

"This is all about you, Cami."

"Me?"

I nod and glance over. She's not touching herself.

"Are you shy?"

"Kind of. I've never—"

"Are you saying you've never masturbated?"

"No, but not in front of someone."

"I'll help." I lightly drag my fingertips up her thigh, then follow the crease of where her leg meets her center, and she gasps. "Your skin is so damn soft."

She swallows hard as I gently run my fingers through her lips, up to her clit, then back down again. She's already sopping wet, which only makes me that much harder.

I'm going to fuck her brainless.

My middle finger presses on her clit and her back arches.

"Damn, you're good at that," she says breathlessly, giving my ego one hell of a boost.

I simply love to touch her. "You're so responsive," I mutter.

"Of course I am." She bites her lip and then exhales. "You're touching me."

My finger slips from her clit to her opening and slides

inside. I shake my hand, pressing the pad of my thumb against her most sensitive spot, and grin when she simply explodes against my hand.

I pull into my driveway—finally—and before she can pull herself together, I help her out of the car, pull her skirt down far enough that I won't have to kill someone if they happen to look outside, and rush her inside.

I slam the door closed and spin her around, her back against the door, and sink to my knees so I can bury my face in her.

"Holy fucking shit!" she exclaims, and fists her hands in my hair, not gently in the least. I pull one leg over my shoulder to give myself better access and eat her like she's a buffet and I've been starved for years.

Because it feels like I have.

"Landon!"

I growl, but don't stop. Her lips are in my mouth, my tongue is inside her, and she comes again, shuddering. I grip her ass, making sure she doesn't fall, and when she's done, I stand and hitch her up, her legs around my waist.

"I need you," I say before devouring her mouth. I manage to unzip my pants and free my cock, then slide home.

"Oh God," she moans against my mouth. "So good."

"So good," I agree, and begin to pound into her, praying my door doesn't give.

Explaining that to the landlord would be interesting.

"Grab on," I instruct her, and when she loops her arms around my neck, I carry her, still inside her, to the staircase.

But we don't get far up before I lower her to the stairs. I can't help it. I need to *move.*

"I love this, but the stairs aren't comfy," she says breathlessly.

I pull back, turn her over, slap her ass, and plunge back inside her. "Better?"

"Holy fuck," she groans.

"I'll take that as a yes." Neither of us speaks for long minutes as I fuck her, hard, primal, not able to get enough of her. When I feel her come for the third time, I pull out and lead her the rest of the way up the stairs and to my bedroom.

I strip us of the rest of our clothes and tumble her onto my bed. I can't help but stare at her. Jesus, have I ever seen anything more beautiful than Cami spread out on my bed, wearing only moonshine?

No. No, I haven't.

"You're so damn beautiful," I say, panting, my hands in fists. I still want to fuck her, hard, but damn it, I want to be gentle with her too. I want to make love to her.

"Need you," she says, holding her hand out for me. "Come here."

I crawl onto the bed and kiss up her leg, kiss her center, and up her body until I'm covering her. I take both of her hands and hold them in one of mine above her head, then guide my cock inside her.

I stop, buried as deep as I can go, and stare down into her deep green eyes. She's everything I ever wanted.

She's everything I ever needed.

"Landon?" She circles her hips, trying to get me to move.

"Yes, my love?"

She stills and her eyes find mine. "I like that."

"Which part?" I grin and pull out to the tip, then push back in. "This?"

"Yes."

"This?" I lower my face and pull her nipple into my mouth, teasing it with my teeth.

"God, yes."

"What else, my love?"

"That." I rest on my elbows at either side of her head, let go of her hands, and grin when she immediately grabs on to my ass.

"Calling you my love?"

She nods.

"You are." I kiss her nose and move my hips slowly. "My love."

"You're *my* love," she says softly. She drags her foot up the back of my leg and hitches it over my hip, making my eyes cross with how deep I can go. "And I need you to move, babe."

"I *am* moving."

"Faster."

"No."

She cocks a brow. "Why?"

I don't answer. I just kiss her, saying without words everything she needs to hear. Because I need to make this last. Because she's amazing and I need to show her just how incredible she is.

Because while fucking her was and is some of the best damn sex I've ever had, it's nothing compared to what it feels like to revel in her.

So I keep this slow, steady pace and make her feel things she never has before.

"TELL ME AGAIN why I have to go to your girls' brunch." I pull into a parking space outside of the popular breakfast joint in Northwest Portland on Sunday and look over at Cami, who looks soft and still a little sleepy.

"Because you're taking me to the movies after this," she says, her voice perfectly reasonable. "There's no need for you to go do your own thing, just to meet up with me in two hours. Plus, you're hungry."

"I'm always hungry," I reply as I take her hand in mine and lead her down the sidewalk and inside the restaurant. It's not as busy as usual, but then, it's almost noon.

The girls slept in this morning.

"They're back here," Cami says, pointing. She leads us to the far side of the restaurant, where Riley, Mia, Kat, and Addie are already munching on fresh fruit.

"Hi!" Riley says, smiling. "We haven't ordered yet. Addie was just starving, so we had them bring some fruit."

"I'm telling you," Addie says after I kiss her cheek and sit between her and Cami. "This baby is going to be a football player. All I do is eat. He's going to make me gain a hundred pounds."

"Not if you eat the right things," Riley says, and spears a strawberry.

"I don't want celery, Ri," Addie says.

"How are you, big brother?" Mia asks.

"Good." I glance around and notice that all five pairs of eyes are on me. "What?"

"Glad you could join girls' breakfast," Kat says with a smirk.

"She made me come," I insist, pointing at Cami. "Tell them."

"I did," she admits, and chews on a slice of melon. "We're going to the movies later, so it seemed logical to bring him."

"But I can leave," I offer, and push my chair back, secretly hoping they'll let me escape, but they just laugh.

"No, we're just flipping you shit," Kat says. "Just beware that there will be girl talk. We're too comfortable with you to censor ourselves."

"There's no alcohol here," I reply. "I think I'm safe."

But my stomach clenches when they all snicker.

I'm in trouble.

"So, as I was saying," Addie continues. "This baby is sucking the life out of me."

"I think that's a bit dramatic," Cami says.

"No, it's true. My boobs hurt *so bad*. Jake and I were having sex, and he had me bent over the bed, and he reached down to grab my tits and I almost kicked him in the balls."

"And there it is," Mia says with a laugh. "Welcome to girl talk, big brother."

I simply shrug and study my menu. These women are a lot of fun, and maybe slightly crazy. I'd rather be anywhere but here, but if Cami wants me here, I'll stay.

I'll do just about anything that Cami wants me to, and I'm not ashamed to admit it.

The waitress comes to take our orders and refresh our drinks.

"So, we hear you dropped the L-bomb," Riley says, and sips her orange juice.

"Riley!" Cami hisses, then hides her face in her napkin.

"What? Is it a secret?"

"It's not a secret," I reply, and laugh, rubbing Cami's leg under the table.

"We tell each other everything," Addie says, almost apologetically. "To be fair, she didn't text us until yesterday."

"Yeah, it's not like she texted us while you were in the heat of the moment," Kat says. "That would just take it too far."

"Ew," Mia says. "You know, talking about sex before was all well and good until you started banging my brother."

"And boy, do we bang," Cami says with a smug smile. "A lot. Like, over and over again."

The other girls all laugh their asses off while Mia makes gagging sounds.

"Did you just shudder?" Riley asks Mia.

"Hell yes. I don't want to ever have a reason to think of my brother naked."

"He's impressive naked," Cami says.

"I can see that," Kat says as her eyes travel up and down my torso. "You should take your shirt off, just to give us a sneak peek."

"I'm not sharing him," Cami replies, rolling her eyes. "You'll just have to take my word for it."

"Thank the baby Jesus," Mia mutters just as my phone rings. I glance down and recognize the number.

"I've gotta take this." I kiss Cami's cheek and excuse myself. "Hello."

"Hey, Palazzo," my old Navy buddy Ringo says. "Sorry, I know it's Sunday, but my day is jammed tomorrow, so I thought I'd get a head start."

"No worries. What's up?"

"I spoke with Lucas last week, and he mentioned that you might be interested in a flight instructor position."

I take a deep breath and shove my hand through my hair. "I can't fly." My voice is flat, and the rage and sense of loss boils up the way it always does when I think about the fact that I'll never pilot another plane.

"Not in the air," he clarifies. "I'd like you to teach in the classroom, and oversee the program up there for me. You'd be the boss, which you're good at."

I frown. "You want me to stand in a classroom and bore the fuck out of people? If anything, I should be in the air."

"But you can't be," Ringo says softly. "You got a shitty deal, man. I'm just thankful that you're okay. And I could seriously use you. I'm expanding the private flight school from San Diego up to Portland. You wouldn't have to travel at all."

"That's awesome, Ringo, but classroom work?"

"Sleep on it. Think it over and call me back this week. I'm not in a huge hurry for an answer, but the only answer I'll accept is yes. You'd be excellent at keeping everything in order, and you're a good speaker. You're not going to bore the shit out of anyone." I hear him sigh. "How are you, man?"

"Better," I admit. "Physically, pretty much all healed up. I've been working for my dad and keeping busy. I have a girlfriend."

"So you're settling down."

I stare blindly as a kid picks his nose in his stroller, his mom hurrying down the sidewalk. Am I settling down?

I guess I am.

"I suppose you could put it like that."

"Perfect. Call me this week."

And with that, he's gone. The thought of working in a classroom doesn't get my blood flowing, but I like that I wouldn't be a peon. I'd be running the show, and God knows I have plenty of experience running shows.

Come to think of it, teaching people who are excited about flying doesn't sound like a bad gig.

I'll think about it later, but the truth is, I just can't see myself working in construction forever. I like it fine, but it doesn't excite me.

Everything about flying excites me.

I make my way back through the restaurant and am almost to the table when I hear Kat say, "This period is killing me. Like, instead of it raining men, it's raining red."

"That's so gross," Cami says, but she's laughing as she takes a bite of her bacon. She glances up and sees me. "Hey, babe. Your food's here."

"Good. I'm hungry."

"I'm telling you," Kat continues without missing a beat. "I'm gonna have to invest in an industrial-sized box of tampons or something."

"Oh my God! Do you remember when we went to that party our senior year with Cami?" Mia says, pointing to Addie.

"Aw, poor Cami," Addie says, hiding a giggle behind her hand. "She wore white pants."

"And didn't expect Mother Nature to show up that night," Cami adds, shaking her head. "It was so mortifying."

"You recovered," Riley says. "You're wearing white pants today."

"Do you know how long it took me to wear white pants again?" Cami demands. "I didn't wear them until just a couple of years ago, and now with this reminder, I'm re-thinking it all over again."

"I hear you," Kat says, nodding. "It's like Subway."

"Subway?" Mia asks with a frown.

"Yep, I ate at Subway and got food poisoning when I was like twelve, and I've been afraid to eat there ever since. Whenever I drive past there, my butt clenches."

The girls all erupt in laughter, and I can't help but join them.

"I'm so glad that my gastrointestinal issues make you laugh," Kat says, her shoulders straight. She eats her eggs. "It was horrific."

"I can imagine," Mia replies, and frowns at her eggs. "Like these eggs. I ordered them over medium, and the yolks are runny. If these are over medium, I'm Selena Gomez."

"You always order the most difficult thing in the world to cook," Riley accuses her. "And I think you do it on purpose."

"Of course I do," Mia replies with a sniff. "What if that twit applies for a job with me? I need to know if they can actually cook. And if you know what you're doing, it's not the hardest thing in the world to cook. You just have to pay attention and not fuck it up."

"Are you going to send them back?" Cami asks.

"No. I actually like the yolks runny." Mia grins and takes a bite of one of them. "But now I know that the idiot in the kitchen doesn't know how to cook eggs."

"We don't even have eggs on our menu," Cami reminds her.

"That doesn't matter," Mia says. "If they can't cook eggs the way I ask, how can they be expected to cook a steak the correct way?"

"Whatever you say," Riley says, and rolls her eyes at me. "Has she always been this difficult?"

"She's always been demanding. Mia knows what she wants, and she gets it. It's as simple as that."

"She's a pain in the ass," Kat says, but winks at Mia. "But we love her."

"Yes, that's pretty much always been the consensus." I chuckle, looking at my sister fondly. "But, with that comes a woman who's excellent at her job. Do you get many complaints about what comes out of the kitchen?"

"Hardly ever," Addie says. "We don't ever want you to change, Mia."

"Good. Because I'm not going to." Her lips twist. "I wasn't willing to change for a man. There's no way in hell I'm changing for you bitches."

"Wait." I lean forward, frowning. "A man wanted you to change?"

This is news to me.

"It was a very long time ago," Mia replies, waving me off. "And it was never going to happen." She shakes her head at me, telling me to kill the subject, but I don't like this. I know that I was gone for a long time, and I missed a lot, but I'm just now realizing that I was gone for some very big moments in my sister's life.

I should have been here to cut that dick's balls off.

"I'm full," Cami says, leaning back in her chair and rubbing her belly. "Take me to the movies now so I can gorge myself on popcorn."

I grin down at her. "Anything you want, babe."

"Ugh." Mia rolls her eyes. "You guys are disgusting."

Chapter 13

~Cami~

"*J* love sleeping in," I say with a big yawn, and smile at Scoot, who is perched on my vanity desk, watching me get ready for my day.

Landon just left for work, after bringing me a mug of coffee and then letting it get cold while he reminded me just how much he loves me in the shower. Of course, then he was late and had to dash out the door, but I don't have to hurry today. My work is caught up and I don't have any meetings or calls until noon.

I sip my now cool coffee, not caring in the least that it's not hot, and run a comb through my damp hair, slather on some face moisturizer, and while that soaks in, I lift my blow dryer.

I close my eyes and enjoy the warm air, sighing content-edly. My body feels . . . well loved and sated, which sounds corny even to me, like something out of a book, but that's the best way to describe it. I have sore muscles in places I never even knew I had muscles.

Good job, Landon.

I grin and set the dryer down, then frown when I can't find the eye shadow I just pulled out of a drawer a minute ago. I glance to the floor, then glare at Scoot.

"Stop pushing my stuff on the floor, you little menace."

Scoot simply blinks at me with those big, yellow eyes. He's too adorable to get mad at. At least, now that my wounds have healed, that is. As I reach for a brush to start applying makeup, my package of pills catches my eye.

"Can't forget this," I say, and push a pill out of the packet, then wash it down with a sip of the cold coffee. "And I'm almost out. Don't let me forget to call in for a refill." I scratch Scoot behind the ears. "You're the only baby I need around here for a while."

"Meow," he says, as if he agrees, and pushes his face into my hand.

"Aw, you're coming around, little guy." I grin and return my attention to the mirror, just as Scoot bats an eye shadow back onto the floor. "You're coming around just in time to irritate me."

I bend and pick up my favorite Urban Decay. "Stop that."

Scoot goes to work bathing his tail, as if he doesn't have any idea what I'm talking about. "Yeah, you're not innocent."

I give him one last stern look, which doesn't seem to faze him in the least, and set to work on my makeup, which on a day like today takes only a few minutes.

But it gives me quiet time to think, and there hasn't been a lot of that lately.

My life has changed in the last few months. I mean, for the most part it's the same. My friends, my job, my home are all the same. But with Landon in my life, it feels so much *bigger*. Full.

Just when I think I can't love him more, he says or does something like this morning that tips me over into that *more* category.

Suddenly, out of the corner of my eye, I see Scoot reach his little paw out and bat at my mascara until *clunk*, it's on the floor.

"I saw that," I say without looking directly at him. He watches me for a heartbeat, then bats my eye shadow onto the floor, and without a pause, sends my blush over for good measure. "Who taught you to be such a pain in the ass?"

"*Meow.*"

"Yeah, meow yourself." I pick him up and put him on the floor and point at his face. "Stay down."

I reach for my mascara and decide to hurry before Scoot jumps back up to wreak more havoc, then sit back and stare at my own reflection. "You're being bullied by your *cat*." I shake my head. "Sad."

Apparently, that's his cue to jump back up again and sit, his tail swooshing over the side. "You're a bad cat."

"*Meow.*"

"Well, as long as you know." I quickly finish my makeup and stow it away before Scoot can use it for hockey practice again. "Come on, bad cat. Let's get dressed. I have some shoes you can hide behind, but if you so much as lay a paw on them, it's off to the pound for you."

"Why do you have bite marks on your Jimmy Choos?" Riley asks as she sits next to me at the bar. Kat's pouring us both some wine.

"Because I have a suicidal cat," I reply, and sip the cool, crisp Chardonnay. Leave it to Riley to see the tiny marks on my heel.

"Excuse me?" Riley says.

"I warned him not to touch them, but I screwed up and left them on the floor and I went to the bathroom, and when I came back, there he was, nibbling."

"Maybe your cat doesn't speak English," Kat says. "Maybe he's Spanish. Or French."

"Well, then I'm screwed because I don't know either of those languages," I reply, and frown as I stare down in my glass. "He's just going to eat all of the shoes."

"Who's eating what shoes?" Landon asks as he wraps his arms around me and buries his nose in my neck. "You smell delicious."

I grin as Kat rolls her eyes. "Her cat apparently eats shoes for breakfast."

"Scoot ate your shoes?" He rests his chin on my shoulder.

"He gnawed on them," I reply with a sigh. "And they're designer."

"Maybe it's because you pile all of your shoes in a mountain in the middle of your microscopic closet," Riley says.

"I keep most of them in boxes, but the ones that I wear a lot do end up on the floor."

"I'm building your closet," Landon says, his voice pure silk next to my ear. He could be reciting the freaking alphabet for all I care. My imaginary panties are sopping wet.

"Oh God, she's biting her lip," Kat says to Riley. "Stop turning her on while she's working."

"I'm not working," I whisper, and close my eyes. "Say something else."

I feel his lips curl into a grin against my ear. "I'm going to make you dinner tonight."

"We're meeting Brian and his new girlfriend for dinner." But hot damn, my nipples are hard.

"Brian has a new girlfriend?" Riley asks.

"And I'm going to run you a hot bath when we get home," he continues, as if no one said anything at all, "and then I'm going to wash you from head to toe."

"I need another drink," Riley mutters as Landon plants his lips against my ear and whispers.

"And then I'm going to fuck you against the vanity in your bathroom."

Oh God.

I swallow hard as he kisses my cheek and pulls away from me, my back suddenly cold where he had been pressing against me.

"You seduced her into a coma," Kat says. "Good one."

"It's been way too long since I last got laid," Riley grumbles as I blink my eyes open and swallow hard, shifting on my stool.

"Well, I guess we should go," I stammer, needing to clear my throat twice.

"Can you walk?" Kat asks with a smirk.

"Of course I can walk," I reply. *Jesus, I hope I can walk.*

"Ready?" Landon asks, offering me his hand. When my gaze climb up his body, his eyes are hot, watching me carefully with not a little humor.

"Are you enjoying this?" I ask as I take his hand and scoot off the stool.

"More than you can ever imagine," he says, and chuckles. "Come on, I'll buy you dinner."

Before he can lead me out of the room, I lean in, gesturing for him to bend down so I can whisper in his ear. "I'm not wearing any underwear under this skirt. That ought to give you something to think about."

I pull away as Kat and Riley bust out laughing. Landon's lips twitch, his eyes are no less hot.

"How could you hear that? I was whispering!"

"Sweetheart," Kat says, saluting me with a glass, "you must have learned to whisper while riding in a helicopter in the middle of a hurricane."

"Are you saying I'm not subtle?"

"You've never been subtle," Landon says, hitching a stray strand of hair behind my ear. "Come on, let's get to dinner before I pull you into your office and take your desk for a spin."

"Ew. We work in there, Landon." Riley frowns as Kat just laughs and waves at us. Landon guides me out to his car, and when we're both inside, before I can buckle my seat belt, he leans over and slides his hand up my leg and under my skirt, and directly to my dripping-wet pussy.

"Mm, you're really not wearing any underwear," he says, his lips centimeters from mine.

"I don't lie about underwear."

"So I see." His finger slides over my clit and through my folds, then slips all the way inside me.

"Oh, fuck."

"I'm going to put a lot more than my finger in here tonight, Cami," he whispers. "I want you to stay wet, just like this, all night."

"Well, you're doing a good job of making sure that happens," I reply, and push my hips against his hand. "You're good at that."

"I know."

Suddenly he's gone, starting the car, but before he can pull into traffic, I grab his wrist and pull his finger to my mouth, licking it clean.

"Do we really have to go to this dinner?" he asks, watching me intently.

"Yep." I release his hand and buckle in, trying to look cool and unfazed, but my heart is beating overtime and my core is pulsing with pure need. Jesus, he turns me on. I swallow hard and try to distract us both. "How was your day? What's new and exciting?"

"Day was fine," he says, checking his blind spot and pulling out behind a Volvo. "I got my travel itinerary for next week, finally."

"Wait. What travel itinerary?" This is news to me.

"Damn, I forgot to tell you." He smiles over at me and pats my knee. "You have a habit of distracting me."

"Okay, tell me now." *Is this where he tells me that he's leaving?* It's no secret that Landon loves to travel, to experience different places.

"I have to go to San Diego next week to meet up with an old friend of mine who's offered me a job."

He's taking a job in freaking San Diego?

I frown and cross my arms over my chest.

"When are you moving?"

"Moving?" I close my eyes and pray that the tears don't fall while he's watching. "Cami, I'm not moving."

He's not moving this week. But next week he's going to San Diego for a potential job.

"Cami, look at me."

But I can't. I can't look him in the eye, when I'm still hot and wet, craving him, as he tells me that it's been fun but it's almost time for him to move on.

Suddenly he pulls into a parking lot and throws the car out of gear.

"Camille, look at me."

"You know, maybe we don't have to go out for dinner with Brian and his girlfriend after all. You can just take me home."

He takes my shoulders in his hands and forces me to face him, a frown on his handsome face. "I'm not moving, Cam."

"You've been here longer than you have been in the past, and I know you like to travel, Landon."

"So you're just waiting for me to bail?" he asks, shaking his head. "No. I'm going down to train for a job that I can do *here*."

"Here?"

"Yes, as a flight instructor."

I stare at him in disbelief, and then, as his words sink in, I let out a loud laugh. "Right."

"Why is the thought of me teaching people to fly so funny?"

"You *can't* fly. You're not medically cleared for it."

His jaw ticks before he says, "In a classroom."

I still and watch him carefully for a long moment. "You're okay with teaching people to fly in a classroom?"

He nods once and looks down at my lap. "It's still teaching, and it's being around planes, and people passionate about them. I miss it, babe. But the job is here, not in Southern California. I'll be managing the whole operation."

"Wow." I take a deep breath, my whole body ready to sag with relief. "You'd be great at running an operation like that."

He drags his fingertips down my cheek. "Are you okay?"

"Yes." I nod and smile, but part of me is still hesitant.

"I'll only be gone for a few days, Cami."

"I'm fine. Really." I sit back and lick my lips. "Congratulations. This is great news."

"Thank you." He watches me for a minute, then starts the car again. "I have no interest in leaving here. I'm happy."

"Good." I grin over at him and take his hand in mine, linking our fingers. "I'm happy too."

"So, THE LADY gave us the keys to the room, and then she said, 'Don't mind the ghost. She doesn't take up much room.'" Stephanie, Brian's new and completely adorable girlfriend, shakes her auburn head and smiles as she takes a bite of her salad. "I mean, I don't believe in ghosts, so I was like, *okay!* But I think Brian was a little creeped out."

"I was not creeped out," Brian says as he watches the adorable Stephanie with big love-sick eyes as she continues to tell us all about their trip to Victoria Island for the weekend.

"He kind of was," she says, leaning toward me like we're conspiring against him. "But we didn't see or hear any ghosts."

"I'm pretty sure I heard a door slam in the middle of the night," Brian says as he butters another piece of bread.

"You were snoring like crazy," Stephanie replies. "You didn't hear anything."

"I don't snore," he insists.

"Yes, you do," I reply, and roll my eyes.

"See!" Stephanie exclaims, pointing at me. "You do."

"Takes one to know one," Landon mutters, earning an elbow in his side.

"You know, I think it's great that y'all are friends," Stephanie says, the South thick in her voice.

"You do?" I ask, surprised.

"Sure. I mean, so many of my divorced friends are bitter

and angry and have nothing but shit to say about their exes. It's refreshing to know a couple who realized they just weren't right for each other and moved on. No bitterness, no anger, just friendship."

"It took us a little while to get here," I reply, holding Brian's eyes with mine. There was a time when Brian was angry, and for good reason. "But you're right, we *are* good friends."

"Well, I like it," Stephanie says, and raises her glass. "To friendship."

"To friendship."

Dinner is relaxed and fun, and I find myself really enjoying Stephanie, and Brian as well. He's different with her. More laid-back. More attentive.

Better.

And I couldn't be happier for them.

After we've demolished dinner and dessert, we go our separate ways, and Landon drives us back to my place.

"Tonight was interesting," he says thoughtfully.

"I had fun."

"That's why it was interesting," he replies as he parks at my house and walks me to the door.

"Me having fun is interesting?" I push inside and toss my keys and bag on the table beside the door.

"You just had dinner with your boyfriend, your ex-husband, and his new girlfriend."

"Thanks for the recap, but I was there." I kiss Landon's bicep, then walk toward the kitchen.

"You seem pretty chipper for someone whose ex is moving on with someone new."

"I moved on with someone new." I shrug and grab a bottle of water out of the fridge. "Landon, Brian and I have been over for a very long time."

"Mia mentioned that you used to try to set him up with women."

"All the time," I confirm.

"Why?"

This makes me pause and frown at my bottle of water. Landon and I have been together long enough that I can come clean about my relationship with Brian. So I take a deep breath and raise my eyes to his.

"I felt so guilty I thought I'd die with it."

"What? Why?"

"Because I left." I shrug and begin pacing the kitchen. I always pace when I think. "Honestly, Brian and I got married because we'd dated in college and it seemed like that was the logical next step. He's a nice guy, has a decent job, good credit score. On paper, we're an excellent match.

"But I shouldn't have married him in the first place. He was madly in love, and I *did* and still do care for him, but I wasn't in love with him the way I should have been to get married. And after a few years, it became apparent to me that I never would love him the way a woman should love her husband."

"Why not?" Landon asks softly, but I just keep talking.

"So I told him that I wanted a divorce, and he acted like it was this big shock, but I don't see how it could have been. There was no passion, no adventure in our relationship. And at first he was so hurt that he couldn't even stand to be in the same room as me. But over time, we talked more and we both agreed that ours wasn't what a marriage should be. And I just couldn't bear the thought of Brian being alone, so I started trying to set him up, which he hated."

I laugh and look over at Landon, who's sitting at the island, watching me pace.

"Why weren't you in love with him, Cami?"

I shake my head and continue. "But it's clear that he didn't need my help at all. Stephanie is great. I like her. She's pretty, and funny, and honestly, I think she's someone that I could be friends with. And did you see how he looks at her? He's so happy. And that just makes me happy."

Having run out of steam, and things to say, I lean back against the counter and cross my arms.

"Why?" he asks again, holding my gaze.

"You know why," I whisper, and bite my lip, horrified that I'll cry.

Landon stands and walks over to me, caging me in the way he did in this very spot weeks ago when he first kissed me.

"Tell me," he whispers, pushing my hair over my shoulder and cupping my neck in his palm, his thumb grazing over the skin of my chin.

"I've always been in love with you, Landon."

He exhales slowly and leans into me, but rather than kiss me passionately and boost me up on the countertop to fuck me senseless, he brushes his lips gently over my forehead and pulls me into his arms, hugging me softly. "Same here, sweetheart."

Chapter 14

~Landon~

"So, this is a surprise?" Steven, Cami's nephew, asks two weeks later. We're in Cami's house, upstairs in the storage bedroom that I'm now turning into her closet.

"Yep," I reply, and spackle where the doorframe was.

"Won't she see the mess when she gets home from work?" he asks with a smirk.

"She and Kat are in Seattle for a couple of days on a wine-buying trip. So I have today and tomorrow to finish this up."

"Cool," Steven says, surveying our work. "She's gonna go apeshit when she sees it."

"I hope so." I grin over at him. "She needs better storage for all of those shoes."

"Why do girls have to buy so many shoes in the first place?" He frowns, like women are as much a mystery as aliens.

"It's not our job to understand them," I reply with a sigh, and clap him on the shoulder. "We just try our best to keep them happy."

"That's a mystery too," he says, shaking his head in disgust. "I've been living with this girl, Melissa, since my folks moved up to Seattle. I like her, but damn, she's a head case."

"How long have you dated her?"

"A couple years, I guess." He shrugs. "We get along okay for the most part, but damn, she's so jealous. I can't even be polite to a waitress without her losing her shit on me."

"That sounds exhausting," I murmur, not envious of his plight in the least. I've dated girls like that before. Hell, most of us have. They're emotionally draining.

"I was so glad you called me to come help with this," Steven continues. "She was ranting and nagging about something this morning. Wanted me to mow the grass or something, which is fine, but I just mowed it two days ago. Sometimes I think she just needs to nag me about anything to feel good."

I nod, not sure what to say. I can see that he's frustrated, but we're not really close friends. After a pause, he glances at me, and looks like he's about to say something, but then turns away and begins stirring the paint we're going to use on two of the walls.

"Go ahead and ask."

He waits a minute, and then surprises the shit out of me when he asks, "Do you regret doing the Navy thing?"

I blink for a minute, mentally switching gears. "Not at all."

He simply nods.

"Why do you ask?"

"Well, I've been thinking about enlisting."

"In the Navy?"

"Yeah." He shrugs. "I think it could be a good opportunity for me."

I think so too. But I don't want to push the military on him. The decision has to be his own.

"Have you talked to a recruiter?"

"A few times, yes. I don't think I can be a pilot because of my eyes."

"What's wrong with your eyes?"

"Glasses. I don't have Navy pilot eyes, but there are a million other things I can do."

"Absolutely." I shove my hands in my pockets and wait, expecting him to start asking more questions, and I don't have to wait long.

"Was it hard, being away from your family all of the time?"

"I'd get homesick a bit in the beginning," I reply, and rub my chin, thinking back to that time. Mostly, I was homesick for Cami, but I don't tell him that. "But they'll keep you busy with training. You'll get leave so you can come home to visit."

He nods. "And maybe I can get stationed in some cool places. See things I wouldn't get to see otherwise."

He's a smart kid.

"That's one of the things I loved about it."

"I've heard girls like a guy in uniform." His young face lights up at that thought, making me smile.

"I thought you already had a girl?"

"Come on, you and I both know that's not going to last. I'm not married to her, and I can't wait to get away from her every day. That's not how I want to live my life."

"No. You don't." I've been there too, and I'm so thankful that I don't have that now. I love being with Cami. I could talk to her all day and never tire of her.

"You're not sick of my aunt," Steven says pointedly, looking me in the eye.

"No. I'm not."

"So, her parents died a while back, and my folks moved away, and I'm the only family she has here, not counting the girls, so I feel like I should ask you some questions."

He's holding my gaze, his shoulders are square, and his hands are fisted. He's a good young man who loves his aunt, and I couldn't have more respect for him than I do right now.

"Ask away."

"What are your intentions with her?" He crosses his arms over his chest.

"Are you asking if I intend to marry her?"

"Do you?"

I nod, finally able to voice aloud what's been running through my head for weeks. "I love your aunt, Steven. She's an amazing woman. I would be the luckiest man in the world if she agreed to marry me."

"Aunt Cami is the best." He nods and looks around the empty room. "She deserves the best that life has to offer.

Someone to love her and spoil her some. Maybe buy her some of the fancy shoes she likes to wear, and just take care of her when she doesn't feel good, you know?"

"I agree."

"I didn't want to move to Seattle with my folks, and Aunt Cami didn't even blink when I asked her if she'd help me out sometimes, like if I needed a place to crash or a ride to school or something. She's always been a good friend to me. She's like a big sister." His voice cracks and he clears his throat with a chuckle. "It's stupid to get all emotional, but I love her, and I just wanted to make sure that you're not just dicking with her, you know?"

"I'm not just dicking with her. And it's not dumb to get emotional when you're talking about someone you love."

Steven nods. "Are you going to make her move away?"

"I don't think anyone makes Cami do anything," I reply with a laugh. "She's much too headstrong for that."

"You know what I mean. If you get married and stuff, and you want to move away, are you going to take her with you?"

I frown and shake my head. "Her business is here. I'm pretty sure that Portland is going to be our home for quite some time."

"Good."

"Do you have more questions, or can we get to work and finish this closet before she gets back tomorrow night?"

He laughs. "I'm done with the third degree. Oh, but don't

tell her anything about the Navy stuff. She won't take it well, and I want to be the one to tell her."

"I won't say anything."

"JESUS, THIS IS incredible," Riley says the next day as she wanders into the closet and turns a circle, her eyes wide in awe. "Seriously, guys, this is fantastic. I should marry you both, right now, just for this closet."

"I'm too young for you," Steven says, his face bright pink. "But yeah, she's gonna love it."

"And I'm taken," I reply happily. "So, we did good?"

"You did great. This is more than a closet, it's a dressing room! I love that you brought her vanity in here with her makeup. There is so much hanging space in here." She turns to examine the shelves. "And she'll have space for new shoes and bags too."

"Yeah, because she needs those," Steven says, rolling his eyes.

"If having too many shoes is wrong, I don't wanna be right," Riley says, then turns to me. "Okay, what can I do?"

"Help us fill it up. I don't know how she'd want her clothes and other things organized, but you will."

"I know exactly what to do." She marches out of the room and returns a few minutes later with her arms full of clothes. "We need to bring her dressers in here too."

"There's not enough wall space in here," I reply, but she shakes her head.

"We're going to put them in the middle of the room, back-to-back, and she can use the top for jewelry and her hair stuff. Trust me."

Steven and I eye each other dubiously, but we wrestle the matching six-drawer dressers into the room, set them back-to-back, and I grin. She's right. They're the perfect height for her to use them, and they leave plenty of space for her to walk around them.

"I'll be right back," Steven says, and runs out of the room as Riley passes me a stack of shoe boxes.

"You can start unboxing those and placing them on the shelves, and I'll come behind you and organize them based on color and style."

"This is really involved," I reply.

"You have no idea," Riley says, nodding. "But it'll be so worth it. It'll get you laid for days."

"Gross," Steven says as he comes back in the room carrying an ottoman from her office. "She doesn't use this, and it'll look great next to the dressers. She can use it to sit on to put shoes on and stuff."

"Brilliant!" Riley says, clapping her hands. "That chandelier is a great touch."

"I thought it made the space feel more feminine," I reply, happy that we've done a good job.

"This is Girl Central," Steven says. "I'm gonna have to go play football or something, just to get the girl germs off of me."

"What are you, nine?" I ask, and throw a sparkly shoe at him, hitting him in the shoulder when he dodges.

"No, I'm out of here," he says, and grins. "Have fun touching all the girl stuff, man, but this is above my pay grade." And with that, he escapes.

"Punk," I mutter, but can't help but smile. "She's going to be surprised."

"This might be the nicest thing anyone has ever done for her," Riley says, and pats my shoulder. "You did good. When will she be home?"

"In about two hours. Kat texted and said they were just leaving a few minutes ago. She's going to text again when they're about a half hour out so I can order a pizza."

"Swanky," Riley says with a wink. "And FYI, don't give her wine tonight. She's been drinking wine for two days."

"Yeah, I figured."

EVERYTHING IS READY for her when she walks through the doors. Sunflowers are set out, candles lit, pizza waiting on the coffee table. And Scoot, who thankfully wasn't interested in the construction process, thus staying out from under foot, is curled in a ball on the back of the couch.

She steps inside and immediately kicks off her shoes, sighs, and glances up, surprised to see me standing in her house.

"Hi," she says, and smiles. "I didn't expect to see you here."

"I haven't seen you in two days," I remind her, and step to her, taking her overnight bag from her, her purse, and helping her out of her coat. "There's nowhere else I'd rather be."

"Do I smell pizza?"

"Mm," I reply, and kiss her on the forehead, breathing her in. Damn, I've missed her. "Come eat."

"You're a prince," she says, and flops on the couch, scrubbing her hands over her face.

"You know you're always beautiful, but you look tired tonight."

"God, I'm exhausted."

I pass her a slice of pizza and she immediately takes a big bite and sighs in happiness. "So good."

I'm going to be inside her later when she makes that same exact sound.

Rather than grab a slice for myself, I pull her feet into my lap and get to work rubbing her arches, and making her purr while she munches happily on her dinner.

"I could seriously get used to this."

I smile. "Me too."

"I think I'm getting the better end of it."

"That's up for debate," I reply. "I get to touch you, talk to you. I think I'm in pretty good shape here."

"You say some really sweet things, you know." She watches me with tired green eyes.

"I don't say anything that I don't mean," I reply. I pass her another slice of pizza and switch to the other foot, paying it as much attention as I did the first. "How did it go?"

"It was great," she replies. "Cuppa Di Vita has a few new wines in their cellar, and we tasted them all." She frowns. "But for some reason it didn't sit well with me, so I tasted, then spit. I didn't swallow." She giggles, making me grin. "I always thought spitters were quitters, but . . ." She shrugs and giggles again.

"Are you coming down with something?"

"Maybe." Her hands are resting on her belly now as she watches me rub her feet. "You have great hands."

"They enjoy touching you."

She smiles softly. Her hair was once in a tight bun, but it's loosened and soft tendrils frame her sweet face. Her makeup is simple, like she usually wears it, and her lips are bare and kissable.

"How are you?" she asks.

Anxious to take you upstairs. "I'm great. It was pretty uneventful around here while you were gone."

"Uneventful is good." She yawns. "I should take my stuff upstairs and get some comfier clothes on."

"I'll go with you," I reply, and hold my hand out to help her up. She's so tired it seems that just lifting her feet up each of the stairs is a challenge. When we get to the bedroom, she crosses to where her dressers used to be, then comes up short.

"I've been burgled," she says. "By a burglar that has a thing for yoga pants and bras."

"I'm sure those exist," I reply with a chuckle, and take her hand again. "But I think I have another explanation."

"I hope so. I was really looking forward to those yoga pants. And why is there a door in that wall?"

"Come on, Sherlock, I'll show you." I lead her through the door and she simply stops and stares, her jaw dropped, trying to look everywhere at once.

"Oh my God."

I hang back and watch as she slowly steps inside and touches the edges of her hanging clothes, runs her hand over the top of a dresser, and sits at her vanity, as if she's never seen any of those things before.

"It's beautiful," she whispers. I walk up behind her and massage her shoulders, watching her face in the mirror.

She's not smiling. She's not clapping.

She's crying.

Fuck.

"I need you to talk to me, sweetheart," I murmur, kneading her tense muscles.

"I love it all so much," she says, and sniffs, completely confusing the hell out of me.

"But you don't like the color?"

"No, the color is perfect," she says, and reaches for a tissue.

"If you love it, why are you crying?" I squat next to her and take the tissue out of her hand, gently blotting at the tears on her cheeks.

"Because it's just so sweet," she says, her green eyes swimming. God, she's killing me here.

"I was hoping it would make you happy."

"I *am* happy."

I chuckle and reach for another tissue. "So these are happy tears?"

"Yeah." She sniffs again. "Landon, it's seriously great. Did you find my closet Pinterest page?"

"Honey, I don't know what a Pinterest is," I reply honestly. "I just built what I thought you'd like, and what I thought would be functional."

She turns in her chair and takes it all in again. "The light is pretty. How did you do all of this in two days?"

"Steven helped me," I reply, and feel completely helpless as she breaks down in tears again. "And Riley came to help me organize it."

"You all went to a lot of trouble."

This is happy?

"Hey." I pull her into my arms and rock her back and forth. "Stop with the waterworks, baby."

"I'm just tired," she says. "I've been really tired lately."

"Maybe you're coming down with something," I reply, rubbing circles on the middle of her back.

"I hope not. I have a lot of work to do." She pulls back and smiles through the tears now as she gazes at her rows and rows of fancy shoes. "I can finally see them all at the same time."

"Are you sure you like it?"

She throws her arms around my neck and hugs me tightly. "I couldn't love anything more."

My thoughts exactly.

"Thank you so much, Landon. This is better than anything I could have imagined."

"You're welcome." I kiss her forehead, then pull her to her feet. "Come on, I'm going to put you in a hot bath, and then bed."

"God, that sounds like heaven."

I smile as I help her sit on the bed, then march into the bathroom to run the water, making sure it's not too hot, then return to the bedroom, laughing when I see that she hasn't even flopped back on the bed, she's simply sleeping sitting up.

Her eyes blink open when I start to undress her.

"Do you think you can sit in the bath for a few minutes without drowning?"

"I can't guarantee anything," she says, her smile soft and a bit shy. "I'm sorry that I'm so sleepy."

"You're adorable." And if the truth be told, I don't mind taking care of her in the least. "But because you're exhausted, I'm going to get in with you so I can revive you if you go under."

"You're the cutest lifeguard I've ever seen," she says around a big yawn.

"Thanks," I reply, and lead us, both naked, into the bathroom, and into the steaming-hot water. She leans against me and sighs deeply.

"Mm, this is delightful."

"I missed you," I murmur against her ear, and watch as water glides over her skin, skimming her breasts. Her light brown nipples are puckered, begging for my fingers to graze over them gently.

"I missed you too." She kisses my arm. "Thank you for my closet."

"You're welcome, baby."

"I bet Riley was jealous."

"I believe she proposed to me at least three times this afternoon."

Cami laughs. "She can get her own man."

"That's what I told her."

She tips her face back, gazing up at me with sleepy eyes, but her lips are slanted up in a grin. "I love you."

And there it is. Every time she says those words, it's as if my world is kicked off its axis and I have to catch my breath.

I am one lucky son of a bitch.

I lean in and sweep my lips across hers. "I love you too, Cami."

Chapter 15

~Cami~

"Breakfast is our thing," I announce as we sit in my kitchen the next morning, sipping coffee and eating pancakes that Landon whipped up before I even left the bed this morning.

"We have a thing?" he asks, his brow raised.

"Yep, we do. And it's breakfast."

"Huh." He seems to think this over before flipping a pancake on the griddle that I'm pretty sure I didn't have yesterday. The man keeps adding to my kitchen appliance collection. "I thought our thing was hot sex."

"Okay, we have two things."

He smirks. "How are you feeling this morning?"

"Better. These pancakes were the perfect medicine." Before I can slip the forkful of sweet pancake into my mouth, Landon grips my wrist and steals the bite for himself.

"Stealing a woman's food isn't a smart thing to do, you know."

"You've never seemed to mind before," he says with an unconcerned shrug, and pours the last of the batter onto the griddle.

"Are you home?" We hear Steven call out before he shuts the front door.

"In the kitchen!" I yell back, and glance down at what I'm wearing, relieved that I pulled on pants before coming downstairs for breakfast.

"I'm just in time," Steven says with a smile, and sits next to me at the breakfast bar. "You never told me Landon could cook."

"I didn't think he could," I reply around a full mouth.

"That's polite," Steven says, but I just smile at him, then open my mouth wide so he can see my half-chewed food. "And classy."

"I'm a classy girl," I reply as Landon slips some pancakes on a plate for Steven. "What's up?"

"I came to find out if you liked your surprise."

My closet!

I jump off my stool and wrap my arms around my nephew, then gross him out by kissing his face. "I love it. Thank you, thank you, thank you."

"I should have called," Steven says, trying to push me away. "Help."

Landon, laughing, just shakes his head. "You're on your own."

"So much for men sticking together," Steven says, pushing my face away. "Seriously, I'm almost losing my appetite."

I take mercy on him and bounce back onto my own stool.

"I really love it, sweetie. Thank you so much for all of your hard work."

He shrugs one shoulder, his eyes trained on his food. His cheeks redden under the praise. "It wasn't a big deal."

"It was a big deal to me," I reply. "Also, you need a haircut."

"God, you're a nag," he says, and scowls at me, then Landon. "Does she nag you like this?"

"He doesn't need a haircut," I say before Landon can reply.

"You're worse than Mom," he informs me, but his lips twitch and I can tell that he doesn't really mind the tiny amount of parenting I dish out.

"No one is worse than your mom, but she loves you," I say, suddenly missing my older sister, and make a mental note to give her a call later.

"Have you talked to her?" he asks me, his eyes suddenly wary. He glances up to Landon, making me look at Landon too, but he's not watching us, he's stuffing pancake in his mouth and cleaning up the breakfast mess.

"Not recently, why?"

"Good." Steven lets out a gusty breath in relief. "Because I wanted to tell you myself."

"Tell me what?"

He's silent as he finishes his food. I'm convinced he's doing this to me on purpose. All I can think is that he's gotten his girlfriend pregnant, or they kicked him out and he's going to ask to move in here, or he's flunking out of school.

Please don't let the girlfriend, whom I've never met, mind you, be pregnant.

"Killing me here, Steve."

"Okay, but first you have to promise not to be mad."

"Was your mom mad when you told her?" I ask, still racking my brain.

"No," he says, and shakes his head.

"I can't promise, but I'll do my best." I glance over at Landon, who's now leaning back against the sink, his face impassive, completely calm.

Why do I get the feeling that I'm not going to be calm in about 3.2 seconds?

"I'm joining the Navy," Steven blurts out, still not meeting my gaze.

I blink at him, then narrow my eyes in confusion. "Excuse me?"

"You know, the Navy?"

"I'm familiar with it, yes, but for a second there I thought you said that you're *joining* it."

"I did," he says, and looks me in the eyes. "I already signed the paperwork. I ship off to basic in three weeks."

My mouth won't work. I'm pretty sure my lips have fallen off because I can't find them. Steven is *leaving*?

Finally, Steven rolls his eyes and says, "You're freaking out."

"No," I say, my voice breaking. "I'm not freaking out."

I'm totally freaking out.

"Look, I think it's a good idea. They'll put me through school—"

"You're going to school now," I interrupt.

"But they'll *pay* for it, Aunt Cami. I've been thinking about it for a long time, and when I talked to Landon about it the other day, he had lots of great things to say, and—"

He keeps talking, but my head has whipped around and I'm staring at my not-so-innocent boyfriend, who just holds my gaze with perfect calm.

"What did you do?" I demand, standing up and shoving my stool away.

"I answered some of his questions," Landon says, and crosses his arms over his chest.

I refuse to think about how great his arms look when he does that. Because right now he's not my hot boyfriend, he's the person who is encouraging the *only* family member I have to leave me.

"Aunt Cami, it's really a great thing."

"No." I spin and point my finger in Steven's chest. "It's not a great thing. It's dangerous, and it takes you far away from home, and in case you've missed it, world affairs are more than a little shaky right now, Steven. Are you telling me you want to run off to *war*?"

"He's not running off to war," Landon says, and I spin on him now.

"*You* are not helping! Why would you encourage this?"

"Why wouldn't I?" he asks, his voice rising with mine. His ice-blue eyes are flashing with annoyance. "What in the hell is wrong with the Navy, Cami? In case you've forgotten, it more than paid my bills and took care of me very nicely for a decade!"

"Yes, and it also took you far away from all of the people who gave a shit about you! You came home every other year to say hi, and then you were off again, until one day we got a phone call and you'd almost *died!*"

"I'm not going to be a pilot," Steven says, surprisingly calmly.

"You're not going to be *anything* in the goddamned Navy," I say, my voice hard. I'm panting. I can't catch my breath. "You're going to stay here and—"

"And what?" Landon demands, on a roll now. "Do what *you* tell him he can do? He may be young, but he's an adult, Cami. You can't make him do anything. You're not his mother. And even if you were, this is not an irresponsible decision."

"How the fuck do you know?" I ask, yelling now. "You were always *gone.*"

Landon visibly takes a deep breath, then walks around the island and toward the kitchen door.

"You're leaving?" I demand. "I piss you off, so you bail?"

He stops cold, then turns around, and before I can react, grabs my face in his hands and kisses me hard. Still holding me, he pulls back and says, "We're both too pissed off to resolve this right now. I need some space and you need to talk to your nephew and calm the fuck down."

With that, he kisses me once more then stomps out, slamming the front door behind him.

"Aunt Cami." Steven's voice is gentle, and to be honest, he sounds disappointed, and that just breaks my heart in two.

"Steven—"

"No, just take a breath and listen to me. This is a good thing, Cami. I need to get my feet under me."

"You're a kid. No one your age has their feet under them."

"I will *not* be a freeloader for the rest of my life," he says, and begins to pace the kitchen. "I'm living with a girl that I don't even particularly like because I don't have anywhere else to go."

"You can come here."

"And mooch off you? No. It's time for me to be on my own."

"Once you finish school and get a good job—"

"I'm flunking out," he says quietly. "I didn't want to tell you because I knew you'd be disappointed in me, but school isn't going well, Cami. Shit, I don't even know what I want to do, and the classes I'm taking are a waste of time. My whole life feels like a waste of time right now."

"You are *not* a waste of time."

"I love you too," he says, and makes my eyes fill. "I know that I owe you a lot."

"You don't owe me anything. Family helps family because we love each other."

"I know. But it's time for me to help myself too."

I take a long, deep breath and try to clear my head. All I can think is, he's going to leave and I'll hardly ever see him from now on, and that just breaks my heart.

"The Navy is a good place to start, Cami. I'll make decent money, have a place to live, see a bit of the world, and when I figure out what I want to be when I grow up"—a smile tickles his lips, making him look so much younger—"I'll have school paid for. I don't want to bus tables forever, I know that."

I chew my lip and stare at the boy whose diapers I used to change. I taught him how to drive. I took him to see movies his mom wouldn't let him see. He's been one of my closest friends his whole life, and now he wants to leave me and make a life of his own.

If this is what it feels like to be a parent, I might just pass on the whole fucking deal because it's nothing but heartache.

"When did you get smart and stuff?" I sniff loudly.

"I'm a smart guy," he says with a shrug. "And why are you all . . ." He waves his hands around like he can't find the words.

"Wonderful? Gorgeous? Your favorite person in the world?"

"Spazzy."

"*Spazzy?*"

"Yeah. I expected this from Mom, but I thought you'd be cooler about it."

"That's why you looked so nervous to tell me?"

"Okay, I thought you'd be calmer than you were. You don't usually act like that."

He's right. What the hell has been wrong with me lately?

I shrug, and Steven starts talking about where he'll be completing basic training, and how a friend of his is enlisting with him, and I nod, but his voice fades as I start thinking.

What *is* wrong with me? First, the wine upset my stomach in Seattle, making for two days of the icks. In fact, Landon's pancakes were the first thing to sit well on my stomach all week.

I'm exhausted too. Even though I just got out of bed an hour ago, I could already use a nap. Some of that might be emotional exhaustion, but it's very unusual for me.

"Aunt Cami?"

"What?" I shake my head, pulling myself out of my thoughts.

"I asked you a question."

"Sorry, can you ask again?"

He frowns. "You're seriously weird today."

"I guess I might be about to get a visit from Mother Nature," I reply with a shrug, and that makes him raise his hands in surrender and back toward the front door.

"And, I'm out. Girl talk like that is disgusting."

I laugh and shake my head as he leaves. That's most likely the solution. I do sometimes get sleepy around that time of the month, and Lord knows I can be bitchy.

That's got to be it.

I take our plates to the sink and rinse them, then stop cold. *Wait.*

"Oh God, no." I run out of the kitchen and up the stairs to the bedroom and fish around in the vanity drawer for my pills.

I finished the pack almost two weeks ago. But I never got my period. Which means I didn't refill them and start taking the new ones because I didn't get my period, which reminds me to get the motherfucking pills.

"I can't be pregnant," I say to Scoot, who has just wandered into the room behind me to see what in the world I'm doing. "I would have had to get pregnant while I was still taking the pills, and that's not possible."

I bite my thumbnail and pace my bedroom.

"Is it?"

Oh God.

"Okay, Cami, calm down. You're not a teenager for God sake. You're a grown woman in a loving relationship."

Don't tell Landon!

I shake my head. No way. What if it pisses him off? Scares him?

Wait.

He's also an adult.

"Go talk to Landon," I tell myself, and swiftly change my clothes, paying no attention in the least to whether or not what I'm wearing matches. I'm wearing a bra and pants, for fuck sake, that's all that matters.

This is a good plan. Landon will know what to do. Or maybe I should just call one of the girls because if it's a false alarm, there's no reason to freak Landon out.

But if the tables were turned and he went to a *friend* before he came to *me*, I'd be pissed.

So I should just go. Right now.

I slide my feet into flip-flops, not giving two shits that it's mid-March in Portland, grab my purse and keys, and drive the short distance to Landon's house.

I march up to the door and knock before I chicken out and run back home.

After what feels like hours, Landon opens the door.

"I think I fucked up."

His face softens and he shakes his head while opening the door wider so I can come inside. "No, babe. It's okay. We're going to fight now and then, and I know that you love Steven."

"What?" I look around, like he's talking to someone else, then realize that we've already had a doozy of a fight this morning. "Oh, that! No. I mean, yes, I shouldn't have said what I did to you, but that's not why I'm here."

"Are you wearing flip-flops?"

"Will you please focus?" I demand, and pace into his living room.

"What's going on?"

"I'm late."

"For what?" He frowns. "And if you're late, why are you here?"

"We are having a serious communication issue today," I mutter, and scrub my fingers over my forehead. "I'm *late*."

His jaw drops for a moment, but he recovers quickly, swallows, and says, "Okay, we need to go to the pharmacy."

"For what?"

He smiles gently, and I'm pretty sure he doesn't understand the gravity of the situation.

"We need to get a test, baby. I don't have any rabbits handy and I'm not psychic."

"Oh! Right." I nod. "Why are you so calm?"

He smiles and takes my hand, kissing my knuckles, and

leads me out to his car. "Because there's no need to be any-thing but calm."

Except, there could be. And then what?

"WE'VE BEEN STANDING in this aisle for ten minutes," I say as Landon reads the back of a purple box. He's read every single brand there is. "They're all pretty much the same, Landon."

"How many have you taken in the past?" he asks, not looking up from the box.

"None."

"Right, so you're an expert."

I roll my eyes. "I'm a woman."

"I've noticed."

Okay, now he's just being difficult.

Finally, he drops one of each brand into the basket and guides me to the check out.

"You're getting *all of them*?"

"Yes."

I keep my mouth shut as we make our way to the register.

"That's a lot of pregnancy tests," the older woman says with a laugh as she begins ringing them up and tossing them in bags. "You know, they're all basically the same."

"That's what I said!"

Landon just smiles and shakes his head at the lady. "We're fine."

"It's your money," she says with a shrug. "That'll be ninety-six sixteen."

Almost a hundred dollars for pregnancy tests!

That's ridiculous. I roll my eyes again, but Landon pays without a word. When we're in the car, he turns to me and drags his knuckles down my cheek, immediately calming me. "Would you feel more comfortable at my place or yours?"

"My car is at your house."

"That wasn't my question."

I chew my lip for a moment. "I'd rather go to mine. That's where we've spent most of our time together."

He smiles gently. "Your place it is, sweetheart."

He's quiet on the ride to my place, but he keeps my hand tightly in his, our fingers linked. His composure has calmed me and I'm finally able to take a deep breath.

"That's better," he murmurs, and kisses my hand. "Just breathe."

I nod and hold my breath for the length of a block before he laughs.

"You're not breathing."

"Oops."

He finally pulls into my driveway, grabs the two bags of tests, and once we're inside, I take them from him. "You can stay down here."

"I'm coming up."

"Okay, but you can't come in the bathroom with me."

He cocks a brow. "Why not."

"I'm not going to *pee* in front of you!"

He simply chuckles and gestures for me to lead the way upstairs.

When we get to the bathroom, I turn around and hug

him hard around the middle. "Before I go in, I just want you to know that I love you."

"Cami," he says, and kisses my head. "You're coming out alive, I promise."

"I know I'm being dramatic." I sigh and pull back. "But this is kind of freaking me out."

"I see that." He smiles reassuringly and kisses my forehead. "We got this, babe."

I nod, not reassured in the least. "Right. We totally got this."

I walk into the bathroom, close and lock the door, and turn to the mirror. I step out of my flip-flops and frown when I realize that my feet aren't just wet, they're muddy.

Because it's March in Portland, Einstein.

"You don't have to lock it!" Landon calls out. "I'm not going to burst in on you while you pee!"

"Go far enough away so you can't hear me pee either!"

I hear him mutter something about women, but I can't make anything else out when I turn the faucet on, just in case.

Peeing when you know someone is waiting for you is harder than it sounds.

I take a deep breath and lean on the counter, looking at myself in the mirror.

"This could be a mess," I whisper, "and I'm not just talking about the pee mess. I'm talking about everything, but you are a big girl. It's going to be okay."

Do I actually *want* to be pregnant? I really don't have to ponder that question. I don't. Well, I *do*, eventually, but not yet. Things with Landon are still relatively new, and I want to be selfish and just let it be the two of us for a while before we think about bringing little people into the mix. I want to plan a wedding, if he asks, and I want to maybe take a trip or two with him. Maybe he can show me Italy or Ireland or even Florida.

I've never been to Florida.

But when I think of the possibility of having kids, Landon is the only one that I want to have them with. He's the only man that I want to be the father of my children, and if it turns out that I am pregnant, well, I guess we'll deal with it.

It can be as easy or as difficult as we make it.

I stare at myself for an extra few seconds, and then shrug in resignation because I am so not convincing myself here.

I dump the contents of both bags onto the counter and stare at all of them in disbelief. How in the world am I supposed to pick one? One tells you if you're pregnant five days before the others. Or at least, that's what it claims. That should be good, right?

But another one actually has the words *pregnant* and *not pregnant*, instead of the blue lines, so an idiot can figure it out.

And I sure feel like an idiot right now, so I choose that one, open the box and pull the stick out, uncap it, and wrinkle my nose.

"What's taking so long?" Landon calls.

"You bought four hundred tests!" I shake my head and then I can't help it. I bust up laughing at the hilarity of it all.

"Why are you laughing?"

"Because this is ridiculous!"

"Did you pee?"

"No, and I won't if you keep yelling at me through the door." I shake my head. What in the hell ever happened to privacy?

Although, if this puppy is positive, I'm going to do a lot more in front of Landon than just pee. That'll be the least of my worries.

And why am I being such a damn sissy?

Because that's the only part of this that I have any control over, at this stage in the game anyway.

So, with a quick prayer, I unzip my jeans.

Chapter 16

~Landon~

$\mathcal{I}$ know for a fact that it doesn't take this much time to pee on a stick. Granted, I've personally never peed on a stick, but it can't be that hard.

I hate this door separating us. I should be in there with her.

I shove my hands through my hair and force myself to take a deep breath. I held it together for Cami. I can't lose my cool now.

Because at the heart of it, the thought of having a baby with Cami doesn't scare me in the least. It would have in the past; if any of the women I dated before had mentioned that she might be carrying my child, I would not have been okay with the idea.

What concerns me is *her.*

We've never talked about this stuff. We just haven't gotten

there yet. I thought we'd have plenty of time to discuss what our goals were regarding family and kids and marriage. Because I do plan to marry her.

Not marrying her isn't an option.

I just don't know what's happening in her head, and that's the part that makes *me* nervous. Maybe she doesn't want a baby at all. I just assume that she does, but what if kids aren't in her vision for her life? Or maybe this isn't the right time. She's just started her business, and it takes up a large chunk of her time.

What I do know is that she's scared, and that leaves a hole the size of Oregon in the pit of my stomach. I can't bear to see the fear on her beautiful face.

Fucking door.

I finally lean my forehead on the bathroom door and close my eyes, willing her to come out.

"Cami, did you fall in?"

I can hear rustling, but there's no answer. She's so damn stubborn.

"I can hear you moving around in there. Just tell me that you're okay."

Or I'll bust this fucking door in.

Just when I'm about to reach for the handle, the door opens, sending me off balance, and Cami startles.

"Have you been standing there this whole time with your ear pressed to the door like Mrs. Kravitz?"

"Who's Mrs. Kravitz?" She's still pale. Her eyes are round and a little glassy.

"You know, the crazy neighbor on *Bewitched*."

I grin and shake my head. "No, I wasn't listening the whole time. But you do realize that I've seen people pee before."

"Not me," she mutters, and looks to the floor. "It says it takes three minutes to process."

"Which one?"

"All of them," she says with a laugh. I take her hand and pull her into her bedroom, then into my arms, and simply rock us gently back and forth.

"Cami," I whisper, and kiss the top of her head, breathing in the fruity scent of her shampoo. My hands glide up and down her back, soothing us both. "You don't need to worry. Everything will be fine. *We* will be fine."

"How do you know?" she whispers.

"Because I do. Regardless of the results of that test, we are going to be just fine."

She takes a deep breath, then tips her head back and looks up into my eyes. Her gaze travels over my face as her hands cling to my back.

"I think it's been three minutes."

"Where is the test?"

"On the bathroom sink."

I kiss her forehead. "Do you want me to get it?"

"We should look together."

"Okay."

"But wait." She stops us when I move to walk to the bathroom. "I just want to say thank you. For today. Thank you for being the kind of man that I can go to when I'm scared, and for not making me feel like I had to keep it from you because I was scared that you might be mad."

"We're a team, Cami. I will never be mad at you for the way you feel. And if you'd hid this from me, well, you wouldn't be the woman that I've come to love so much it takes my breath away."

Her eyes fill, and she bites her lip. "Love you."

"I love you too." I hug her tightly once more, then take her hand and we walk into the bathroom together, then stare in awe when we see the word *pregnant* staring back at us from the white stick on the vanity.

"Well, I guess it's positive," she finally says, then glances up at me and blinks. I'm grinning down at her, suddenly relieved and so fucking happy. I didn't realize until this moment that this was the result that I'd been hoping for.

"You're sure you're not mad?" she asks.

"Do I look mad?"

She studies me for a minute, and then smiles softly. "No, you have a goofy smile all over your face."

"How could I be upset about this, Cam? The woman I love more than anything is going to have my *baby*. We made something amazing." Suddenly I lift her in my arms and spin us in a circle, making her laugh, and kiss her hard on the mouth. "We're having a *baby*!"

"Maybe I should take another test, just to be sure."

"Take all of them, I don't care," I reply, and hold her close. "Are you okay with this?"

"I don't have a choice."

I shake my head and guide us downstairs and sit on the couch facing her. "That's not the answer to my question. We've never talked about this stuff. Do you even *want* kids?"

She frowns when Scoot jumps into her lap and curls into a ball, not even batting an eye when she starts to rub his belly. "I do want kids," she says slowly. "I just always thought they would come later." She bites her lip and glances up at me, then continues when I nod. "I was so relieved when Brian and I didn't ever get pregnant, or even have a scare."

The thought of her having a baby with anyone else makes my blood boil, but I sit silently and listen.

"And that was just one more thing that I felt bad about. Brian wanted kids, and I refused to go off the pill because I knew, deep down, that our marriage wasn't going to last, and I didn't want to have a baby with him. It would have just complicated things.

"So thinking about kids has never been an exciting thought for me." She stops and swallows, still petting Scoot, who's purring happily. "I have some mixed emotions."

"I think that's perfectly natural when it comes as a surprise," I say quietly, and rub her thigh gently. "But I have to ask you if you are tempted to . . . *not* have the baby."

"Like, abort it?" she asks with a scowl.

"Yes." I'm holding my breath.

"No, I don't want to do that."

And, I can breathe again.

"I'm nervous and surprised, and I might need a day or two to wrap my head around it all, but I don't want to get rid of it." She takes my hand and kisses my palm, then snuggles her cheek into it. "It's you, Landon."

I grin and pull her in for a soft kiss.

"It's us."

"Hey, Mia, I need you to do me a favor," I say as I drive to my parents' house the next afternoon.

"I'm working," she says, then pulls the phone away from her mouth so she can yell at someone who didn't toss the Caesar salad enough. "I'm working with idiots."

"You hired them," I remind her.

"And what does that say about me?" She sighs. "What do you need?"

"I need you to set up a table in the new space and get it all pretty."

"Pretty?"

"Yeah, you know, candles, flowers, stuff like that."

"Do you need food for this romantic getaway you're taking yourself on?" Her voice is dry, making me smile.

"It's for Cami."

"What's the occasion?"

"Can you just do it for me?"

"When do you need it done?"

"In an hour."

"An hour?" she shrieks. "I'm running a kitchen here, Landon."

"I knew you'd do it for me. Thanks!" I hang up on her, still grinning, and pull up to my folks' house. I've never knocked on the door before going in, even after I'd grown up and left. I'm not about to start now.

I walk through the door and am immediately enveloped

in home. Mama's cooking something for dinner. The furniture hasn't changed much since I was a kid. The only difference being a new TV for Dad to watch football on.

And then it hits me: this is my childhood home, but it's not *home*. Cami is my home.

"Mama?" I call out, and make my way to the kitchen.

"Landon!" She comes around the corner, wiping her hands on her apron, and gives me a hug and a kiss on the cheek. "This is a surprise. I don't see you enough. Are you hungry?"

I laugh and shake my head. "No, and I can't stay too long. I need a favor."

"Oh?" She picks up a spoon and stirs the pot of red sauce on the stove. "What can I do?"

I lean against the counter and watch her for a moment. She's my mother, and that's how I've always looked at her, but now I wonder if my father looks at her the way I do Cami. Does she take his breath away? Her hair has some gray in it now, and her hands are more frail than they used to be, but she's the same woman that I remember from my childhood, holding me when I was sick and loving me when it felt like I didn't deserve it. She's an amazing woman.

"I'm going to propose to Cami."

Her eyes fly to mine and immediately fill. "Oh, my sweet boy."

"It's time," I say, purposely not telling her about the baby. I want to tell her and Dad when Cami and I are together. "I was hoping I could have Nonna's ring for her."

She pats my cheeks as the tears start to roll down her

own. "Of course you can. She promised it to you, after all. You stay here and I'll get it."

She rushes from the room to her bedroom and is back quickly, carrying a small black box.

"Your nonna wore this ring for sixty-four years," she says as she passes it to me. I lift the lid and stare down at the vintage diamond-and-sapphire ring. "But even more special than that, your nonna knew."

"Knew what?"

"That it would be Cami who would wear it one day."

I frown. "What do you mean?"

"She said to me one day, 'Cami is for our Landon. She will make him a good wife one day.'"

"How did she know?"

"We all have eyes, don't we?" Mama asks with a smile. "You've always looked at her differently than anyone else. She is for you."

"Yes." I swallow and close the box. "She's the only one for me."

I MANAGE TO sneak into the new construction side of the restaurant without Cami knowing and sigh in relief. Mia is putting the finishing touches on some sunflowers on a small table, adorned with a red tablecloth and flickering candles.

"So what's the big secret?" she asks when she sees me. "You're acting weird. Cami's acting weird. Based on the flowers and candles, I'm led to believe you fucked up big-time and are about to beg for forgiveness."

I smirk. "No, we aren't fighting. I guess Cami didn't say

anything to you yet, but you're my sister, and I have to tell someone, but I need you to keep this on the down low."

Her brows climb into her hairline. "Okay."

"I'm going to ask her to marry me."

"Holy shit!"

"And we're going to have a baby."

Her mouth drops, and then, to my utter shock, she starts to laugh. "You always surprise me," she says when she can breathe again. "Life is never dull with you around, Landon."

"True." I smile and tap the box in my pocket, suddenly nervous. "I hope Cami's okay with the thought of that for the rest of her life."

"You already know the answer to that," she says with a smile, and gives me a hug before heading back to the kitchen. "Break a leg!"

I'm hoping I don't get a broken heart.

I take a minute to look around the new space. The booths are already in and ready to go. All that's left is some trim work and decorations and it'll be ready.

Who would have thought three months ago when this project started that this is where I'd be?

Definitely not me.

"Oh my God."

I spin around at the sound of Cami's voice. She's in a sexy black skirt with a blue blouse tucked into it and she's in her sexy heels. Her hair is up and her face is beautifully surprised.

"Hi."

Her eyes find mine.

"Hi. Mia said you needed to see me over here."

"She was right," I reply, and cross to her. "How do you feel?"

"Curious." She pokes her head around me so she can see the table again. "Are we having lunch over here?"

"That wasn't really my plan," I reply, and lead her to a chair at the table. She sits, and stares at me when I sit next to her, keeping her hand clutched in mine. "It's funny how you can know someone for so long, and then one day you realize that you never really knew them at all. Our friendship has always been important to me, Cami, but it's only been in the past few months that I've truly grown to know *you*. Inside and out. What makes you tick. What makes you laugh and what scares you and that you're bad at buying things for your kitchen."

She laughs and tilts her head, listening intently.

"Loving you has always come as easy as breathing for me, and falling in love with you is no different. I admire you. Your strength of character. Your humor. Your intelligence. You are impressive and not a little scary, Cami.

"I didn't think I believed in soul mates," I continue, the words flowing effortlessly out of me now. "It's always sounded like a romantic notion for movies and books, but I've realized that a soul mate isn't someone who just slips into your life and one day you realize, *Oh, there you are.* It's the person that you measure time against."

I swallow and she leans closer to me.

"All I know is, there was my life before knowing that you're my world, and this is my life after, and everything before just seems so . . . *small*. You have shaken up my life. You make it brighter, and we're about to be in for the adventure of our lives, and I can't wait for it. I want to start this chapter with you as my wife."

I slide down to one knee and pull the box out of my pocket, open it, and look up into the most beautiful green eyes I've ever seen.

"Please marry me, Camille."

She's staring down at the ring, then closes her eyes and impatiently wipes tears off her cheeks.

"You don't have to do this just because I'm pregnant, Landon. We can—"

"That's not what this is," I say immediately, and set the ring on the table so I can cup her face in my hands and look her in the eye. "The baby may have sped it up a bit, but, Cami, I've been thinking about proposing for a while. I just thought I'd have more time to make it more romantic than this."

"This is pretty romantic," she murmurs, more tears spilling from her eyes. "Are you sure?"

"Sweetheart, I've never been more sure of anything in my life. I want you. I *need* you." God, I've never felt more vulnerable in my life. She's holding my heart in her hands.

She bites her lip and then she nods and smiles brightly.

"Is that a yes?"

"It's a yes."

I sigh in relief, then kiss her, softly at first, but I can't hold back. I deepen the kiss, exploring her mouth, nibbling her lips. My hands are brushing up and down her sides, and then I just pull her into my arms and hold her against me.

Finally, I pull away and show her the ring.

"This was my mother's mother's ring," I begin. "If you don't like it, we can find you something new."

"It's beautiful."

"Cami, you've been a part of my family for so long, it just seems right that you wear her ring. And I know that she'd be proud for you to wear it."

"Landon, it's beautiful. I loved your nonna," she says, and stares down at the ring. "I remember admiring this ring when I was a kid and I would come over to your house for Sunday dinners. She was always so kind to me."

I slip it out of the box and onto her finger.

"It's so pretty," she says quietly, staring down at the ring. "Can we tell the girls right away?"

"I already told Mia I was going to ask you. She helped me set this up."

She nods and grins widely. "She's going to be my sister."

"She's been your sister for a long time, sweetheart."

She starts to cry again. "My hormones are all over the place. It makes my eyes leak." She looks up at me. "Are you crying too?"

"No," I lie, and wipe my eyes. "I must have gotten something in my eye."

"Starting this whole thing with lies," she says, and stands. "I see how it's going to be."

She's joking, but I yank her against me and press my lips to hers. "You take my breath away. And I'm so happy you said yes."

"I'm happy you asked."

Chapter 17

~Cami~

*D*id that seriously just happen?

I glance down at my left hand, and yep, it sure did. Landon proposed. I'm wearing the ring I'd admired on his nonna for years. The ring is classic, vintage, and because of the sentimental value it holds, it's absolutely perfect.

But the words that came along with it?

Holy. Crap.

"Let's go tell the others," he says, and takes my hand in his, then leads me into the restaurant and back to the bar, where Mia, Kat, Addie, and Riley are all sitting. They break into applause as we walk in. Kat is already pouring drinks.

"We're getting married!" I announce.

"And having a baby," Riley says, and throws her arms around me.

"So much for keeping it on the down low," Landon mutters beside me.

"Yeah, like I'm going to keep information like that to myself," Mia says, rolling her eyes. "Did you say yes?"

"Of course she said yes. I'm a catch," Landon says. We all gather around the bar as Kat passes out the drinks, passing nonalcoholic ones to Addie and me, then she raises her glass in a toast.

"To Cami and Landon. May you have many years of great sex together."

"I'll drink to that," I say with a laugh, and sip my drink, the bubbles from the cider matching my mood. I feel light and happy. I can't stop smiling.

I glance up at Landon and see that he's already watching me, a grin also spread over his lips.

Love you, he mouths. I tug him down so I can kiss his cheek and whisper the sentiment in his ear.

"We get to start planning a wedding," Addie says. "We should go dress-shopping right away."

"Why? I'm going to be huge," I reply with a frown, and then pout. "I don't want to be one of those pregnant brides the size of a house in a huge white dress." Jesus, just the thought of it is depressing.

"You don't have to be," Mia says. "You could get married before you start to show."

"That's fast," I reply, but the idea doesn't sound bad at all.

"You should just go to the courthouse in a couple of weeks," Riley says. "Then you can still wear any dress you want."

"A couple of weeks?!" I ask, as if she's lost her mind. "We can't pull a wedding off in a couple of weeks, even if it is at the courthouse."

"Why not?" Kat adds. "We have a reception hall right here with the best chef in the city. We buy some flowers and a cake, and there you have it."

"You've never wanted a big, fancy wedding," Riley says, nodding. "Your sister and her family can easily come down from Seattle for it, and we'll all be there."

I'm looking around the room, trying to take it all in. Finally, I glance up at Landon.

"What do you think? Is it too fast?"

"I think it's a great idea," he says. "If I had my way, I'd fly us down to Vegas tonight."

"No. No eloping. Mom and Dad would never forgive you," Mia says.

"Sounds like it's the courthouse in a couple of weeks, then," Landon says with a grin. "Unless it's too fast for you?"

"It's a lot to take in," I reply, and glance around the room at my best friends. They're smiling and Landon's hand on the small of my back is reassuring. Wow, this is overwhelming.

But, it's what I've always wanted.

"Okay," I say, and shrug. "Let's do it!"

"Right on!" Kat says, clinking her glass to mine.

"I know I'm a selfish bitch," Addie says, and laughs, "but I'm a little happy you're doing this before I'm the size of a house too."

"Oh my God, our babies are going to grow up together!" I wrap my arms around her and hug her tight. "And we get to go baby-shopping and stuff too!"

"I know, I'm so happy," she says, sniffling. "And I'm warning you, everything makes me cry. Everything. I heard a Britney Spears song in the car this morning and had to pull over because I couldn't see the road anymore."

"I'm already a little weepy," I say with a nod.

"Oh, goodie," Mia says, rolling her eyes. "We're going to have two emotional pregnant women on our hands for the next nine months."

"But then we get two babies to snuggle," Riley says with a smile. "And I didn't have to give birth to them."

"Me neither," Kat says, fist-bumping Riley. "I'm not having kids. Y'all can just keep shooting them out for me and I'll spoil them like crazy. Aunt Kat is going to be their favorite."

"One at a time," I say firmly.

"Unless there's two," Landon says thoughtfully.

"What?" My gaze whips up to his. "You don't have twins in your family."

"On my dad's side," Mia says with a nod. "There are a few sets. So good luck."

"You're mean," I reply, looking back and forth between the two. "And if there's even a tiny possibility of that, we definitely need to do this before I really do look like a house."

"It's okay, baby, you'll be a beautiful house."

THE FIVE OF us all took the day off from the restaurant just a few days later to go shopping. That's unprecedented. We've only ever left it unattended once or twice before, and that was for Addie's dress shopping and her wedding.

It's a nice tradition.

We walk into a boutique wedding-dress store in downtown Portland, just down the block from the mall, and I am immediately overwhelmed. The girls all split off, oohing and aahing over frilly dresses in every corner of the store, calling out suggestions for which ones I should try on.

And I'm just . . . paralyzed. There's so much to take in. There are mannequins in white dresses with veils and flowers. There's a display table with a guest book and a basket full of pink rose petals.

Chandeliers dripping with crystals float overhead, casting the space in soft light, and there are deep, soft couches placed strategically before trifold mirrors with a pedestal where the bride can show off the gown she's chosen to try on.

Holy fucking shit! I'm getting married.

"You must be Cami," a middle-aged blond woman says with a smile as she approaches me and shakes my hand. "I'm Lori, your consultant. We spoke on the phone."

"It's nice to meet you," I reply, surprised that my lips even work.

"Are these your bridesmaids?"

"No," I reply, still feeling a bit guilty about this. "My fiancé and I decided to just have one person stand up with us, and I could never choose between these four, so I'm having my sister as my matron of honor."

"It's perfect," Addie says, pulling dresses out to study them. "You need to stop feeling guilty. None of us are mad at you."

"If I say I'm mad at you, can I pick out the dress?" Kat asks with a laugh. "Just kidding; I'm totally not mad."

"You look a little intimidated," Lori says with a sympathetic pat on the shoulder.

"This is all happening a little fast," I say with a smile.

"How long have you been engaged?"

"Two days."

She raises a brow. "And when is the wedding?"

"In eleven days."

Now her jaw drops. "Afraid he'll change his mind?"

"No." I laugh now, starting to loosen up a bit. "It's a long story."

"Okay, well, the important thing is that you're here now. You gave me a description of what you think you'd like over the phone."

"She wants to try on a few different things," Addie informs Lori from across the room.

"They're making me," I correct her, rolling my eyes.

"Trying on a few things is a good idea," Lori assures me. "Wedding gowns are very different from other dresses. Plus, this is the fun part."

"I found one," Kat announces.

"I'm not wearing black," I reply, rolling my eyes.

"Don't judge," Kat says, scowling. "It's pretty."

"Help," I whisper to Lori, who just laughs.

"This is just like *Say Yes to the Dress*," Riley says. "I love that show."

"Do you have a Randy?" Addie asks hopefully.

"Unfortunately no," Lori says, laughing at the mention of the man in the TV show, "but we will make up for that with some champagne."

"I really like it here," Kat says with a satisfied smile.

"I hope you have cider for Cami and me," Addie says.

"Certainly," Lori replies.

After drinks are poured, Lori leads me back to a dressing room, carrying three dresses that the girls chose. I immediately shake my head when she holds up one that Kat pulled off the rack.

"No. I'm not a frilly person." I stare at the fluffy dress, then sigh. "But because it's Kat, I'll try it on for her."

"That's the spirit." Lori helps me step into the dress, zips me up, and when I turn to the mirror, I have to admit, it's not bad.

"Let's go show them."

I walk barefoot into the showroom and climb onto the pedestal, facing the girls.

"It's pretty," Mia says, her head tilted.

"It makes your ass look fantastic," Riley adds.

"I think it's awesome," Kat says with a wide smile. "And it's totally *not* your style."

"No, it's your style," Addie tells her with a grin. "So now we know what to go for when it's your turn."

"Marriage is in the same category as babies for me," she says, shaking her red head. "So I'll just admire it from here. Thank you for putting it on."

I swish in a circle, enjoying the way the fabric feels against my legs. "It's actually a fun dress. It would feel good to dance in."

With that, I go back to the dressing room and change into a mermaid-style dress that Addie chose. I want something more demure, appropriate for a courthouse wedding, but I have to say, the bling on the bodice of this dress is awesome.

"This is perfect for your figure," Addie says when I return to the pedestal. "It hugs your body perfectly."

"And the sweetheart neckline makes your boobs look bigger," Riley says.

"But it's too much dress for my small wedding," I reply with a sigh. "I like it, but it just isn't *the one*."

"I think I saw one," Mia says, jumping up off her couch and handing her drink to Kat, who immediately takes a sip of it because she's already finished her own.

"Girls, I wish you could drink so you could taste how bad this stuff is."

"Yet you're inhaling it," Riley says. Kat simply shrugs as Mia returns with a dress covered in lace.

"Oh, good, she can be a doily," Addie says, rolling her eyes.

"Actually, I think you'll be surprised when she puts it on," Lori replies with a smile. "That's a nice choice."

"Okay, let's do it."

Once I'm changed, I return to the girls, and rather than face them, I face the mirrors, my eyes pinned to myself.

"Wow." Now, this dress is exactly what I had in mind. It hugs my curves in all the right places, the hem hitting the toe of my shoes. The sweetheart neckline still shows off my boobs, and the simple lace cap sleeve give it a soft touch.

It's not puffy or too much.

"What do you think?" Addie asks. I can hear sniffling behind me, so it must look great from the rear as well.

I turn to look at my girls, who all have soft smiles on their pretty faces. "I really like this one."

"It's great," Riley says, wiping her eyes.

"You look so happy," Mia adds, also wiping tears. "And I just realized that you're going to be my sister by marriage."

"I know," I reply, not even bothering to stop the tears rolling down my cheeks. Addie is in full-on pregnancy sob mode, and Kat is the only one simply sporting a wide, happy smile.

"It's perfect," Kat says. "It's you."

"Let's add this," Lori says, clipping a veil in my hair and turning me back to the mirror.

Holy crap, I'm getting married.

"Cami," Riley says, standing dramatically. "Are you saying yes to this dress?"

I laugh, wipe a tear from my cheek, and say, "Yes!"

"We are so good at this," Addie says before blowing her nose in a tissue. "Like, really good at it."

"What, being friends, or finding wedding dresses?"

"Both."

"THEY MADE ME try on some of the most hideous dresses," I tell Landon that night as we lounge on my couch. His head is in my lap and I'm combing my fingers through his soft, dark hair. His eyes are closed. "Even after I found *my* dress, they made me try on others that were just ridiculous. I'm sure the saleslady was happy to see the back of us."

"I'm just happy you found something you like," he says, then sighs in happiness when I use my nails to scratch his scalp, grip his hair in my fist, and give a little pull. "That feels good."

"Mm," I reply. "Then we had lunch, and I was tired after that, but the others insisted that they needed pretty new dresses for the big day too, so we spent a few hours in the mall."

"Did they find something?"

"Yes, they all found some great stuff. At one point, Kat tried on this jumpsuit and walked out the dressing room and was all like, 'I'm gonna go like this.' and Addie said, 'Oh, no, you are *not* going to fuck up the pictures wearing that.'"

I chuckle at the memory.

"Sounds like you had fun."

"We did."

"Good." He turns on his side, facing my belly. "Don't worry, buddy, Mommy and her friends might be a little crazy, but I have your back."

Mommy. My breath catches at his words. Oh my God, I'm going to be someone's *mommy.*

If that isn't enough to strike terror in my heart, I don't know what is.

Suddenly Landon pushes his hand under my T-shirt and drags his fingertips up my rib cage, making me catch my breath for a whole different reason.

Jesus, all he has to do is barely touch me and I'm on fire. He leans in and kisses my bare stomach, pushing my shirt up, gesturing for me to lift it over my head and toss it aside.

"Your skin is so soft," he says quietly, his lips traveling

over my ribs and up to my bare nipples. "I love that you weren't wearing a bra."

"I took it off when I changed clothes when I got home," I reply, and tip my head back against the couch, when he tweaks one nipple with his fingers and the other with his tongue. "It came in handy."

"Very," he replies. His hand dips under the waistband of my yoga pants, but before he can make me too crazy, I move, urging him to sit up, and I straddle his lap, grinding my still-covered core over him. "Fuck, I never stop wanting you." His voice is raw and his breath is coming in short pants. He drags his nails up my back and buries his fingers in my hair, fisting them and pulling.

"Oh, yeah," I moan.

"You like that?"

"You know I do." He lets go and I look down at him to find him grinning wickedly.

I love it when he looks at me like that. Very good things happen when he's in this mood.

Wicked things.

Naughty things.

I can't wait.

"I want to suck on you," I murmur against his lips. Suddenly he palms my ass, flexing his fingers hard, and lifts me. I wrap my legs around his waist and hold on as he walks to the stairs.

"I have a better idea," he replies, then kisses me as he climbs the stairs and gets us both settled, naked, on the bed.

"We're never going to have sex on the couch." I pout, then laugh when he bites the ball of my shoulder.

"Eventually," he says. His tongue glides over my collarbone, and then he places a wet kiss at the hollow of my throat. "But for right now I want to make love to my fiancée in our bed."

"I support that wholeheartedly." I gasp when his hand glides down my stomach and his fingers find their way to my pussy. "You're really great with your hands."

"Just my hands?"

"So far."

"Hmm." He licks my neck, tugs my ear between his teeth, then proceeds to kiss me madly. His hand is playing me like an instrument, and I'm making sounds I didn't know I was capable of. My hips are moving, rocking against him, and just when I'm about to fall over the ledge, he stops. "Not yet."

"I'm so close," I say, reaching for him. He captures my hands in one of his and pins them over my head.

"I'm in control here," he says, his voice hard, but his eyes are happy and bright with lust. His gaze slowly slides from my face, down my torso to my wet pussy, and back up again. "You're stunning."

"You're sexy as fuck and I want you."

"God, I love it when you talk like that." He lowers his pelvis to rest against mine. His cock is hard and heavy, resting against my wetness, and he begins to move in small pulses, rubbing the head against my clit. "How does that feel?"

"Shit, Landon."

"Tell me."

"I don't know how," I reply honestly. I can't form words, and if he stops now, I'll die. I bite my lip and gasp as my world splinters, sending me into an intense orgasm, and just when it's almost over, he rears back and pushes inside me, burying himself to the hilt, and the orgasm starts all over again.

"Landon!"

"Yes, baby," he growls. "Look at me."

I open my eyes. I'm blind at first, but then there he is, above me, watching me with those ice-blue eyes, so full of love and lust and admiration. He releases my hands and lifts my left leg, hitching it over his shoulder, and opening me up so wide, plunging so deep, I can hardly stand it.

"You are so fucking sweet," he whispers roughly, and begins to pound me in earnest, our hips rocking and meeting in a rhythm as old as time. I can't take my eyes off of him now. His muscles are flexed, sweat has beaded on his brow and neck, and he's the most incredible thing I've ever seen.

Just when I think it can't get any better, he slips his hand between us and circles my clit with his thumb, and suddenly my muscles flex, squeezing him, and I come undone, shaking, trembling, unable to control myself.

He cries out as he comes, pushing into me once, then again, and holding himself there as he empties himself into me.

When he covers me, bracing himself on his elbows, we're both out of breath. I can barely move.

"Love you so much," he whispers, his hands in my hair. I find the strength to drag my hands up his back and down his arms, and then circle back around to his ass, where I give him a little squeeze.

"I love you too."

Chapter 18

~Landon~

$\mathcal{J}$'m in heaven. There is a cat, curled up and purring, next to my hip and a beautiful woman draped around me, her head on my chest and arm around my waist. We're snuggled up under the covers early in the morning one week later.

"I don't want you to go," Cami says softly. She hugs me tighter, clinging to me, and buries her sweet face in my neck.

"I'll only be gone for a couple of days, baby."

She nods, but I know she's not convinced. This will be my second trip down to San Diego for meetings about the new flight school.

My traveling makes her nervous. I don't know how to reassure her that it's not permanent. That traveling full-time no longer interests me.

I guess only time will truly prove it to her.

I move to get out of bed, but she coils tighter, throwing

her leg over mine now, and holds on tight. "Three more minutes."

I chuckle and kiss her head. "I don't want to miss my flight."

She tips her head back so she can look up at me and pouts. "Stay."

"Turn your dimple off, sweetheart," I say with a laugh, and trace the spot in her cheek. "You know I can't resist it."

"That's my evil plan," she says, and drags her hand down my stomach to my cock. "Don't you have a little time?"

"Once we get started, it's never for a little time," I reply, and take her hand in mine, then kiss her fingers. "I do need to jump in the shower."

"Okay." She kisses me softly and burrows down in the covers when I roll away. Scoot meows moodily, not happy to be moved, then snuggles in next to Cami and falls back to sleep.

I walk into the bathroom and shave quickly before starting the shower and stepping into the hot, steamy water. Just when I finish rinsing the soap from my hair, I feel cool air rush around me and hear the door of the shower close, and then a soft, warm body wraps her arms around me from behind.

"Hi," Cami says softly before placing a kiss on my shoulder.

"Hi yourself." Her hands glide down my stomach, then she clutches my cock firmly in her small hand and begins to jack me off slowly. "Oh God, that's a thing."

"This is a thing?" There's a satisfied smile in her voice.

"Oh, yeah." I swallow hard and take her hand in mine, pour shampoo in her palm, and guide her back to me, making me slick so she glides easily. "You can go harder."

"I don't want to hurt you."

"You can't hurt me," I say, barely able to talk now. Her grip tightens and she presses herself to me, her other hand joining in the fun, and my knees want to buckle.

"This is fun." Her voice is happy. "But I need more soap. I'm not sliding as easy now."

Rather than give in to her request, I spin around and boost her up against the wall. She immediately wraps her legs around my waist, and I slide home. My forehead is against hers. I kiss her hard before fisting my hand in her hair and pulling her head back so I can bite and suck on her neck. I'm fucking her, as hard as I can, against the cold tile of the shower, but it doesn't seem to bother her. She's digging her nails into my shoulders and the noises coming out of her sexy mouth drive me on, fucking her harder and harder until my balls tighten and lift and I come harder than I can remember ever doing before.

As I come down to earth, she's squeezing me, her muscles spasming from her own orgasm.

"That was fun," she breathes. "I should join you in the shower more often."

"You have an open invitation, sweetheart."

I lower her to her feet, make sure she's steady, then quickly clean up and leave her in the shower so I can hurry up and get out of here.

"Did I make you late?" she asks.

"No, I'll make the flight."

"I'll drive you to the airport."

Leaving her is hard enough. I hate it. But watching her drive away at the airport would be pure torture.

"I'd rather you didn't drive to the airport during rush hour," I reply, and smile when she steps out of the shower, looking all damp and flushed, and well fucked. "And this way, my car will be waiting for me when I get home."

"Okay." She puckers up and turns her lips up to me. "Kiss me before you go."

"Happily." I grip her shoulders and lift her to her tiptoes so I can kiss her senseless. "How was that?"

"That was good." Her eyes are glassy. "Really good."

"I'll give you plenty more of those when I get home. Be good."

"*You* be good."

I grin. "I'm always good, baby."

I'VE BEEN IN San Diego for twenty-four hours and I already miss Cami so much it hurts. Jesus, I've become a heartsick moron.

And you know what? I don't give a fuck.

After a long, intense meeting this morning, I'm ready for a break and a call home. I dial Cami's cell and frown when she doesn't answer.

That's not like her.

I try her home line and she answers on the fourth ring, sounding sleepy.

"Did I wake you up?" I glance at my phone, frowning when I see that it's one in the afternoon.

"Yeah, I was taking a nap."

"I'm sorry, babe. I was just calling to hear your voice."

"How's it going down there?"

"Not bad. There's a lot of information to absorb, and the meetings are long, but it's great to be around these guys again. It feels really good."

"That's good."

She's saying the right words, but her voice is flat and she sounds . . . *wrong.*

"Are you okay?"

"I'm sorry." She sighs. "I'm actually not feeling great today. I'm nauseous and a little crampy, which my doctor assures me is normal for this stage, and I must have slept on my shoulder weird because it's killing me. That's when I slept, because I don't sleep well without you."

"I know. I'm so sorry that you're not feeling well, sweetheart. I hate that I'm not there to take care of you."

"Well, you're not. And I don't mean that as snarky as it sounds. I'm just bitchy."

"I get bitchy when I don't feel good too; trust me."

"Oh, I'm sure I'll find that out firsthand eventually," she says, sounding a bit like herself. "I'll wear a sexy nurse outfit to help you feel better."

"That sounds like a great deal to me."

Ringo sticks his head out of the conference room door, indicating they're ready to get back to work.

"Baby, I have to go. I'm sorry. I'll be home as soon as I can."

"I know." She yawns. "Love you."

I hang up, feeling guilty as fuck for not being at home with her. I don't like that she's having cramps. Even if her doctor says it's normal, it doesn't sound good at all. I send Mia a quick text and ask her to look in on Cami for me, then turn my ringer off and return to the meeting.

"Everything okay?" Ringo asks.

"I think so," I reply, and sit across from him. "How much more do we have to discuss?"

"We should be able to wrap things up here in a few hours, and you can be on a flight home this evening."

"That would be great." I nod and open my laptop. "Cami's not feeling great."

"Civilian life sure is different, isn't it?"

"Man, that's the truth." I nod and look over at my old friend and former wingman. "Priorities change so much. Two years ago, all I could think about was getting in the air and maybe getting laid once in a while."

"And now you just want to stay home and be with your girl," Ringo says with a grin. He mindlessly fiddles with the ring on his left hand. "I understand. I loved the Navy. I loved the travel and the rush of the flying, the thrill of it all. But then I met Suzanne, and the thrill changed."

"Exactly." It occurs to me that I haven't picked my ring up from the jeweler yet and mentally put it on my calendar for this week. It seems there's a lot to do before we get married in less than a week, but I can't wait. "I was so pissed after the wreck," I say quietly. "I didn't want my flying career to end. Not like that."

"Like I said before, you got a shitty deal."

"I didn't even really want to come home. I felt so lost when I was still in the hospital and they told me that I couldn't fly anymore. But there was nothing else to do. So I came home, and worked with my dad. I'm thankful that he gave me the work, but it didn't drive me. It was Cami that really healed me. I may have been fine physically when I first got home, but she's the one that helped me get my head on straight."

"Well, let's wrap this up so we can get you home to her."

"Sounds like a plan."

We dig in for several hours, going over potential employees, looking through résumés, and deciding who I'll call in for interviews next week when Linda, Ringo's assistant, pokes her head in the door.

"I'm sorry to interrupt, but, Landon, you have an urgent call from a Mia."

I frown and my gaze immediately meets Ringo's.

"You can take it on this phone," he says, and hands me the receiver, punching the button for the correct line.

"Mia?"

"Landon, I'm sorry to call like this, but your cell kept sending me to voice mail."

"It's fine, what's up?"

"First, I don't want to freak you out. I went to Cami's to check on her like you asked, and she looked horrible. She started throwing up and couldn't stop, and kept complaining about her shoulder. I finally talked her into going to the ER, and she's been admitted. I really think you should come home as soon as possible."

Ringo, who can hear everything, says, "I can fly you up."

"I'm on my way. Is she okay now?"

"They're still assessing," she says. "Just come home."

"Can I talk to her?"

There's silence for a minute, then Mia returns. "No, she's talking to the doctor."

"Mia, what aren't you telling me?"

"Nothing. Just get here."

"Tell her I love her." I hang up and immediately gather my things. "How fast can you have me up there?"

"Three hours, max."

"That's too long."

"Sorry, man, I can't control geography, and I'm flying a Cessna, not a Navy jet."

"Fuck," I mutter, and rush behind him out of the building. "She didn't sound good when I spoke to her."

"Beating yourself up won't solve anything." Ringo pulls out his phone. "I need the Cessna ready to go in fifteen minutes. I don't give a shit, make it happen. There's an emergency."

He clicks off and leads me to his car.

"I appreciate you doing this."

"You're my friend, Landon. This is the least I can do. We'll get there."

I nod and stare at my phone, praying Cami's okay.

BECAUSE OF THE fucking weather, it took us almost four hours to get to Portland, then it was another thirty minutes of finding my car and busting ass to get to the hospital.

When I finally find Mia and the others, I'm going crazy with worry.

"Landon!"

Mia jumps out of her chair and rushes to me, hugging me tight.

"Where is she?"

"She's in surgery," Riley says. Her eyes look tired. Steven is sitting with Addie and Jake, and Kat is on her phone.

"Your mom and dad are on their way down," she says to Steven, who nods wearily.

"What the fuck is happening?" I demand.

"They won't tell us much," Mia says. "But there really wasn't time."

"Why?"

"Right after I hung up with you, the doctor told me that they needed to take Cami in for emergency surgery, and then everything happened so fast, before I knew it, they all rushed off, and I was escorted in here. I called the others, and that's really all I know."

"They didn't say if the baby was okay? Or what she was having surgery for?"

"No," she replies, visibly frustrated. She pulls Cami's ring out of her pocket and passes it to me.

"Why do you have this?"

"They wouldn't let her wear it in surgery."

I march over to the registration desk.

"I'm here regarding Cami LaRue. She's been in surgery for a few hours. Can you give me any information?"

The woman smiles. "Let me call back." She speaks with someone briefly, then hangs up the phone. "The doctor should be out shortly. Cami was just taken to recovery."

I sigh in relief. If she's in recovery, she must be okay. "Thank you." I return to the others. "She's out of surgery."

"Thank God," Riley says just as a man in green scrubs comes through the electronic doors.

"Are you friends of Cami's?"

"Yes," I say immediately. "I'm her fiancé."

He shakes my hand and frowns slightly. "Cami's surgery went well, and she's in recovery. As soon as we make sure she's handled the anesthesia well and she's settled in a room, you'll be able to see her."

"Thank you. What happened? Is the baby okay?"

He sighs. "Cami came in with symptoms of an ectopic pregnancy, meaning the embryo had implanted in her fallopian tube rather than her uterus. We did an ultrasound to confirm. Unfortunately, her tube ruptured and we had to perform emergency surgery. She lost her fallopian tube and the baby."

I drop into a chair and stare at my feet.

We lost the baby.

"The good news is, the surgery went well and we were able to clean up all of the infection. She'll have some recovery time of a few weeks, but she's going to be just fine."

"Thank you," Riley says.

"I'm very sorry for your loss."

Someone is rubbing circles on my back. The girls are talking about making calls and what they can do for her once she's home.

It's all just noise to me. I need to see her.

Finally, after what seems like hours, a nurse comes to get me and leads me to Cami's room. She's asleep, and I'm told that she's been given a strong dose of pain medicine so she'll probably sleep for a couple of hours.

I sit next to her and take her hand in mine. Jesus, she looks so small in this hospital bed. Aside from some circles under her eyes and the IV in her arm, she looks no different from when I left her yesterday morning.

And yet, our whole world just changed.

She'll be devastated. Fuck, *I'm* devastated. After the shock wore off, we were both excited about the baby.

But we can have another. We have our whole lives ahead of us. I pull her ring out of my pocket and slip it onto her finger.

"I'm so sorry, baby," I whisper as tears fall down my cheeks. Suddenly there's a hand on my shoulder, startling me.

"She's a strong girl," my mother says, tears falling from her own eyes. "I'm so sorry about your bambino." She kisses my head and sits across from me.

"Me too." I can't take my eyes off of Cami. "Why did this happen? And I don't want to hear that everything happens for a reason, because that's bullshit."

"Watch your mouth," Mama orders, making my lips twitch. "We don't know why this happened, and I know that makes you angry. Did you know that your father and I lost a baby after Mia?"

My eyes whip over to hers. The room is softly lit, making it difficult to see her face. "What?"

"We did," she says softly. "And there was no logical

explanation. It just happens, Landon. And it breaks your heart."

I nod and lean my forehead against Cami's hand. I'm ready for her to wake up. I want to see her beautiful eyes and kiss her. I need her.

"It will make you stronger, and one day, when you are blessed with other children, it will make you that much more thankful for them."

"I just need to make sure that Cami's okay," I reply. "As long as she's healthy, that's all that matters."

"She's a strong girl," Mama repeats, and reaches across to pat my hand over Cami's. "And she loves you more than anything in this world. She always has. She'll blame herself."

"It's not her fault." I frown and shake my head. "That's silly."

"Grief isn't logical. She'll blame herself and she'll feel that she's let you down. Be careful with her for a little while."

I nod. "Thank you, Mama. Will you tell the others that they can come in to see her after she wakes up?"

"I guess that's my dismissal, then," she says with a smile. "I'll leave you with your girl." She circles the bed and stops to kiss me once more. "I'm so sorry for your hurt, my sweet boy."

I want to weep in her arms, comforted the way only a mother can, but I nod and gruffly say, "Thank you."

Mama leaves, and I lean on the bed, Cami's hand firmly in mine, and close my eyes, listening to the rhythm of her breathing until I'm lulled to sleep beside her.

Chapter 19

~Cami~

*E*verything is fuzzy. My head, my thoughts, even my fingers feel fuzzy, but someone is holding my left hand.

I think I'm sore. I try to open my eyes, but they're so damn heavy. Everything is fuzzy and heavy.

"Cami?"

Landon! Landon's here. But he's not supposed to be here. I frown and fight harder to open my eyes, but they're fuzzy too.

I blink and turn my head, relieved to see that it's Landon holding my hand. He looks tired, and his blue eyes are worried.

"Hi, baby," he whispers, and kisses my cheek.

"Hi," I reply, but my throat is dry. "Water."

"Here." He lifts a straw to my lips and I drink eagerly, so damn thirsty. I drain the glass and settle back against the bed again. "How do you feel?"

"Fuzzy," I reply, my voice more normal, but weak. "Sore."
I frown when tears fill Landon's eyes, and then it all comes
back to me. All of the pain and the fear, and the doctor tell-
ing me that I'd have to lose the baby. Oh God, did they tell
Landon? I grip his hand in mine and he leans toward me.
"Did they tell you?"

He nods.

"I lost our baby," I whisper. "I'm so sorry." Tears fill my
eyes now and fall on my cheeks, but I don't care. Our baby is
gone. But Landon just folds me in his arms so I can bury my
face in his shoulder, and gently hugs me, running his fingers through my hair and murmuring sweet words to me.

"It's not your fault," he says. "And I'm sorry too. I was
excited for the baby too."

I know, and I've disappointed you. I can't bear it. I didn't get
the chance to feel it, or hold it, and we'd only known about it
for a short time, but I was already so excited to meet him or
her, and now we never will.

The tears come in earnest now, and I cling to him, sob-
bing against him. Finally, he pulls back and wipes my tears.
"I'm sorry I wasn't here for you."

"There's nothing you could have done," I reply, and cup
his cheek in my hand. His stubble scratches my palm, but I
like it. "There wasn't anything anyone could do."

"I could have taken you to the hospital sooner," he says
gruffly. "I should have taken care of you."

"I'm okay," I reply, and pull him in for a sweet kiss. "I'm
sad, but I'm going to be just fine. But I'm so very sorry that I
lost our baby."

"Sweetheart, we'll have more babies. We'll have as many as you want."

Before I can answer him, there's a knock on the door and a doctor walks into the room.

"It's good to see you're awake," he says, and smiles kindly. "How is your pain?"

"I'm sore," I reply, and flinch when I try to shift my hips.

"We'll get you some more pain meds so you sleep through the night. You'll be sore for a few days, but your recovery time should be fairly fast. You're a healthy woman."

"Before surgery, you told me you'd do your best to save the tube," I say, and see Landon's gaze whip up to the doctor's. "Were you able to?"

The doctor sighs and shakes his head.

"I'm sorry, Cami. The damage was too great, and there was already infection setting in. I had to remove the tube."

"Oh," I breathe, and close my eyes. "So this means it'll be more difficult to get pregnant later."

"I'm sorry," he repeats. "But it's not impossible. Your uterus and the other tube are perfectly healthy."

But I've stopped listening to him. Not only did I lose the baby, but now it's going to be a challenge to get pregnant again. We can't have as many babies as I want. We'll be lucky to have any babies at all.

"Cami?" The doctor frowns when I look back up at him. "I'm going to order that medication for you. I think a good night's sleep will do you good, and you'll feel better tomorrow. You're lucky that you came in when you did. If you'd waited longer . . . well, the outcome could have been very grave."

"Thank you, Doctor," Landon says, and shakes his hand, then sits next to me again. "Why did you wait so long to go?"

"I thought I was just not feeling well," I reply shortly. I'm sad, but now I'm getting angry too. Why did this happen? Everything that I've ever wanted was in the palm of my hand, and in the span of a heartbeat, it was ripped away.

I need a few minutes alone. To gather my thoughts, to grieve for just a few minutes on my own.

"Landon, can you please go?"

"What?" he asks, surprised. My voice is calm. I'm not being mean or hurtful. Hurting him any more is the last thing I want.

"I just need to be alone for a little while."

"Cami, I really don't want to leave you by yourself." The hurt in his eyes is killing me.

"I only want a few minutes of privacy. Please."

But he stubbornly shakes his head.

"Maybe we should go somewhere when you're feeling up to traveling," he says, and I immediately close my eyes. "Somewhere warm," he continues. "You can take a couple of weeks away from the restaurant and put your feet up. I'll bring you cocktails and you can soak in some sun."

"I don't need to *leave*," I whisper, and suddenly I'm just so fucking *mad*. At Landon. At the doctor. At Mia for not coming sooner.

At every fucking thing.

"Okay, well, you can take some time to stay home—"

"You know what," I reply, and glare at Landon. "Maybe this was a blessing."

"What?" He scowls and sits back in the chair, surprised.

"I mean, it's good that it happened now rather than after the wedding because now you're off the hook. You don't have to be saddled with a wife and a kid that just slow you down.

"All you can talk about is leaving. Take me to San Diego. Take me somewhere warm. Well, you know what, Landon? I don't want to leave. *You* do. You've never wanted to be here. All your life you've done everything you can to *not* be here. But I love it here. This is my home, and this is where my business is, and this is where I'm fucking happy.

"So maybe you should just go."

"You want me to go," he says, perfectly calmly.

"Yes, that's what I've been telling you. I need some time alone."

I shake my head. I'm not crying. I'm boiling mad. I don't think I've ever been this pissed off in all of my life.

"Just get out."

"I don't want to leave you, Cami. Not like this."

Not like this.

"I'm fine, Landon. I was just fine before you, and I'll be great after you. *You* don't determine my happiness."

He stands, but stays at the side of my bed for a few moments, just watching me, until I pick up my empty water cup and throw it at him.

"Get the fuck out!"

He blinks, and then he turns and walks out the door just as Riley walks in. She frowns back at him before approaching the bed. "Hey sugar."

"Hey."

"Where is Landon going?"

"I don't give a fuck where Landon's going. I told him to get the hell out."

She's silently surprised for a heartbeat, then drops into the chair Landon was in and says, "Excuse me?"

I stare at my best friend, blinking, thinking about everything I just said to her, and I can't believe it.

"I sent him away."

And now the tears come again. It feels like my heart is being ripped out of my chest. I bury my face in my hands and sob, barely aware of Riley petting my hair.

"Why did you do that?"

"Because I'm so sad and pissed off and confused!" I wail into my hands. "I lost our baby, and he's talking about having all the babies I want, but I can't do that, Riley. I can't give him lots of babies. I don't think I ever wanted lots of babies, and if he wants them, he should have them.

"And he's always talking about going away!" I'm babbling now, barely making sense through my tears, and I don't care. "He doesn't want to be here, he was just here because he felt obligated to me."

"I don't think that's true."

"It's fucking true! And now he doesn't have to stay here. I don't want him to go, but I don't want him to be sad. And every time he looks at me, I'll just be a reminder that I lost his baby." I'm hiccuping now with the tears. Riley's stopped petting my head, leaving me be to cry and rant and just purge all of this bullshit out of my body.

"I wanted that baby so much," I say, quieting a bit now, but keeping my face in my hands because I'm just so embarrassed and ashamed. "I loved him already, and I was hoping he'd look like his daddy. And Landon is everything I've ever wanted and I screwed that up too. I'm just not supposed to have a husband and a family, Ri. And it's good that this happened now, before the wedding."

I'm rubbing my swollen eyes. I need a cold cloth, but I don't want to ask for one. I just want to call Landon back, but that's dumb. I already fucked that up.

Suddenly a cold cloth is pressed to my neck, and I take it and push it against my eyes, crying into the cotton, making it warm.

"I can't stop crying."

"Shhh."

"It's so much more than just losing the baby," I say, quieting a bit now. "We lost all of it. His first steps, swimming lessons, the first day of school." I shake my head. "I won't get to straighten his tie on prom night, or dance with him at his wedding." She puts her hand on my ankle over the covers and sits silently, letting me cry it out and then just breathe, taking long, jagged breaths until I'm calm enough to wipe my face and glance up.

But it's not Riley sitting next to me.

It's Landon.

"You didn't leave."

He doesn't smile at me, and he takes the cloth out of my hands, runs it under the faucet to get it cold again, and passes it back to me. It feels like heaven on my face and neck.

Landon just watches, calm as can be. His eyes show the hurt, and that makes my eyes well up again. Of course he's hurting too. I don't want him to hurt. I never want that.

"I loved her too," he says quietly, and leans in to rest his elbows on the bed, taking my hand in his. His touch always feels wonderful, but this is better than anything I've ever felt. "And I'm so sad that we'll never get to hold her and love her, and do all of the things you just said. It's tragic, Cami."

I nod and bite my lip. "I'm sorry."

"Losing her *isn't your fault*," he says firmly. "Look at me."

My gaze finds his. "None of this is anyone's fault. I don't know why it happened. But I do know this: I'm not about to lose my child and the love of my life in the same day. You are convinced that I don't want to be here, but, Cami, I've never said that. Yes, the Navy took me away for a long time, but when that was over, I didn't have to come home. I could have relocated and started over anywhere. I *chose* to come back to Portland, and I'm so damn glad I did because it brought me to *you*. Will I want to travel with you? Of course. But this is our home.

"I can't spend the next fifty years proving it to you over and over again, just to have you mistrust me. You know me well enough that I don't do anything that I don't want to do."

I smile and nod softly, hope burning brightly in my chest.

"I'm sorry I said that. I don't know what's wrong with me. I don't say things to deliberately hurt people, and I'd never try to hurt you."

"You're sad, and you're angry. And, please don't throw something at me again, but your hormones are probably all over the place."

My lips twitch, and I simply nod again. I'm just relieved that he didn't actually leave when I told him to.

Thank God.

"I told you before, and I'll say it again, I didn't propose to you because of the baby. Cami, I've wanted you for as long as I can remember. I want you to be my wife, with or without the baby. You are *mine*, do you understand me?"

"Yes," I murmur, and take a long, deep breath. "I'm a pain in the ass."

"Oh, for sure," he says, finally smiling. "But you're a pain in *my* ass, and I wouldn't have it any other way. We're going to get through this, the same way that we'll get through every other difficult time that crosses our path: as a team."

"I don't deserve you."

"Yes, you do. You deserve every wonderful thing that life has to offer. You deserve better than me, but this is what you're stuck with."

"Thank God."

He tips his forehead against mine.

"I love you so much."

"I love you too, you beautiful pain in the ass."

"If the dairy guy is late with my cheese one more time, I'm going to fire his ass and look for someone else."

"Organic dairy isn't easy to find," I remind Mia the next morning. "Especially not at the prices he gives us. Everyone else charges an arm and a leg, and I'm not going to approve the funds for a more expensive dairy just because you and this guy don't get along. Did you sleep with him or something?"

She just shrugs, not looking up from her phone.

"You slept with the *dairy guy*?" I demand, my voice a little shrill.

"He's good-looking," she says defensively. "And he's not an idiot."

"But apparently he's late all of the time," Landon says, crossing his arms over his chest. "Do I have to beat him up?"

"No," Mia replies, rolling her eyes. "I know you don't like to hear this, but I'm not a virgin. I do have sex. Not as often as I'd like, but it does happen."

"I'm not going to pay more for dairy just because you boned the dairy guy and don't want to deal with him," I say firmly. "You're an adult. You can deal with it."

"*He's* the one being difficult," she says. "He wasn't late before."

"Maybe he's trying to get your attention," Landon suggests. "If you have to talk to him about his tardiness, you have to deal with him."

"I don't have to deal with him," she says, just as stubborn as I am. "I can just send him an e-mail telling him I'm firing him."

"No firing him until we find someone else for the same price." I sigh and shift in the bed. "When is the doctor coming in?"

"What's your doctor's name again?" Mia asks. We are waiting, impatiently, for him to come in and discharge me so I can go home. I'm still sore, but I will be for a while. I just want to get home and recover there.

"I keep forgetting," I reply, and look over at Landon, who

is boxing up flowers that arrived this morning. "What's his name?"

"Dr. Holmes," the man himself says when he walks in the room and smiles. "You look better this morning."

"I feel a little better." He pulls my chart up on his laptop and sits next to me. In the light of day, without powerful pain meds to fog up my brain, I can see that Dr. Holmes is a hottie. I glance up at Mia and wiggle my eyebrows.

"Your blood pressure is great. All of your labs came back normal this morning, and your hormone levels are decreasing like they should." He glances up at me and offers me a smile, and if I wasn't already engaged to the hottest man in the universe, I might melt just a little. "So I hear you want to go home."

Suddenly the flash on Mia's phone goes off, blinding all of us.

"What the hell is wrong with this shitty phone?" she says, but she's blushing. She was trying to get an incognito photo of Dr. Hottie.

Landon just glares at her, and I have to cover my giggle with a cough. Dr. Hottie just keeps talking, like this happens to him every day.

Because it probably does. If any doctor were to get selfie requests, it would be this one.

"I think we can let you go home, but I want you to follow up with your primary doctor in a couple of days."

"I can do that."

"Okay, I'll get your paperwork finished up and a nurse will be in shortly with your prescriptions and some instructions, and we'll get you out of here."

"Thank you."

"You're welcome." He nods, shakes Landon's hand, and winks at Mia on his way out.

"What in the hell was that?" Landon demands as Mia and I bust out in laughter.

"I'd texted Kat and told her that Cami's doctor was the sexiest doctor I'd ever seen and she dared me to sneak a picture and send it to her. But I forgot to turn the flash off."

"Seriously?" Landon says.

"Oh, come on." I jump in to Mia's defense. "Kat *dared* her."

"If she dared you to jump off a bridge, would you do that too?"

"Possibly. Depends on the circumstances," Mia says with a sassy smile. "Like you've ever passed up a dare in your life, brother."

"I didn't flash my camera in the doctor's face."

"That doctor has seen your fiancée naked," she reminds him.

"Yeah, he's lucky I didn't punch him," Landon says, and kisses my forehead. "Are you ready to go home?"

"So ready." I nod and scoot over so he can join me on the bed. "Snuggle me."

"That bed is kind of small for snuggling," Mia says, then rolls her eyes when Landon complies. He cuddles me close and kisses my cheek. "You guys are disgusting."

"You need a man to cuddle," I say, and laugh when she shakes her head.

"I don't need to cuddle."

"Cuddling is nice," I reply with a sigh, and lean against my firm, strong man.

Chapter 20

~Landon~

"It's about fucking time you got married," Lucas says a month later. We're in the room I grew up in at my parents' house, getting dressed for the wedding.

"You're not married, and we're the same age, idiot," I reply, and grin. We love slinging insults at each other.

"I'm not the settling-down kind of guy," he says, completely lost as to how to tie his tie. So I walk to him and shove his hands away, doing it myself. "A wild man like me can't be tamed."

"Or you're too ugly for any woman to want to look at you for the rest of her life." I laugh and cinch up the tie, too tight, of course.

"Ha ha," he replies, and walks to the mirror to adjust his tie and slip into his jacket. "So you guys decided against going to the courthouse?"

"Yeah." I nod and grin, remembering Cami's face when I suggested the church. "Even if it's still a small thing, she deserved something more special. She's always had a soft spot for that old church down the street. You know, the tiny one that our moms used to drag us to for Sunday school when we were little?"

"I know the one." Lucas's face sobers. "How is she?"

"She's doing better," I reply, and nod, thinking of my strong girl. "She suggested us going to therapy right after she lost the baby."

"Really?" he asks with surprise. "You're in therapy? Has hell frozen over?"

"I was surprised too, but I'm glad she did. We've had some interesting conversations, that's for sure. It's been good for both of us." I shrug and smile at my longtime friend. "You could use some therapy yourself."

"Nah, I'm happy with all of my dysfunctional ways."

"How's it going in here?" Jake asks as he and Steven walk into the room. "Aw, don't you just clean up all pretty like?"

"Fuck you," I reply calmly, but my palms are sweaty and I'm more than a little nervous. Not at the thought of marrying Cami. There's nothing I want more in the world. I'm just antsy. I'm ready to get this all over with, so she's finally my wife and we can move forward with our lives. "Why are you guys here?"

"Because we've been banned from the girls' domain," Steven says. "And I'm sick of seeing Aunt Cami cry. Girls are so sentimental."

"Get used to it, kid," Lucas says, slapping Steven on the back.

"Also, she kept telling me I look *so cute,* like I'm twelve or something." He shudders. "It's gross."

"Awww, you're just so cute," I say, and pinch Steven's cheek, then slap it lightly. "Let's get this show on the road."

"I should warn you," Jake says as we stomp down the stairs and out to our cars. My parents left for the church earlier to help with any finishing touches. "They've been drinking champagne like it's going out of style, since Addie can drive. Let's just hope they can stumble into the church."

"They'll be fine," I reply. "You bozos are taking your own ride. I'm not giving you a lift to the restaurant after the ceremony."

"You're so selfish, wanting your bride all to yourself," Lucas says with a grin. I just wave them off and drive my own car down the street, then take a deep breath and walk inside. The church is so charming all on its own that it didn't require much for decoration. There are some candles lit, and a bouquet of flowers on the altar, but that's it. All of the girls are already sitting, along with Cami's siblings, who traveled for the occasion, Ringo and his wife, and my family.

We wanted to keep the guest list small, inviting only those we're truly close to to share our day.

Steven disappears into a side room, and Jake joins Addie in the front row as Lucas and I walk to the front of the church where the minister is already standing.

"Are you ready?" he asks me.

"I've been ready for weeks," I reply truthfully. He smiles and nods at the pianist, queuing him to begin the "Wedding March."

Cami's sister, Amanda, walks slowly down the aisle, smiling brightly, and then finally, there is my gorgeous bride.

Cami's all smiles as Steven escorts her down the aisle. Her dress is lacy and hugs her curves perfectly. Her eyes are pinned to mine as she walks slowly to me, and finally, Steven passes her hand to mine.

"Who gives this woman to this man?" the minister asks.

"I do," Steven says proudly, kisses Cami's cheek, and joins his family.

God, she's beautiful.

And she's mine.

The minister begins speaking about the sanctity of marriage. The promise. And I can't take my eyes off her.

Cami and I chose to exchange traditional wedding vows, and before I know it, her sweet voice fills the small chapel as she begins to recite them.

"I, Cami, take you Landon to be my husband. To have and to hold, from this day forward, for better, for worse, for richer, for poorer, in sickness and in health, to love and to cherish, forsaking all others, till death do us part."

A tear slips down her cheek when the minister says, "And now, with the authority vested in me through the state of Oregon, I now pronounce you husband and wife. You may kiss your bride."

But I don't just kiss her. No, that would be damn boring. I dip her deeply and kiss her the same way, showing God and all of our nearest and dearest just how much I love this woman.

When we stand, the chapel erupts in applause, and we are enveloped in hugs and well-wishes from our families.

Finally, the photographer says, "Well, since all of the guests will be in photos, let's go ahead and get them out of the way so we can get you all to dinner at the restaurant."

"Who knew that photos with only twenty people could take so long?" Lucas asks an hour later after we've been posed in every way you can imagine. "That made me damn hungry. Let's go."

"We'll be right behind you!" I call out to everyone as they file out. "I want a minute with my girl."

Cami frowns up at me as everyone leaves, and when we're alone, I turn to her, standing in the same places where we exchanged our vows an hour ago, and take her hands in mine.

"I needed a few minutes alone with you. How are you?"

"I'm wonderful," she replies with a wide smile, her green eyes shining with happiness. "How are you?"

"I can't even tell you how happy I am," I reply, and kiss her hands. "I'm glad that we decided to exchange the traditional vows because we're traditional people, but there are a few other things that I want to say that I didn't want everyone else to hear and I wanted to say them here."

I swallow, clear my throat, and continue to hold her gaze.

"The first time I saw you, something inside me said, *That's the one*. Of course, I was a kid, but through all of the years that passed after, that voice was still there. Sometimes it was a whisper, and other times it was a shout. No one and nothing compares to you and what I feel for you, Cami. You aren't just my other half, you're the best part of me. There is nothing you can ever do to lose my love, my sweet. It is endless. And while I will love you until my last breath, I will love you beyond that, into whatever that may be. You are a permanent part of me, and for that I will always be grateful because there is nothing in this world that is better than you. I'm humbled to be yours."

She's smiling so brightly, and yet so gently at the same time. She boosts up on her toes to kiss my lips, and then, to my surprise, begins to speak.

"I'm so glad you did this because I have something to say too." She blinks and seems to gather her thoughts, and then turns those bright green eyes up to mine. "*Wuthering Heights* is my favorite book, and the best line in it says this: *If he loved you with all of the power of his soul for a whole lifetime, he couldn't love you as much as I do in a single day.*

"I've always felt that that line was written for me, about you. I've watched you from a distance for years, caring for you, worrying about you, thinking of you. I've felt pulled to you my entire life, Landon. I couldn't explain it, and I couldn't wish it away even when I tried. You've never left me. I've carried you with me always. It's a constant surprise to me that you're mine now. It feels like the best dream I've ever had, and I find myself wishing and praying that I don't wake up.

"But, I'm not dreaming. And for better or worse, you are finally mine. I have a feeling that ours is going to be a life that's a little bit messy, with lots of laughs and some tears, but that is what makes it great. It's passionate and whole and true. And I can tell you for certain that it's forever. Because it's already been forever."

She reaches up and gently catches a tear that has escaped my eyes.

"I am so blessed."

I pull her in and wrap my arms around her, and kiss her tenderly.

"Now that we've finished our vows, are you ready to go celebrate?"

"I'm ready for all of it."

"IF THEY DON'T stop putting parsley on the plates, I'll—"

"Mia," Cami says with a laugh, and hugs her tightly. "Relax. I don't care about the parsley. And you're supposed to be enjoying yourself. This is a *party*."

"You're right." Mia shrugs. "I'll give them a refresher course on garnishes later."

"Atta girl," I reply happily as Lucas and Addie both stand and Lucas taps his water glass to get all of our attention.

"Hi, everyone," Lucas says. "So, it's tradition for the best man to give a toast, but instead, Addie and I are going to tell a story."

"It's a really great story," Addie adds with a nod.

"Picture if you will," Lucas begins, raising his hand for dramatic effect, "a hot summer in 2003."

"Cami was seventeen and Landon was in his early twenties, home for the summer before he shipped off to join the Navy." Addie glances over at us, grinning widely. "And we had a big cookout in Landon's backyard."

"But Cami didn't come alone," Lucas continues. "No, Cami showed up to the cookout with some dude, none of us can remember his name. Now, what I do remember is seeing Landon's face when Cami walked into the backyard with that bozo on her arm. It wasn't pretty. In fact, I do believe that Landon proceeded to glare at the guy all night."

Please don't tell them about how drunk I got that night.

"What he didn't know," Addie says, picking up the story, "was that Cami was so *not* into Mr. No-name. Frankly, she just brought him along in hopes that Landon would get jealous and *finally* make a move. It was her last-ditch effort, if you will, before Landon left."

"Oh, he was jealous all right," Lucas says with a laugh. "And I won't even get into how much beer he drank that night."

"Thank you!" I call out.

"But he didn't make a move on our Cami," Addie says, and everyone in the room says "aw" in sympathy. "I believe her exact words after that night were 'screw him.'"

"Awww!" everyone says again. I reach under the table and take her hand in mine, and when I look down at her, she's laughing with the others, not embarrassed in the least.

"But the story gets better," Lucas says. "Not long after Landon moved back home, I came to town to see how he was doing, and I was shocked when he bailed on a night of debauchery with me to take Cami out on a date."

"It was their first official date," Addie says with a smile. "And it may have been years later, but they finally got it right. That first date led us here, and all we can say is, it's about time, you guys."

"To Landon and Cami," Lucas says, raising his glass. "And to a long life together."

Everyone cheers and I lean in to whisper in Cami's ear. "This moment is thirteen years in the making, and I couldn't have pictured it any better than this."

Epilogue

Three months later . . .

~Cami~

"*I* have wedding photos!" I announce, and pull an album out of my purse. The five of us are enjoying Sunday-morning brunch at our usual place in Northwest Portland.

"Oh! Fun," Riley says, and reaches for the album and she and Kat huddle together to look through the photos.

"Why didn't anyone tell me that you could see my belly through my dress?" Addie asks with a scowl. "I would have showcased it more."

"No one can miss it now," Mia says, and reaches out to rub Addie's stomach. "Are you ever going to tell us what you're having?"

"No. Jake and I want it to be a surprise."

"I don't like surprises," Kat says, and then points to one of the photos. "Aw, Cami, this candid shot is awesome. When was this?" She turns the album to show me and I smile at the memory.

"That was after everyone else had left the church and Landon wanted to say a few things to me privately. We didn't realize that the photographer stayed to take a couple photos, but I'm so glad she did. That's one of my favorites."

"What did he want to talk about?" Addie asks.

"That's one of the few things that I'm not going to share with you guys," I reply. Those words were too important to share them with anyone else.

"Well, it's a great picture," Kat says. "She did a really good job."

"Thanks, I think so too."

"Hey, Kat, did you buy your airline tickets for your trip yet?" Mia asks, making Kat frown again.

"Yes, but I'm telling you guys, I don't want to go."

"You *do* want to go," I correct her. "You just don't want to fly."

"I don't need to go," Kat says.

"It's a freaking wine convention in the Sonoma Valley. Of course you need to go," Riley says with a laugh. "It's shocking that you've never been down there before."

"I've never had time to drive down there before," Kat says.

"You're one of the most badass women I know," Addie says, and shoves a chunk of pineapple in her mouth. "I don't know why you're so damn afraid of flying."

"Because I just don't like it," Kat snaps. "You don't like things. Sometimes people just don't like things."

"Okay, look." Riley looks back and forth between them, warning them to chill out. "Kat, it's not going to suck. It's not a long flight from here."

"Did you book an aisle seat?" Mia asks. "That will help. Looking out the window might freak you out."

"I got an aisle seat," Kat says. "Can I get drunk before I get on the plane?"

"I don't see why not," I reply with a shrug. "Also, think of all of the hot guys that will be down there for the convention."

"Sexcation!" Addie exclaims, and claps her hands happily. "There's your silver lining. You can go down there and hook up with some hot wine dude. You can have lots of hot sex in the rows of grapes."

"Ew," Riley says, wrinkling her nose. "Don't have sex in the grapes. Someone is going to end up drinking those."

"That's kind of sexy," Kat says, sitting back to think it over. "It has been about six months since I last got laid. A sexcation sounds damn good."

"See?" Addie says, proud of herself. "I knew someone would end up taking advantage of the sexcation idea. It's a really brilliant idea."

"So to recap," Kat says thoughtfully, "I can get drunk for the flight and have no-expectations sex all week?"

"Yeah, that pretty much covers it," I reply with a nod. "You should totally do it."

"Okay, I'm in. But I have to be really drunk for that flight."

"We can do that."

Menu

Buttermilk Pancakes

Topped with *Banana*, Granola, and *Honey*

Frittata

Asparagus, Sausage, Cheese, Sage, and Cherry Tomato

Tangerine Mimosa with *Strawberries and Pomegranate Seeds*

Chandon

Buttermilk Pancakes

Serves 2

1 cup all-purpose flour
1 t. baking powder
¼ t. baking soda
¼ t. salt
3 T. granulated white sugar
1 large egg, lightly beaten
1 cup buttermilk
3 T. unsalted butter, melted
Plus extra butter for greasing the pan

Toppings:
Granola
Banana, sliced
Honey for drizzling

1. In a large bowl, whisk together the dry ingredients:
   flour, baking powder, baking soda, salt, and sugar.
2. In a separate bowl, whisk together the egg, buttermilk,
   and melted butter.
3. Make a small well in the center of the dry ingredients
   and pour in the egg mixture all at once. Stir together

until just combined (there will be small lumps). Be careful not to overmix the batter or the pancakes will be tough.

4. Heat a frying pan or griddle over medium high heat. Adjust flame as necessary to keep even heat.

5. Using a pastry brush, lightly brush the pan with melted butter. Carefully ladle about ¼ cup of pancake batter onto the hot pan, spacing the pancakes a few inches apart. The batter will be thick, so it may be necessary to move the ladle in a circle for a thinner pancake.

6. When the bottoms are brown and small bubbles appear around the perimeter of the pancake (about 2–3 minutes), turn over. Cook an additional 1–2 minutes until lightly browned. Repeat with remaining batter until all pancakes are cooked.

7. To serve, spread with additional butter and top with granola and sliced bananas. Drizzle with honey to taste.

Sausage, Asparagus, Cheese, Sage, and Tomato Frittata

Serves 2

6 large eggs
1 T. heavy cream
Salt and pepper
¾ cup Gruyère or other sharp cheese, set aside ¼ cup for topping
4 breakfast sausages, roughly chopped
1 T. olive oil
6 stalks asparagus, cut into bite sized pieces
¾ cup cherry tomatoes

1. Heat broiler and adjust oven rack to approximately 5 inches from the broiler element.
2. Whisk eggs, heavy cream, ½ t. salt and ¼ t. pepper. Add ½ cup of cheese and mix together. Set aside.
3. Over medium heat, place a non-stick, heavy bottom, oven safe skillet. Add breakfast sausage and cook until browned. Drain excess fat, but do not clean skillet. Heat 1 T. olive oil, add sausage, asparagus, and cherry

tomatoes back into pan. Cook for an additional 2–3 minutes until asparagus is bright green and the skin on the tomatoes begin to blister.

4. Add egg mixture to hot pan with sausage and asparagus. Gently move eggs around in pan until large curds form, about 1 minute (this helps to cook the eggs, but not scramble them). Shake the skillet to distribute the eggs and to let the bottom set. The top will not be set at this point.

5. Top with remaining ¼ cup of grated cheese and place under broiler and cook until surface is puffed and slightly browned and top is mostly set.

6. Remove from oven and let stand for 5 minutes. Using a spatula, loosen frittata around the edges and slide onto plate. Cut into wedges and serve with an additional drizzle of olive oil and sprinkle of sea salt.

Tangerine Mimosa with Strawberries and Pomegranate Seeds

3 cups chilled tangerine juice
Grand Marnier or other orange liqueur
Strawberries, hulled and sliced
Pomegranate seeds
1 bottle of chilled sparkling wine
For each drink:
Equal amounts of juice and sparkling wine
Dash of Grand Marnier

1. Pour tangerine juice into each champagne flute, about half full.
2. Add splash of Grand Marnier and strawberries and pomegranate seeds.
3. Top off each drink with sparkling wine.
4. Serve immediately.

Jake's song for Addie, "If I Had Never Met You,"
specially written and recorded for *Listen to Me,* is
available for purchase from music retailers!

Kristenproby.com/listentomesong

Make your reservation for the next deliciously sexy novel in Kristen Proby's *New York Times* bestselling Fusion series,

BLUSH FOR ME

As the take-charge wine bar manager of Seduction, Portland's hottest new restaurant, Kat Meyers is the definition of no-nonsense, and she isn't afraid of anything. Well, almost anything: she hates to fly. When she's forced to travel on a death trap with wings, the turbulence from hell has her reaching for any safe haven—including the incredibly handsome guy sitting next to her.

Ryan "Mac" MacKenzie hasn't been able to get his sexy seatmate out of his head. The way she clung to him stirred something inside him he didn't think existed: tenderness. As the owner of a successful wine touring company, Mac thinks he's got a handle on what life can throw at him and he's not prepared for any surprises, especially in the feelings department. And when he brings a tour into Seduction, he sees the petite spitfire he just can't forget.

Mac is determined to discover what else they have in common besides fine wine and the inability to keep their hands off each other. But what will it take for two stubborn people to realize that what they have is so much more than a hot chemistry between the sheets and to admit to falling in love . . . ?

Pre-order now!

About the Author

*N*ew *York Times* and *USA Today* bestselling author KRISTEN PROBY is the author of the bestselling With Me in Seattle and Love Under the Big Sky series. She has a passion for a good love story and humorous characters with a strong sense of loyalty and family. Her men are the alpha type, fiercely protective and a bit bossy; and her ladies are fun and not afraid to stand up for themselves.

Kristen lives in Montana, where she enjoys coffee, chocolate, and sunshine. And naps.

BOOKS BY **KRISTEN PROBY**

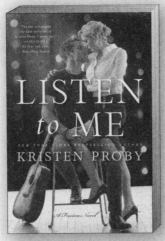

LISTEN TO ME
A Fusion Novel
Book One

Seduction is quickly becoming the hottest new restaurant in Portland, and Addison Wade is proud to claim her share of the credit. But when former rock star Jake Keller swaggers through the doors to apply for the weekend gig, she knows she's in trouble. He's all bad boy . . . exactly her type and exactly what she doesn't need.

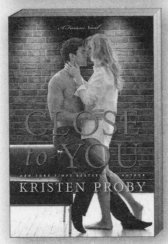

CLOSE TO YOU
A Fusion Novel
Book Two

Since the day she met Landon Palazzo, Camilla LaRue, part owner of the wildly popular restaurant Seduction, has been head-over-heels in love. And when Landon joined the Navy right after high school, Cami thought her heart would never recover. But it did, and all these years later, she's managed to not only survive, but thrive. But now, Landon is back and he looks better than ever.

COMING WINTER 2017
BLUSH FOR ME
A Fusion Novel; Book Three

When Kat, the fearless, no-nonsense bar manager of Seduction, and Mac, a successful but stubborn business owner, find themselves unable to play nice or even keep their hands off each other, it'll take some fine wine and even hotter chemistry for them to admit they just might be falling in love.